Clocking 90
on the road to
Cloughjordan

and other stories

Leo Cullen

ACKNOWLEDGEMENTS

...nety on the road to Cloughjordan', 'The funeral of Canon ... and 'The view from College Hill' were previously published ...e *Irish Press*; 'Clouds over Suez' and 'The spoils of war' were previously published in *Spark* magazine.

First published in 1994 by Blackstaff Press Limited
with the assistance of The Arts Council of Northern Ireland

This edition first published in 2002 by Beeline
an imprint of Blackstaff Press Limited
Wildflower Way, Apollo Road
Belfast BT12 6TA, Northern Ireland

Printed and bound in Great Britain by Omnia Books Ltd, Glasgow

A CIP catalogue record for this book
is available from the British Library

ISBN 0-85640-722-4

www.blackstaffpress.com

Contents

CLOCKING NINETY ON THE ROAD TO CLOUGHJORDAN

THEY SET OFF AT NOON ON A bright March day: Connaughton, two of his men and his two eldest children, to find out how fast his new Fiat car could travel. The town slept on, even this raw morning could not awaken it, while they whined away on the dry quiet roads.

Fanning was in the front passenger seat; he smelled of hard lardy carcase exteriors; he wore his white coat and blood-streaked apron; this would be a short trip. Barry sat in the back seat with the children: a small girl with a big white ribbon tightly bowed yet slipping off its tail of hair, and a small boy with greased and neatly parted scalp.

Barry would have preferred had he been left in the hearse. He had been quietly relaxing there in the half-light within the coffin shed when Fanning came looking for him. It was where he liked to relax between jobs of helping Taylor with his coffin making and his own jobs of polishing coffin handles, dusting the hearse and driving it. He liked the glassed-off silence, the faint residue of pine, of life itself within the hearse. He had noted a long time ago he could talk to himself, he could even shout in there and nobody would notice.

Was Barry free for an hour or two? Fanning had called over the rasp of wood-planing in the loft above. Would he like to accompany the boss and himself?

Yes, he was free, Taylor had shouted down for him from the loft – in the workshop Barry took his orders from Taylor. On the road it was the other way around: Barry at the wheel, Taylor, the bowler-hatted acolyte, sitting helpless alongside him. Taylor had not yet recovered from a trip they had recently been on.

Yes, said Taylor vengefully, Barry was definitely free. The outing would do him good. His only obligation was the delivery of a funeral habit to the County Home in Roscrea.

So the crew had set off. They brought the habit with them in the car.

It was a compact car, unpretentious. It had a boxy appearance, but the feature that had taken Connaughton's fancy when he first saw it was its little oblong-shaped speedometer: were the car to travel as fast as that indicated, it would do ninety miles an hour.

'You need a good fast car, boss,' Barry said by way of agreement with Connaughton's choice that first day he drove it home from the garage.

'Connaughton has the right car now,' all the street's passersby nodded as they looked into it, studied its dashboard. Connaughton often had to cover a funeral, a race meeting, buy cattle for his butcher shop, hire a maid for his hotel, all on the same evening.

'He has the right car now all right. He'll kill himself in that.' Connaughton ran a part-time hackney service: to Rineanna, to Collinstown Airport – services for a fee; and to Knock shrine – no fee. Knock he saw as religious duty. He was deeply devoted to the Virgin Mary.

'Not that much room in there though, is there?' they agreed with one another. 'Can't see it lasting that long.' Connaughton drove on his clutch. No car lasted him that long.

When the car swerved into the County Home the high-pitched whine of its engine startled some inmates. One old man in slippers, carrying a wide white enamel tray across the yard, stopped in the centre and did not then know what to do. Two others, slumped on an iron bench in the lee of a massive limestone building of windows and fire escapes, pulled their heads behind coat flaps. The burial habit was quickly delivered, and circling the man with the tray in the yard's centre the car took off again for open country. Approaching the straight stretch outside Cloughjordan, its needle already almost touching eighty, its whirr still rang in the ears of the man holding the tray five miles behind.

'Think she'll top the eighty, boss?' said Barry, who every now and then peered anxiously over the high dividing seat as the car sped along the raised road like that little aeroplane they had all gone out to see on College Hill the previous summer.

'Think she'll top the eighty, boss?' – the question hummed in the children's ears as they tried to count poles rushing by and couldn't.

'Think she'll top the eighty?' said Connaughton, more to himself than to the others. He looked in the driver's mirror, asked the girl to sit steady behind, not to be giddy; told Barry, with a wink at Fanning, to tighten his safety belt and said they were coming up to the straight stretch.

Connaughton then blessed himself. It was not taken by the others as a sign of fear; he was a pious man. They blessed themselves also. The doors were checked. All locked. A pallor began to spread from Fanning's face to his hands. His left hand searched beneath the upholstery for a solid grip. He wished he could be at home: walking through the yard maybe, from the slaughterhouse, carrying a carcase on his back; hearing the mare Judy whinny maybe in her box as he passed. 'There's my girl,' he would say. Reassuring her.

Barry's voice cracked into a note somewhere in the middle of the musical scale and then into a strangled falsetto: 'Come ba'ack...' It was the beginning of his one and only song. He repeated it again and again, a hysterically recited mantra. The children urged the car along. Eyes on the speedometer, hands clutching the seats in front of them: 'Go on, Dada, go on!' The straight stretch of road was before them, it was bare, the hedgerows were bare, the fields on either side were bare; not an animal, a car, a person in sight. The steeple of the church rose in the distance before them, there was a cluster of buildings...

'Go on, Dada, go on.'

'Come ba'ack, Paddy Reilly,' Barry quavered.

The wind buffeted the car. The speedometer needle rose steadily and stuck on eighty. It quivered between eighty and eighty-five. It reached eighty-five. Fanning whooped a little hiccup and looked at Connaughton staring grim-faced beside him. 'You've done it, boss' – he shook his head – 'you've done it. Would y'ever think she'd do it, the little beauty?'

'It should do ninety,' Connaughton replied. They streaked past the church. The needle jumped across eighty-five.

'Slow down, boss,' Barry cried. 'We're in the friggin' town, the guards, the civic guards!' He thrust his head beneath the seat as they swept past a few houses and shops and a straggle of head-swivelling figures. Then they were on the other side of the town.

Connaughton's mouth was numb. There was silence in the sealed-off car. A fear, as of being in the presence of something uncontrollable, something beyond their power, gripped each of them.

'Is your foot touchin' the floor, boss?' Barry screamed from beneath his cover in the back. 'Let me take over, boss? Give me the wheel. Where are we now?' He thrust up his head but not long enough to pick out a landmark. Down again he ducked. 'Give me the wheel.'

Then there was one straining second when, as the blur rushed the windscreen, the needle slipped over ninety. Connaughton tried to hold it there, but it would not hold. He did not tell the others.

After that, while time still remained suspended, the car, like a fast-finishing racehorse, was slowly reined in and turned back towards the stands past which it had triumphed. The country-side resumed its familiar aspect of fields, walls, hedges and haybarns. As he returned through Cloughjordan, Connaughton told the children they wouldn't bother stopping for an ice cream but if they waited till Moneygall they'd get one. He promised.

'And for God's sake,' he said, laughing to the men and turn-ing round in the car, 'don't tell your mother what you've been up to.'

Barry broke into song: 'Commmme back Paddy Reilly to Ballyjamesduff...' Other words too he sang to the same air: 'Sheee's the best little car on the ro'oad today.' The children sniggered at him. Fanning thought of how he would tell his wife when he got home to her for dinner in his new house on Park Drive Estate.

'Very irresponsible,' she would answer, turning the wireless down and silencing the baby with a bottle. 'Never happy to leave things as they are ... Very irresponsible taking two small children out like that. He's another child.'

Town was as ever when the motorists returned up the wide street. A few more cars, perhaps, parked outside the high shop fronts. There was the gentle refamiliarising bump of tyre against

THE FUNERAL OF CANON CROSS

TIME CLANGED URGENT BELLS in Barry's ear, for he saw no road forward. Again he changed from top gear down to third, again he changed back up. The bowler was off, discarded as soon as the airport dropped behind. It rested on the drive-shaft hump between his seat and Taylor's, a third head. The flannel cap spread across his head. His off-white racing cap, its flaps danced erratically about his ears.

The lorry allowed him no option but to pass it. Climbing the slow incline for ever, a two-tiered lorry with a load of sleeping pigs, it bullied him into a crawl.

Yet Barry dared not pass. He dared not get close enough even to attempt to pass. A swirling spray of rainbow and mud burst before the hearse. His hearse, his pride; it would destroy it.

For a whole hour this morning he had admired it. A shiny ace of spades, he thought, tucked in beneath the wing of a refuelling aeroplane on the apron. He had contented himself with a silent appraisal. Taylor the coffin maker, his assistant on these trips, who sat beside him right now, who wished like him the lorry would go away, Taylor had been no company this morning. No acknowledgements had been asked for from him.

Taylor had slumped in his passenger seat all the time they awaited the plane's arrival. Hadn't been a word from him since Johnstown, where they had come on the main road on the way up. Where Barry had sauntered out, incautious of on-coming traffic, parrying when Taylor told him what a blind so-and-so he was with: 'There's hardly any traffic on the road at this hour of morning.' And to lend strength to his convic-tion, Connaughton had shot behind him in the big American Chevrolet seemingly unconcerned as he. The whole cortège: military, sergeant, superintendent, clergy, cream of the country, had followed. Yes, Taylor had been silent since then.

And, cream of the country, they had all parked in atten-dant rows behind Barry at the airport.

It had been a slow morning. From time to time mourners staggered out of their cars, walked across to Barry, enquiring, 'What's keeping them?'

'Poor driving conditions overhead,' he answered in his testy, scraping voice, without looking in the direction of the cloud-packed sky into which the bereaved peered.

It was a sense of importance that raised Barry today above the level of all others. It was no ordinary funeral.

'How long will we have to wait?' they asked him.

'Oh, maybe all day before conditions improve up there. And you know what that means – all night maybe as well.'

The Canon was flying home. Canon Cross. Dropped dead while on a tour of the USA with the county's hurling team. The top brass from the town's army barracks, the superinten-dent, sergeant, clergy of most ranks and of both persuasions, today Barry had them all in train: no ordinary funeral. And the hurling team. The All-Ireland champions. Who were fly-ing home with their dead patron; the hurlers too he had in train. And not in the wide-windowed team bus, but in a fleet of hackney cars especially hired by Connaughton from among the hackney drivers of the town. The dramatic element: what so sustained Barry, so dignified his demeanour. No ordinary funeral this.

The plane had duly touched down. Barry and Taylor had boarded; ensured the American coffin was presentable before allowing the full-back and half-back lines of the hurling team to carry it down the gangway to the black pool of the reception party. Taylor, tall, almost stately, had had to doff his bowler as he entered the plane's low doorway. Barry's remained wedged to three or four contact points on his bony skull.

Among the waiting crowd below a conflict had arisen. Some thought the returning champions deserved three cheers: others thought silent reverence in order. Within the plane there had been no such indecision. Following seven hours in the air and the consumption by team and officials of the contents of tiny spirit bottles seemingly endless as the ocean that lay somewhere below them, the coffin, standing, not in the hold where airline regulation normally decreed, but in a space made by the removal of three rows of seats, had long been forgotten. Passing hurlers, en route to the toilets, no longer nodded towards it in reverence. Barry had been shocked: conditions no better than a changing room, discarded clothing flung on the floor. He had set the official tone for the team's reception. Had swept down the aisle. Sidestepped blockages of colourful jackets and shirts, pocket handkerchiefs, blue and gold team ties. 'Johnny Leahy.' He had found his target. 'Order. You're the trainer. Tell them they'll have to be silent going down the stairs, sir,' he rasped, shaking his head at the little man beneath the wide-brimmed American hat. 'The coffin is the first man out, sir.'

Only one arm had risen on the gangway descent. The goalkeeper's. It had not risen in acknowledgement of the waiting supporters – he had gone before the coffin to take its downward tilt, had stumbled and almost lost his footing. And so no adulatory arms had risen from among the mourners.

The cars strung out behind the hearse.

It had belted along at a good lick. Connaughton's instructions. Was to continue doing so – at least as far as Naas. L. W. Connaughton: Undertaker. An entry in the second race of today's racing card at Punchestown followed his name. L. W. Connaughton: Horse Trainer. The plan was the cortège would break at Norton's Hotel in Naas for refreshments while he slipped out the few miles to Punchestown, saddled his interest, injected against its weakness – burst blood vessels – instructed his jockey, and slipped back in time to carry on down the country. Now there was this lorry. Things threatened to come unstuck.

Taylor had abandoned his sulks at about the time the plane touched down on the runway and skimmed like a swan all the way round the airport to where they were parked. Now he advised Barry, 'You'll have to pull past him, driver.' Connaughton too, from behind his windscreen, ushered them forward with wild arm movements. 'Pass him on the inside,' Taylor said. 'He's leaving you space. The boss is in a hurry for the races.'

'Do you want me had up by the guards?' Barry had but one good eye. He punished Taylor with a look of it. 'Don't you know it's dangerous to pass out on the inside. Do you want me locked up?'

Would a police officer in the cortège speed forward, arrest his man, thus arresting the whole funeral . . . ? If Barry did not pause to consider how his lock-up might be achieved it was because he was, at that moment, concentrating on a blind spot with his one good eye to the right of the lorry. For there had suddenly appeared a huge space. No traffic coming against it.

A space like that would not present itself for long. He acted quickly.

'Rushing, that's what kills this job.' He shot across the road onto the empty right-hand side. 'If the aeroplane only came down when it was supposed to . . . I hate rushing.'

Taylor said nothing. The slam of the car seat thrilled into his back. Swept him before his thoughts. The coffin jolted back on its stay pins, stayed put. Smoothing away from the lorryload of awakened, squealing, sodden pigs, Barry first looked across in triumph at Taylor, threads of his cap bobbing furiously up his nose, and then looked into his mirror to see if Connaughton had also rounded the obstacle.

There was nobody behind him. Not even the lorry.

Looking back on the wide empty road he felt abandoned, lonely. 'Better slow down a bit,' he said to Taylor.

Just when he had begun to think the others must somehow have taken a wrong turning he saw Connaughton.

'Jesus Christ, he's on the wrong road,' he said. Connaughton was on the other side, the correct side, of the new dual carriageway.

He looked in his mirror. 'And he's after taking the funeral with him!'

He had not taken all the funeral, however. Taylor, looking back, could see that where the road had divided and where they had taken the right-hand side some of the others were now doing likewise. So far as he could see the first car now in pursuit of the hearse was the sergeant's. There were now two funerals: one following Connaughton in the Chev, one following Barry.

Connaughton drew abreast of Barry. They were separated only by a narrow strip of brown earth. He opened his window, pointed ahead, tried to say something. Barry turned on his wipers as the spray of the Chev leaped at his windscreen.

'What's the boss doing? What's he speeding for?' he asked, in turn speeding up himself. Taylor opened his window. It had never before been opened while the hearse was in motion. Taylor found the handle turning loosely in his hand as the window slid into the body of the door and stayed there. He deciphered nothing of Connaughton's roars. They were lost in his wake with the swirling slipstream.

'I think what he's saying is he has to get to the races.' Taylor turned to Barry. Pearly droplets shone off his bowler hat.

'He wants to kill us all.' Barry felt pain go through him as he opened out the engine that until this day had been his cosseted baby: the hearse had to lead even if the funeral was proceeding on two different roads. Connaughton slid past, receded behind again. They were on a long high elbow. Just then the sun broke through and lit suddenly the whole patch-work of flat green fields that stretched below on either side. Each time Connaughton's black, oiled head drew level he shouted something and then fell behind again. Barry's con-centration was absolute. He held his eye on Connaughton so that he might stay ahead; he also held it on the road on which cars now seemed to be coming against him with increasing regularity and speed.

'Dangerous bloody driving,' Barry gritted, as a car horn pinged urgently past and then receded to distant extinction like the whine of a bee that has lost its sting. A car approached, far too close to his side, attempting to pass another car in fact, giving him very little room, a narrow gap. It veered at the last moment, let the hearse through, the sergeant, half the county's hurling team, some clergy of one persuasion, the Canon's housekeeper in a car driven for her by her niece, some members of the sodality. 'Isn't this a nice carry-on?' Barry steeled.

A race was on. This group on one side, Connaughton in the chief mourner's car containing nobody but himself in the other. Followed by the other half of the team, the super', some far-out relatives of the Canon, clergy of the other persuasion, military, four sisters of the Mercy convent on the grounds of the Canon's former estate.

Connaughton's train should have held the lead: he had the freer passage. Barry had to contend with opposing traffic charging at times two and three abreast.

Connaughton's intention was not, however, to race. He was obliged merely to stay abreast of Barry by a compulsion to shout in horror whenever a vehicle seemed about to extinguish Barry, Taylor and the already extinguished priest to oblivion. Shouts that fell deafly on the slipstream. And for Barry's part, he wished only to remain slightly ahead: all his instincts said that even if they were on different roads, however it happened that they were, it was the position of the hearse to lead.

'I don't remember two roads coming up, driver,' said Taylor.

'That's because you were asleep coming up, sir.' Barry clenched his teeth, avoided an army convoy, held his left hand on the gear stick and steered the wheel with his right as it vibrated from contact on the road of wheels against verge.

Taylor was awake now. He suddenly had a sensation that the Canon was also awake, and that being mildly curious, as he had always been during life of events that awakened him, he had slightly lifted his coffin lid and was poking his head above.

There was an atmosphere in the glassed-in silence behind, he felt sure, but when he did find the courage to look behind he found the coffin lid flat, serenely shut. 'Don't blame him. Probably frightened to death,' he muttered and caught sight through the rear window of the sergeant's car behind hopping along the verge's edge as though its wheels might buckle off and every part of it fall asunder.

Two carloads of hurlers in either lane drew abreast. One player opened his window, signalled his opposite number to do likewise. He unzipped a leather sports bag and one by one pelted its contents of hurling balls at the opened window opposite while the dividing grass space raced between.

Some of the balls found their target. Then there were scuffles within the car for possession. Some hit the car. They hopped on the road and then scuttled about beneath the passing traffic until finally they lay, white mushrooms on the tarmac, inert, as the funeral raged away from them.

Suddenly the two trains converged again – as neatly and as mysteriously as they had first sheared off. Connaughton slotted in behind the hearse, the sergeant behind him, the super' and so on, like a zip. Barry's racing cap came off; bowler and official status were reinstated. Connaughton slumped forward a little in his seat, lit a cigarette, worried over the queue of traffic he imagined on the narrow road to the racecourse and wondered might it be unreasonable to expect that what had just happened could have gone unnoticed.

They slipped unremarkably into Naas. The road was already dry along its centre; moisture shimmered from it as from a hotplate. Barry parked tidily alongside a lorryload of pigs; the others jutted in an assortment of lengths and angles to the road.

There was a room in the hotel, converted into a bar, reserved for them. They moved in its direction, some stiffly, some of the hurlers jostling.

Connaughton raced across to the hearse. His face was creased. Barry checked his door was locked, that all within was secure.

'If I'm not back in an hour,' Connaughton said, 'go on without me. It's a single road from here on so you shouldn't have difficulties. I'll have caught up with you before you turn off the Dublin–Cork road.'

'As you say, boss, just leave it to us.'

Connaughton headed for his car but then turned back, his head shaking so violently that an incredulous laughter rattled from it. 'Could you not see you were on the wrong side of the dual carriageway? You're a lucky man to be alive.'

'You're right, boss,' Barry said. 'Lucky man I am, I must admit.' He hesitated. 'I knew I was on the wrong side. But I said to myself, if I turn round now and go back, the boss is going to miss the off, and I know you're carrying money for nearly everybody here with the exception of the teetotaller in the box.'

'No excuse,' Connaughton said doubtfully as he turned away.

Taylor staggered, a new tremor in his step, in the hotel's direction. It was only with Connaughton's disclosure that the horror of their driving ways had dawned on him.

'And besides,' Barry said to him, 'both you and I know what would have happened if we were to turn around and go back: the sergeant would never be able to U-turn on that road. Bad driver. We'd only show him up badly.'

'You're a blind so-and-so driver,' said Taylor. 'Could you not see them all flashing headlights coming against us. And it broad daylight!'

Connaughton had rushed away to the racecourse, on another death-defying mission. It was not until years later, in the story's retelling, that he permitted himself, that he had the time, to laugh outright.

RACING

K F. SLATTERY ARRIVED AT Connaughton's Hotel early on the night before. Connaughton's children followed him down the long corridor. He was shown his room and retired early. They had seen his riding stick poke out of his travelling bag.

Connaughton had a lot of business to attend to before they set out for the races next morning.

'We'll say a prayer, boss.' Fanning, his butcher, stuck his nose into the car as they left. 'The town is behind you.' He banged his hand down on the roof. And they were gone. As if kick-started. With the town's money.

K.F. Slattery sat motionless in the passenger seat all the drive up. The part in his greased, black hair was as straight down the centre as that in Connaughton's. Together they made a single-gauge railway. The boy and girl sat behind.

The conversation was horses, courses, livestock, bloodstock, land. K.F. enquired about New Hope, but did not ask for his instructions. Connaughton never gave his instructions until just before the off.

'He's a wide, generous horse' was all he would say. 'He likes to go at his own pace. But don't fight with him.'

In the back seat the children ran racing commentaries; they could list the names of all the top steeplechasers. They leaped up and down in the bench seat.

In between commentaries, as was the case on all their trips, both had their private battles with car sickness: Connaughton drove a car like he rode a horse. Spurs in the flanks: clutch, brake, accelerate, nudge, kick, nudge.

Something was up. Even the children were aware: Mama had not come down to say goodbye. She had dressed them for the day but said her goodbye with a wave from the big window of the Commercial Room.

Connaughton caught Holy Communion at a church in one of the small towns – Rathdowney – on the way up. That was nothing new. He always caught Communion; only the town varied. And the jockey did not catch Communion. Connaughton was disappointed but said nothing. He bought a packet of cigarettes; nothing new there either. But something was up.

It was a bright day on the course, mild for early spring. The sun sparkled off the stables, gables, the glass frontage of the weigh room, the bronze dome on the clock above the stewards' room. It shone on the parade-ring railings, separated the impatient horses within from the calculating, murmuring onlookers.

All the horses seemed over-energetic. Each one pushed purposefully against the tail of the one before it. Each handler leaned back on his reins, attempted, like a failing tug-o'-war contestant, to gain footholds in the yielding grass.

A big chestnut mare plunged out of line. First she bruised against the railings, where a section of the gallery jumped backwards in good-humoured alarm, then she leaped into empty space in the centre of the ring. The horse behind quickened its stride, filled the gap that the chestnut had created.

The two children dangled on the rails. They watched the gaps in the chain of horses, watched them fill as new horses entered the ring.

Suddenly, as if at some secret signal, the swirling bracelet of manes, hooves, bit bitings and hanging racing blankets broke. The horses converged on the ring's centre where jockeys, owners and trainers – they seemed to have come from nowhere yet had now become a crowd – awaited them.

'Look.' The girl tugged at her brother's arm. 'I see Uncle Pearse. He's in there in the middle with Dada.' She pointed.

Her brother looked for his father's racing colours: satin green and scarlet sashes; he picked Slattery out. Yes, there was his uncle. Tall, stooping to the jockey, saying something through the side of his mouth. His father was in there too. At the horse's side. Back humped, head hidden beneath the saddle flaps. He tightened the saddle girths. The horse expanded itself as he did so, gave a few backward flicks of its hind legs. Connaughton led it round on his left arm; relaxed it as he would a child. Gently, he slipped the girth buckle, then with one upward tug of his right arm he shot it into its slot.

Jockeys were rising above the crowd. They shortened stirrup leathers, hunched themselves into position. Slattery made a hop; Connaughton legged him on. For a moment he teetered over the saddle, a slither of green and red, almost went over the side. Then he was aboard.

'Slippery Arse Slattery,' said an onlooker close to the children. 'True to his name. What chance New Hope with Slippery Arse on his back?'

'Little,' someone else laughed. 'Little hope for New Hope. You can have twenty-five to one on New Hope.'

'Twenty-five to one.' The children didn't know what

twenty-five to one meant, yet the dismissive tone puzzled them. Somehow, they didn't know how, they had got the impression coming up in the car that New Hope had a chance.

All the horses were mounted. Jockeys bent down in their saddles, received final instructions from trainers. Trainers looked up at them, made arm movements, as though they themselves were riding out the finish.

'Don't give him his head unless he absolutely asks for it,' Connaughton said. 'He has little ways of saying when he is well in himself.' Connaughton darted one side then the other of New Hope's wildly jerking neck. 'And he's been saying it recently.' He did not wish to raise his voice yet the horse's movements made him do so. 'Don't let him off ahead unless he wants to because he can be foolish. Just keep him steady. Keep him on the bit. He's the good old boy today, aren't you?' He slapped his New Hope on the neck and smiled his first smile of the day. 'He can make mistakes when he's like this but keep him there and he'll go for you when you ask him.'

He did not mention the blood vessels. There was no point. What could Slattery do if the horse burst a blood vessel? He had given the injection. He hoped it would take effect. That was all he could do. And say a prayer.

Then the ring was empty. The horses cantered down to the start at the other side of the course. The crowd swirled in all directions at once. Those who did not scramble for vantage points raced to the bookies. It was the biggest steeplechase on the calendar, the Leopardstown Chase, and the bookies were mobbed.

The children ran forward to their uncle Pearse. 'Get up there on the top stand,' he shouted. 'Your auntie Joan is up there.'

They clutched his fists, tried to open out his fingers, searched for the customary parcels of joy, the two half-crowns with which they could buy the incredibly tangy, incredibly yellow, orange squash of the racecourse. Little blue-nosed Willie Browne caught sight of Pearse.

They went into a tangle of words. Browne's words slipped over the brim of his wide hat; Pearse's funnelled down between the collar flaps of his coat.

'You have a great chance, Pearse, today. He looked in the bloom in the parade ring.'

'At twenty-five to one with the books, you must be the only one who thinks so.'

'Come on. You have him in perfect condition. Don't tell me New Hope isn't for this one. You didn't engage a crack jock just to give him the ride.'

Pearse made no reply.

Willie looked down at the children. They knew him, had often seen him with their father.

'Cute buckos, your connections.' Willie grabbed the boy by the arm. 'What do you think yourself, young fellow? Is he going to win?'

'I don't know. I don't know.' The boy bent to his knees as the pain of the little ex-jockey's hold gripped him.

'What about your own chestnut mare, Willie?' Pearse asked. 'What about QED, will she run?'

'Oh she's an old chestnut now! She'll either run well or she'll be tailed off and wheeled up. And if she is wheeled up it will be herself will stop her, if you get what I'm saying. You can't tell. You mightn't go wrong if you back her on the tote each way. Give you an interest in the race.' He laughed.

As they talked people rushed all about them. There was one big man. He laughed all the time he spoke to another man while at the same time craning his neck above the crowd, keeping an eye on everything that was registering on the book-makers' blackboards. He suddenly said, 'Now, make the burst for the bookies.'

Willie Browne disappeared too. The children rushed ahead to find Auntie Joan. Pearse stood at the foot of the stand wondering should he dart back to the tote, lay an insurance on Willie's QED.

On the stand people jostled for positions. The children squirmed between dark tunnels of bodies until suddenly they found themselves at the very front. There was an iron rail before them. As always, they thought they would not grow accustomed to the height, the open space, the drop. Quickly they did.

Joan had her calf-length camel coat on, and her wax imitation cherries. 'On your own today,' her whiskey-mellow voice beamed down at them. 'Pity Mama couldn't make it. The excitement was too much for her, your dad said.' They were pleased to see Joan. They enjoyed race meetings with her. Joan squeezed everything into an outing.

When Connaughton shouldered his way through to them he seemed relieved.

'Did you get it all on?' he asked Pearse.

Pearse nodded.

'At what price?'

'Twenty-fives and twenties.'

'Four to one Amber Point' – a dozen urging roars crisscrossed above the sway of last-minute backers below, vied with one another for the crowd's money – 'Nine to two Amber Point, six to one Knight Errant, and eight to one the field.'

The bookmakers' blackboards were lined out, one beside the next, below them. Whenever one board told a tale of money transactions it registered on all of the others within seconds. They swung on their uprights, figures were rubbed out, new figures appeared, they were in a race of their own.

Pearse studied the prices through his field glasses. 'He's still at twenties. Amber Point clear favourite. There's a bit of money going on old QED.' He laughed and shook his head.

Connaughton was not as dismissive. 'I wonder,' he said.

The girl asked for the glasses. Pearse adjusted them for her. The glasses were her vehicle into another, a cut-off world. They swept her beyond the stands, across the open fields, to the far end of the course. Down there at the start were the horses. She was in that other world with them. It was silent. In a sunny corner of the course. The horses wended about between one another. It seemed to her that over there a great conversation was going on. Such a conversation as might occur between actors, out of audience earshot, before a performance. There was the man with the white flag, the ambulance, a tractor and trailer. The ambulance followed the horses once they had started. She had noticed it before. It had to be on hand for fallen riders.

'What's the tractor doing out there, Dada?' she asked.

'Oh, it's in case a horse has to be put down, dear,' he said. 'It's carried back on the trailer.'

'Put down, what's that?'

'You know, destroyed.' His face pained. It frightened the child. A smell of something hot, very stiff and still, something sweating, overpowered her.

'They're under starter's orders . . .'

'They're off!' The commentary went out over the public address system. The crowd stirred. The public address system screeched and then went dead.

The silent movement on the other side of the course was mirrored by the silence on the stands. The bunched specks, grey in the distance, rose and fell again almost instantly.

'All safe over the first,' someone with field glasses said. One speck began to draw ahead of the others. Over each fence it seemed to quicken.

'New Hope is gone ahead,' Connaughton said grimly to Pearse. Pearse too looked grim. 'I told him not to, I told him.' Connaughton covered his face with his hands in a moment's despair, then picked up his glasses again.

New Hope cantered round the bend at the bottom of the course, into the straight. His tail was out, his ears pricked. Slattery wore goggles. Faceless, motionless on the horse's back, he seemed beyond reach of all human contact.

There was hardly a murmur as he passed before the stands. The hearts beat faster in Connaughton's little group. He was their big, bay-coloured horse. He had to stay ahead now. That head with the blaze of white down the forehead would have to lead all the way round again.

Then the others passed. The thunder of their hooves was immediate, alive. It coursed like brandy into the faces of the onlookers on the stands.

'Look,' one person said, 'New Hope is tiring, he's not travelling like a stayer.'

The favourite and second favourite flashed by. They led the bunch behind the leader.

'Come on, Amber Point,' a hard chorus of calls pleaded. His jockey stood on the stirrups, perfectly balanced, his body angled, parallel with his mount's neck.

It seemed he would sweep all before him.

New Hope made a mistake over the first after the stands. A gasp, like a flock of birds released suddenly through the support beams above, went up from the crowd. He recovered.

'I told you he's tiring.' The same man spoke again, this time with more conviction. 'They'll catch him!'

'That'll teach him a little lesson,' Connaughton whispered to Pearse, 'steady him.'

Then the bunch followed over the first after the stands. There was a rattle of hooves against sticks and they were out in the country.

Everything was quiet again for a few moments. A big bookie in long, grey tweed coat and dickie-bow tie saw his opportunity.

'I'll lay ten to one New Hope,' he shouted. It was a thrill to the children: hearing the name on its own like that, naked, almost as if their own names were called out.

A ripple passed through the stand. 'I'd take that offer,' someone behind them muttered, 'except I wouldn't be back for the finish in time to see him winning. He's threshin' like a steam engine out there.'

'Ah, you would not take it. You'd hold on to your money,' said the fellow who had earlier predicted the eclipse of New Hope, 'and you'd be right too. Any dark horse, as you and I know, ever won a race, never showed his true colours that far out.'

'Maybe not, maybe not.' If the frontrunner's mentor sounded suddenly unsure, New Hope still sailed out there – a sure thing.

The big bookie waited. He boxed his betting dockets in his hand, shuffled, flicked them from one hand to the other as he would a deck of cards. He consulted his clerk. 'Twelve to one New Hope,' he bellowed. 'Gone out to twelves.' Yet no one approached him to lay money on New Hope. He produced his trump: 'And ten to one Amber Point!' He held out his hands; the money came streaming in.

Suddenly the commentator's voice leaped at them out of the public address system. The horses were again out on the far side of the course.

'New Hope leads the field by twenty lengths,' the voice boomed. 'Knight Errant leads the bunch followed by Amber Point.' The voice whipped the crowd into excitement. The horses had another four fences to jump but they were already shouting on the stands: 'Come on Amber Point, make your move!' 'Come on Knight Errant!'

'He's jumping well,' Connaughton said as he watched through the glasses. 'He's jumping like a stag and taking nothing out of himself. K.F. only has to sit there.'

'It's a fast gallop he's set.' Pearse was worried.

'It is,' Connaughton, shaking his head, agreed.

'And New Hope is safely over,' the commentator thundered. 'Knight Errant is gone,' he shouted. 'The second favourite is a faller.' A shock wave blew through the crowd.

Connaughton looked at Pearse. 'Oh that's good, Dada, isn't it?' the boy said.

'And New Hope is safely over the regulation fence. Amber Point leads the rest of the field. But New Hope is full of running. He has two fences to jump.'

As the horses turned into the straight they seemed remote, removed – on a film screen. They plodded up the hill. The crowd roared.

One fence to jump. 'He's home bar a fall.' Pearse suddenly let go all his pent-up emotions.

'Oh come first New Hope,' Auntie Joan's mellow voice tinkled, 'you're winning.'

It was unreal. The children were over the railings. The air flashed black and white. They couldn't hear him. Couldn't hear his hooves, nor the crack of whips against necks from the charge behind. The horses behind didn't even seem to be moving forward.

There was only New Hope. He was coming to the last. It cut his body from view. His head bobbed above it. He was in front. He steadied for the fence. He was wrong-footed. No, he was right. Slattery threw a quick glance around to see how far ahead he was.

He was twenty lengths clear. New Hope rose. He was

taking a mightier leap than ever. The crowd rose to him, rose to the gallant stayer. 'Come on the boy,' somebody whooped. 'Come on the gamble, up the parish of Carrickmore.' He threw up his hat; it skimmed on the air into the bookmakers' tumult below. Then – it was in the flickering of an eyelid it happened – New Hope was on his own.

No one saw what happened, no one saw Slattery lose his seat. The roar rising for New Hope crashed into an even more almighty one. It ploughed like thunder across an overcast sky. It was as though some force from above and outside had suddenly beaten down on the crowd. The crowd was shaken, mercilessly, by its own roar of shock, of despair, of sympathy for the victims, of fear, of dismay. The roar was followed by a measurable moment of silence. In that moment, all the horses charging behind, the riderless one, the jockey on the grass, all stopped still. Life itself seemed to stop. Then the crowd shook its shoulders; the roars began again; the race was on again. The whips swung again with renewed purpose. The children saw New Hope pass the post, bemused, his saddle flaps flaying like rudimentary wings. They saw nothing else; a charge of horses crossed before them – they neither saw nor heard them.

'And QED wins! A length from Amber Point in second place. It's a photo for third.'

It was over. 'Willie Browne's fella, hah!' People ran to collect bets, to place bets, to watch the presentation of the trophy. 'Winner all right.' Connaughton's party stood alone on the stand.

'He took off too early,' Connaughton said to Pearse. 'Slattery shouldn't have looked around.' It was his only word of blame.

A few moments later Connaughton was on the paddock. New Hope was out there, standing perfectly still, reins on the ground, ears pricked, puzzled. Connaughton walked slowly over, reined him in.

Hot air rose from the open sunroof of a hot-dog van outside the stiles. They passed through. Within the van, frying onions sizzled, and weakened by the smell, the children slowed down. But the adults walked on. The last race was in progress. They walked across the car park, between the cars flashing in the evening sun, the public address commentary following them. A few people stood on car roofs, watched the race through field glasses. Once again, as on the five previous occasions, horses drew up to the line. The commentator's voice quickened, exploded and died away.

The buses passing by outside the hotel, swaying up and down the quays where they had parked, were now imagined rather than heard. It was night-time, yet in the dining room it did not seem so. A fluorescent light, set outside the windows, created an artificial daylight.

Every time a waitress appeared through the swing doors she was followed by a clatter of heat and steam.

Heavy hotel cutlery cast but a dull reflection at the eyes lowered about the table.

The children had recovered their spirits. They sought and received permission to go to the toilets again and again, using the opportunity to explore. Joan too felt cheered.

A severe-looking waitress stood above them. She gave off a starchy sound as she moved around the table. Yet her uniform, dampened by the evening on the dining-room floor, was as limp as the napkin held across her arm.

'Would you like to order, sir?'

Connaughton looked pained. He didn't feel like any food, he said.

'Lamb cutlets for Joan, is it?' Pearse enquired with unconvincing bonhomie: Joan liked the cutlets at the Clarence.

'Please,' she nodded. 'With mushrooms and stuffed tomato.'

'And I'll have the mixed grill.' He directed his whisper behind Connaughton's back and handed the menu back to the waitress.

'I'll have steak and chips.' The boy did not go through any intermediaries but called his order directly to the waitress.

'And me too,' said his sister.

It was a shock diversion.

Everybody looked at Connaughton. A light might flicker out of the despair; it might as easily snuff out again.

Unquestioning, as though the children were adults, the waitress took the order down. 'Two steak and chip.' She waited a moment. 'Is da it then?' Her earnest pronouncement fell flatly on the table.

'Yes . . .' The fractures appeared in Connaughton's gloom. 'Yes, we lose the Leopardstown Chase and all they can think of is steaks. Yes, two sirloin steaks. What will you have, K.F.? The mixed grill. And the chicken salad for me.' He chuckled as he gave the order.

K.F. thought deeply as he ate. He felt there was something he should say.

'He took off too early,' he said in the end, shaking his head, 'he was too keen.'

'See that mustard there?' Connaughton pointed at the puckered smather on the side of his plate. 'He was keener than that.'

'I wonder . . .' Connaughton went on after a few minutes. 'I wonder how much that big bookie in the dickie bow stood to lose had Amber Point pipped QED instead of the other way round?'

'Oh, you could ask Willie Browne that one,' Pearse answered.

'You mean they were in it together?'

'Indeed they were. And if you care to walk down the corridor and into the lounge you'll see they still are.'

The seed of another question cracked in Connaughton's brain. He tried to contain it, but instead it grew stronger.

He saw, clearly, New Hope at the top of the course. How effortlessly he had cleared each fence! He saw the bookie call those fantastic odds on Amber Point. The favourite! Twenty lengths behind! How otherwise could he have called those odds? And how otherwise could he have got hold of the backers' money? It was because New Hope had gone so far ahead.

A question continued to burn in his brain.

The question was for K.F., but he did not ask it. How much extra, he wanted to ask, how much extra had that bookie and Browne stood to gain through K.F.'s handling of the race?

Enough to pay for one jockey's fall?

He watched K.F. meekly butter a thin slice of bread.

Hardly.

THE VIEW FROM COLLEGE HILL

TWO TINKER CHILDREN STOOD gazing up at the poster on the wall outside the hotel. They wore outsized overcoats and wellingtons. The girl pointed up while her younger brother pulled her by the hand. The sharp sun pinned their shadowless forms to the pavement.

There was an aeroplane on the poster. Zooming across the top of the page, like the children it stood out in sharp, unsurrounded outline. A man in goggles, with smile as broad as the wingspan, waved out of the open cockpit.

AERIAL DISPLAY AT COLLEGE HILL

it said in big blurred print. 'Take-off time 3 p.m. Sunday 1st July', it said below in handwriting and below that, in print again,

SQUADRON LEADER (BOMBER) SCANLAN (WAR ACE)

Connaughton passed the tinker children as he walked to his car on the kerbside. Something touched him – the sight of these children, dressed for rain in the brightest sun. Any other time they would be in rags. He was reminded again of the burned-out hoop of caravan in the camp at town's edge, the cinder of a baby that had brought the townspeople together and bought new clothes for the tinker children. Connaughton would have liked to drive them out to the air display along with his own children. Yet he did not offer.

Cars turned onto the wide street. Over the hump on the top of the town each car lifted its tail for a moment and then scooted around the bend towards College Hill. With each moment the street became quieter. Connaughton and his children passed cyclists. And, as they drew nearer to College Hill racecourse, walkers. They strode singly and in groups: grown-ups, children and prams.

'What's it like up in an aeroplane, Dada?' Connaughton's two children wanted to know. 'Is it like in the car?' They stood in the back of the car, gripped his seat; excitement would not let them sit still.

He turned round and smiled at them.

'No it's not like in the car. More like in the sitting room. On a sofa. Except you have a better view.'

Connaughton's answer gave the children a few moments' silent thought, allowed him remember his own flying experiences. He had twice flown to Lourdes and loved it. He would always remember one moment in particular. It was when the plane tilted and, looking down, he saw directly beneath him the snow peaks of the Pyrenees. Like teeth. Between him and the mountains there had been nothing. For one frantic second he had thought of what the drop might be like: if the side of the plane he leaned against fell open – one silent, screaming drop. Even now he had to shake his mind free of it. Free of the terrible but luxurious imaginings he kept most of the time under control.

'And are we really going up, Dada?' they wanted to know. The first indication he had given them that they would fly had not been until they had got in the car.

Mother did not know about it. 'They are too young to fly up in an aeroplane?' Her question had been in the form of an imperative.

'Yes,' he had agreed, 'they are.' Yet she had hugged them more fiercely than normally, had waved, as though she would never see them again, until they were out of sight.

'We are,' he now answered the children's question. 'Flying' – he pursed his lips in pleasure as he always did when choosing his phrases, enunciating them clearly, and even for his children he chose them, always laughing as he did so at the thought of young minds grappling with big words – 'flying is an exhilarating experience: an experience neither of you should miss. A wonder of the modern world.'

But for Barry, he would have told them of his European crossings.

A group of men stood on the iron-railed bridge below College Hill racecourse. Ambush Bridge it was known as locally. During the War of Independence it had been the scene of a skirmish in which both sides had casualties. Barry stood among the men: erect, yet leaning against the crossbar of his bicycle – his pulpit – doing all the talking.

Connaughton would not have noticed him – selected rather than random items dominated Connaughton's line of vision (the random items reappeared in his mind only years later, often resurrecting with them vague yet uncontrollable feelings of nostalgia). But as he approached the bridge Barry dashed from the group, a stung bullock from a herd, and flagged him down.

'A funeral in Killea, boss,' he shouted his greeting. 'A Missus Maher. It'll be tomorrow.'

'Which Maher, Barry?' The Killea district was a constant flux into and out of life of Mahers; the two men could not decide on which one of them it might be who had died and therefore on whether the deceased's family would employ Connaughton or the town's other undertaker.

'Come in tomorrow in any case.' Connaughton gave his

hearse driver his instructions and was about to pull away – it was getting hot in the stationary car – when Barry for the first time noticed the children.

'You're not taking them up in the aeroplane?' A bloodshot eye accused him as he thumbed over his shoulder at the hill above.

'I may do, Barry. Why?'

'I don't know why, does their mother know?' Barry looked doubtfully at the children for a moment. 'I suppose ye'll be all right.' In Barry's eyes his own driving was masterful (Connaughton thought otherwise) whereas Connaughton's was downright dangerous. It would still be dangerous once he had left the ground. Even if he was but a passenger.

'I may do, Barry. Why?' Connaughton chuckled. Barry amused him.

It was perfect flying weather on College Hill. The sock balloon tugged at its staypole. It lunged and shied away from Devil's Bit mountain. The northeasterly was cold, clouds rushed by and in the intervals the sun warmed through the dark clothes of the gathering. Shouts and laughter lifted on a wind that made waves in the buttercups and grass, battered nettles. The road below ran straight across the chequerboard country until reaching the little river. Crossing the iron bridge it took a different direction. Cars moved along it, distant and silent, towards the air display. In a roadside field, cows grazed. A few colts threw heads in a small, angular field.

The farmer owner stood in his gate, a leather purse enveloped by his hand. Two rope lengths along the crest of the hill marked off the runway.

Inside the field, car doors were already wide open. People poked into luggage boots, poured tea, balanced sandwiches on car hoods.

The crowd was thickest in a corner of the field to the right
of the gate. There, a three-card-trick man had set himself up
with the equipment of his life's calling: a pack of cards and
a wooden box. There was roulette; the operator spun his wheel,
its numbers raced round and became a blur. Tack atak atak
– nails on the wheel slapped against the staying leather strap.
It slowed – somebody raised a hand: 'That's me number' –
but caught in the wind the wheel started up again, slapped
past the number. A man with a monkey on his back sold raf-
fle tickets. The monkey tore up the duplicates of those he had
sold. Connaughton drove past all of this diversion, over the
flattened grass tracks. Then, making fresh tracks, he drove to
the upper end of the car park and away from everybody else.
As soon as his children jumped from the car they raced back
to the sideshows.

A few people lined up on one side of the ropes, as though
waiting for the end of a point-to-point race as yet out in the
country.

Suddenly, from nowhere, the hum found them. They
scrutinised the sky. Different directions were pointed to.

'Look, there he is.' A man shot his arm in the air. A huge
red-faced man, in one arm he held a large child. He had thrown
up his head and the curly auburn lock, which was all the hair
he had, caught in the wind. It budged a few times, then a gust
lifted it from his forehead. It flew back across the collar of his
coat, a flapping wing.

'There she is,' he roared, 'she's flying out of the mountain.'
He caught the lock, trained it over his poll again. 'Can ye not
see her over there?'

At length everybody could see the aeroplane. It lowered
towards them. The noise grew louder, ever louder, until some,
fearing deafness, wished it would go away.

It headed towards the runway. Everybody now stood well back from the ropes. Its engines slowed, the onlookers could hear them tick over, they seemed to go dead. The plane dropped. 'He's out of petrol,' somebody said. 'He's going to crash.' The wheels bumped against the ground, shuddered into the plane's undercarriage. 'She'll fall apart,' a man said. Then the engines roared back to life, the plane rose sharply. For a second there was the flash of a face behind the perspex but the plane nosed into the air and banked away so quickly that those who thought they had seen the face could not be sure.

The aeroplane looped high in the air. Once. Twice. Three times. With each upward swing its engines belched, on each downward swoop they died away. It climbed a fourth time. But then the engines choked; they died altogether. Like a hawk, it stood directly overhead for a moment. Then, hesitantly, it turned on its wings. It turned, falling, twirled like a swallow, twirled a few more times and then went into freefall. There was silence in the air, silence in the crowd. Then the horror of what was befalling them dawned.

'He's going to crash on top of us,' someone shouted. Like the whorl of hair from the crown of a head the crowd parted away from a centre; became one with the general scatter of cattle and colts. All backs were turned from the flimsy construction that was falling among them. When the engines returned to life again, now almost at their ears, they ran even faster. Some looked around, almost in time to see the plane buoy away and once again complete its loop. Then it landed.

The pilot lifted himself out of the cockpit. A tall, thin man, he stood on the wing, spread his legs and waited. It was some moments before the drift of crowd neared the plane.

'Come closer,' he said when the movement stopped. He had a gentle voice. It surprised people. After the boom of the engines, the clack of the propellers, his voice was as much part of the quietness as the crowd's slow shuffle across the grass.

He leaned down over the fuselage, yanked open a door. 'Feel free,' he said. 'Look inside.' He returned to his stance bestriding the wing, above the wave of bobbing heads that surrounded his plane.

Arguments started. Over the different switches and buttons on the mahogany dashboard, over the dials, the gauges – what each indicated: whether the figures pertained to knots, to miles per hour, windspeed, oil pressure, altitude or air time.

'How much can you knock out of her, lad?' a burly, tractor-tanned man called up through funnelled hands.

'Over two hundred miles per hour, sir, I would expect.' The airman deliberated over his answer. 'Given optimal conditions. Yes, fast enough to get in and out of this place.' He risked a joke, but nobody laughed.

'What did I tell you?' the brown-faced man thumped a person beside him. 'I knew she'd hit the two ton!'

'And how high will she take you?' was the brown man's next question.

'Into an atmosphere thinner than you or I would feel comfortable in.'

The crowd listened quietly to each reply from the airman but a low murmur followed the next remark to come from among them. It came from a thin man who stood close to the brown-faced man and whose pale face was barely visible beneath a slouch hat. 'Atmosphere indeed. Is any atmosphere thin enough, or cold enough, for you English and your blasted war machines? A nerve you have, coming back to this country.'

The airman was the first to recover: 'Well I'm hardly at war now, old chap. Now I'm a circus act. This blasted machine as you call it can just as easily be an instrument of pleasure as of war. Have I ever, in any case, been at war with you? Or with your country?'

His listeners shuffled.

'I have not. And why on earth ever should I?'

The hushed gathering, whipped by the wind, pushed even closer together.

'He's right, he's right, a brave man begod.' The brown-faced man again spoke up. The murmur again rose up, this time, it seemed, in approval.

Connaughton had held well clear of the throng about the plane. Until suddenly the airman raised his voice to a new level.

'It's a four-seater,' he said. 'De Havilland Rapide. Spick. Span. I will take you in threes. Any three of you are welcome. First flight fifteen hundred hours. That is now.' He had thrown down his gauntlet.

In the silence that followed there were a few whisperings. For the first time the click of the engine could be heard. Beneath its slitted hood it tinkled and contracted, like cooling coal clinkers. The wind made musical sounds through the propellers.

'If those of you on the ground would like to watch, I will, with the permission of the first fliers from Carrickmore, demonstrate how a bombing mission is accomplished,' he said. 'You will watch the road down there. And we will assume the bridge you can see of strategic advantage to the enemy. Enemy's only access across the river, yes? What is the river called?'

'The Suir, sir,' someone piped up.

'The Sewer,' he mispronounced. 'The enemy wants to cross the Sewer. On no account can it be allowed. So. We will first fly over the town. An aerial view. Then, on the return journey, a simulated bombing of the bridge.'

The people looked about at one another, moved back a little from the plane, while, above, the airman stood on his wing and gazed beyond the flat countryside at Devil's Bit mountain.

'Ha, a courageous man, make way for the first fliers from Carrickmore,' he said when he saw Connaughton, arm raised, move through the crowd. 'But have no fear. I have flown through one war; crash-landed in France once and have no intention of doing so again. Not on College Hill. Unless I am forced to.' He slid one leather-booted foot forward, brushed it along the tapered wing of his plane as if he were testing the wing's sharpness; the crowd beneath saw the lacing in the vent of his jodhpurs contract. 'Post-world-war bus,' he said. 'Best circus plane, reliable. Make way for my first fliers.'

'It's Connaughton, who owns the hotel,' the tractoring-tanned man said as the crowd stood back and then came together again. They surrounded Connaughton, his children and the aeroplane, at the same time separating themselves from them.

The children were snapped into seats. Preconceived notions of the inside of a plane and its likeness to anything they had imagined, let alone their sitting room, were quickly snatched from their minds. The seats into which they were pinned were in a sort of low comfortable pouch at the rear; the leather upholstery crinkled like an old car's; they had a wing on either side, their father and the pilot before them. The noise of the plane when it started up seemed to be outside rather than within. By lifting their eyes to window level they could see the fields running in a novel manner away from them, on-lookers' faces merged in a scramble of eyes, noses. All was beyond their control. It was safe.

Up front Connaughton felt no such sense of security. He might as well be out there on the bonnet. Takeoff stuck him to his seat. He wanted to see if his children were all right but his neck, weak as those telegraph poles that suddenly rose out of the hill and bent in the middle as they sped by, would not turn his head around.

He could not believe anything could travel so quickly and wondered why the fields rushed all the time up at him instead of away. He closed his eyes. Then he was away. He opened his eyes. He was airborne.

He passed over the backs of a herd of bullocks. College Hill receded. The crowd became a shrinking stain on the hillside.

Everything was changing. All constancy dissolving. He closed his eyes again.

Then the children began pointing. Up there, in that rattling flying structure, a quarter of a mile above their own familiar town, their visions too took flight.

'Look,' they shouted, prodding into the yielding perspex glass.

'Look Dada a car. Look at how slow it goes on the road. I see a person. It's a doll.' They laughed gleefully. 'It's a doll's town. Look at the funny man Dada on the bike.' They couldn't believe it: the cows become dogs, the dogs invisible. It was a toy town.

Connaughton opened his eyes, looked, ruefully, horizontally into space. He looked into the far horizon of clouds and hills. Slowly he neared his gaze. A lightness soared up through the soles of his feet, into the base of his spine, would not let him look directly beneath. Slowly it eased, he settled in his seat. A flood of enjoyment displaced the feeling he had felt of free suspension in space. He identified the town: the wide main street; the church, silent and erect on the town's perimeter; the army barrack square, grey building surrounded; the lake; the hurling pitch.

'What a wonderful view,' he enthused to the pilot. 'Carrickmore, I have always heard told, garrison town.'

Now Connaughton could see it: one straight sweep of road a mile long from the station to the town hall street – straight for

lines of marching men. Another road, straight also, crisscrossing this one. Leaving the steps of the church and finding the
gates of the barracks. He pointed out the features to the pilot.

'Yes,' the pilot nodded, 'military town, well laid out.
Reminds me of a town we levelled in France.

'Hold tight now,' he suddenly announced.

He brought the plane out of its circular glide above the town,
nosed it round towards College Hill. Within moments they
found the straight stretch of road that snaked towards the bridge,
the advance point of an imagined enemy. They raced directly
above it. It drew nearer, nearer; passed beneath faster, faster.
Now the children looked down over the heads of the elders.
Saw the road rise up to meet them. It was their turn to be
scared.

'Stop, stop,' one of them shouted, and again, 'stop, stop,'
hysterical now. 'Stop' – it was the only word he could say.

The onlookers on the hill also thought a crash imminent.
The plane they had watched soar about the sky, inscribe arcs
as graceful as any bird's, now seemed set on a headlong colli-
sion with the earth. The wind buffeted into them, drew at
trouser legs and frock ends, pushed the grass, rushed it against
children's bare legs. They, looking up, moved unconsciously
about in the wind as the plane dived.

When it was but a tree's height above the road it straightened. It straightened and sped parallel with the road.

'He's goin' to drop the bomb on the bridge,' someone
shouted. 'That's what he tould us he's at!'

Bomber Scanlan sighted his target. 'Go easy, for God's sake,'
Connaughton yelled. He pumped furiously at the foot panel
below him. A reflex: he braked, clutched, hammered a quick
tattoo on the boards with his shoe soles but found no pedals.

Then he saw Barry. Barry and the bike on the centre of
the bridge. Transfixed. 'You'll hit him,' Connaughton

bawled. 'For God's sake think of the children.' The plane dropped lower. As it seemed they must spreadeagle him Barry made his move. As fast as the speed of the plane he dived into the undergrowth alongside the end railing of the bridge. And disappeared, leaving the bicycle flat on the roadway.

'Bombs away,' the pilot whooped, pressing his thumb against an imaginary button on the dashboard, and the plane rose, leaving Connaughton's stomach and those of his two children behind, cratered on the road surface.

Now it was silent prayer time. 'Stop,' one of the children continued to sob. Connaughton prayed for an end.

And it came quickly. The landing and the taxi across the grass were as something in a dream – something partaken in only as outsiders, something quickly forgotten but never emptied from the mind.

Yet as soon as the children were hoisted from the cockpit by other would-be passengers they became excited. Words would not string together quickly enough for them to describe all they had seen.

Connaughton said nothing. He had become detached. The grass on which he walked was to him a strange new experience. He felt for his feet on it. College Hill itself, the people's faces, the over-excited colts in the paddock below, they were all things his attention ran out towards. There was so much of everything, all so rich. He wondered how a flight in an aeroplane could have done this to him.

On the way home they stopped at the bridge. The bike was gone. There was a flattened pathway through a forest of head-high nettles. It seemed some crazed bullock must have ploughed through, lay now panting, mortal, on the other side.

An image of the horrified Barry passed through Connaughton's mind. 'Bombs away,' he whispered. He chuckled.

Another image stood before him. This time it would not pass so lightly away. Again it was Barry. But it was not so much Barry, the lovable, slightly dotty Barry he knew, as Barry the image of all men. An image outstretched in terror. The amusement on his face turned to a frown. For he had remembered something else.

'Bombs away,' he said again, this time to the children in the seat behind. 'Can you imagine what it must be like to be bombed?'

He studied them for a moment in his driving mirror. Wondered could they understand what it was he was about to tell them and then began.

'I remember once I was in Dublin.' He looked into his mirror, they were listening, they listened to all his stories. 'It was the day of a famous All-Ireland Hurling Final. The Thunder and Lightning final it was called. 1939. It rained incessantly all through the match. Everyone was drenched' – he shook his shoulders for emphasis – 'and yet the game was so close that not a sinner left the grounds until the final whistle blew.

'Yes, they knocked sparks with the hurleys.' He thought about the match for a few moments and then went on. 'I remember distinctly walking down the city afterwards through the crowds. It was early evening but dark. Thunder still crashed away overhead.

'I saw faces in the street that evening that were frozen with fear. Those poor people.' He paused for a few moments. 'Barry on the bridge just now reminded me of them. And do you know who those people were?' Remembering his listeners, his voice softened. 'They were the first influx of refugees from the bombings in eastern Europe. Poles, burned out of their homes.

'Interesting-looking people, I spoke to a few of them. They had actually been to the match, I don't know how they had got there – the government maybe, trying to decide what to do with them, trying to make up to them for what they had just come through. And they had a surprisingly good command of English. They would have been, I would say . . . ' his lips pursed, anticipating his own choice phrases even in contemplating this sad event. 'They would have been from the upper echelons of Polish society. They spoke but did not look at you. Unsuitably clad, summer clothes on them sizes too big. Huddled in doorways.'

He nodded his head, looked into the mirror at his children's attentive faces, searched within them for comprehension.

'I wasn't a bit scared were you Dada?' one of them burst at length.

'No, not a bit,' he answered.

'Not a bit,' he repeated softly to himself.

He drove home along the flat road, deep a few moments in his reflections. Looking in the mirror again, his own pleading eyes took him by surprise.

WHY DID THE HEN CROSS THE ROAD?

THE PETROL SEEMED TO EMPTY endlessly. And the day was beautiful and long.

These two impressions merged in the child's mind as he watched the vapour rise from the petrol tank, ripple the creeper-covered house behind and disappear in the hot air above the escallonia behind the pumps. He sat in the car's stuffy leather.

Three and elevenpence, four shillings, four and a penny, the figures clanked by the money meter, slow as the dates on a moving-calendar. The meter stuck on fifteen shillings, the grinding noise ended, the woman yanked the petrol gun out of the tank, stumbled backwards as she did so, a hank of lard-blonde hair sliding across her face.

From behind the house there returned the sound of farmyard noises. Then she re-entered the gun. It jumped into emission. The noises were again drowned.

Miss Jackson, so broad a face, blue eyes set so far apart, seemed vacant. Yet, for all her apparent vacancy, Miss Jackson never allowed the pumps to slip petrol a halfpenny-worth beyond the amount requested. Except on the rare occasions when somebody pulled up at the pumps and said, 'Fill her up.' Then she clamped her hand down on the release lever, let the petrol pour and, because no limit had been set at which her mind must return to the present, it wandered away until the petrol gushed upward from the tank, splashed onto the roadway and woke her.

Customers argued over these last pennies of wasted petrol. But it was useless. 'I'm afraid I can't tell how much has spilled, sir,' she always said – her excuse for allowing no deductions for her carelessness.

Connaughton did not say 'Fill her up.' He said, 'See how much it takes' – it was less familiarising, more cautious. The last time he had asked to 'see how much it takes' he had bridled about the spillage. But she was impenetrable. He had remained in bad humour for an hour. 'Goose,' he had pronounced in the end.

He had forgotten. Today, again, because tomorrow he was off to Ballinrobe races, he ordered, 'See how much it takes.'

Miss Jackson, who had been disturbed from her dream at fifteen shillings, now returned to it: to her dog, her fat Jack Russell; to how he ate up his milk and boiled potatoes. She pictured him: his neat little way at first – checking the potatoes were not too hot, in the end gulping – like the wolf that must somewhere be in him. Then she thought of her own dinner. Of her boiled mutton. She hoped her sister would not take it off the boil. Not until it was soft and almost falling off the bone, the grizzle melted and marled into the meat.

She jumped back from the car. Too late; she felt the cold, anaesthetising effect of petrol as it splashed through her summer dress onto her thigh. Then, with a clank that shook the pumps, she stuffed the nozzle in its slot.

'Twenty-three shillings it took, sir.' She studied the money meter. 'And three pence.' He decided not to quibble over the spillage.

The boy was almost asleep in the back of the car. 'Nice day, Miss Jackson.' Connaughton closed the door gently as he stood out on the road to talk to her. 'Good hay weather.'

She looked at him and did not reply. A gust of wind swept under the car, the engine cracked as it cooled down: it was good hay-making weather.

He had decided not to quibble over the wasted petrol because he was on a mission and just now it had occurred to him she ought to be of assistance.

'Have you saved your own?' he asked.

He thought she might have. He had seen hay cut in one of Jackson's fields as he had driven past a few days previously. No rain had fallen since.

'It's still on the ground,' she was about to say. It had been her first reaction. The fact was, however, she and her brother and sister had lifted it into cocks only the previous day – Sunday. And though Catholics often saved hay on Sundays, people of her religion did not, having the Faith in the Lord to wait. She felt a vague sense of wrongdoing, rather of having fallen from a position of superiority. It was she had persuaded the other two. Yes, she'd said. She knew it was the Lord's Day. They had a dairy herd. The town depended on them for milk during the winter months...

Her terrier came ratting through the gravel round the pumps. It stopped beneath Connaughton and straightaway, without looking, straddled one of his legs. 'Oh, you naughty Sydney,' she whispered. 'Devil.' And lifted him with her right arm onto the supportive ledge of her left.

'One field of it is all is saved,' she said.

'Bless the work, good and early. I wondered ...' Connaughton chose his words. '...I seem to have run out of hay... I wondered if I might have a lock from you?'

'A sop, Mr Connaughton?' she questioned him. She had never heard of a lock, wondered if it was more than a sop.

'It's for a horse of mine running tomorrow, Miss Jackson.

I want him content in himself. A lock is enough. He'll go out on summer grass once this race is over.'

Content in himself. Miss Jackson nodded. She understood contentment: its presence in the dairy among her own cows . . . the first, excited head-butting of the hay. Shredding it. Grinding it down. Jaw muscles, like leather purses, filling, emptying, rhythmic. Eyes blindfolded in pleasure. Dribbles of digestion . . .

She wondered would she run into the yard behind, to her brother, ask him what he thought of Connaughton's request. But the vague sense of guilt she still felt about her Sunday labours helped her to her own decision. 'You may,' she said. Give some of it away, it was how her mind worked, give away her guilt. 'Should I . . .' she faltered, ' . . . put some of my money on your horse?'

'Yes,' he joked to himself, knowing that informing her was not going to set the town in a rage of fancy for his horse – upset its market price. For she would have nobody to whom she could pass on the information. 'Yes,' he laughed – the thought of her fortunes on his horse's back – 'but not too much, mind.'

As he drove away his son woke and lifted himself on the back seat. He turned round just in time to see the broad, quizzical face of the woman holding the dog as it shrank behind in the distance.

He strode quickly across the hayfield. The boy bounded along as best he could in his father's wake. His father walked too fast and the grass-stalk stubble scraped his sandalled bare feet. The tossed, tousled look of fresh-made hay had already left the haycocks. They sagged now, sun-settled, their backs sleek as the backs of animals.

Connaughton and his son stopped, in an intensity of heat,

in the centre of a hamlet of haycocks that threw off the scorch of the early afternoon sun.

Connaughton's hand dived into the heart of a cock. He held it there a few moments in silence, a concentrated look on his face as though he were divining something. Then he tugged, withdrawing a wisp of hay from the cock's butt. He shoved his nose in the wisp, shook his head from side to side. As he plundered the hearts, randomly, of other cocks, shaking his head in disappointment, muttering 'heated', a silence yet prevailed. The only sound was the sweep of his feet through the after-grass, the crackle of rattleweed. The boy was overpowered by the apparent permanence of the haycocks. His own presence, and the presence of the hay-cocks, together, in relation to a distant hum, somewhere, very far away but all-encircling and pierced every now and then by dog barks, puzzled him. Connaughton already looked towards the hay in the adjoining field.

The adjoining field was one of the biggest in all that area: three fields, knocked at some time into one. And it was the only field in all that flat area that climbed. It went over the brow of a hill and fell away some distance, how far it was not possible to say, on the far side. The field, as far as the eye could see, was mown.

Connaughton strode across the dividing wall. The boy followed but brought rocks tumbling from the wall.

'Can you not be more careful,' his father said, pained, 'making gaps like that, cattle to walk through.'

It was a cooler field. Hay lay scattered about it, dry but not yet cocked. Its green was as fresh grass, perfumed, herbs and grasses distinguishable from one another, not yet a uniform mass. No heating in it.

Connaughton gathered a double armful and headed, trip-ping – not seeing where he was going – over the swathes on the ground to the car.

A figure stood on the crest of the hill as he returned for his second load. He gathered his armful (he had seen the figure) and heard shouts: 'Who do you think you are?' They were directed, to his intense irritation, at him. Like rocks, they clunked down the hill. 'Who do you think you are? That's my fuckin' hay.'

With but a few footsteps, giant footsteps they seemed to the boy, the man was upon them. Up to this moment the boy had conceived of time as a dawdle. The heat of the car, Miss Jackson's unrestricting face, then the heat of the haycocks, had wafted, hammocked him. Now, with the man's abrupt arrival, everything closed in jerky motion about him. 'Leave that down,' the man shouted. 'Walking in here like that. Who do you think you fuckin' are?' The rape of his property; the man's amazement was uncontainable.

The boy was frightened, Connaughton indignant. 'What do you mean, leave it down? What do you mean, who do I think I am?' he said.

'Oh, I know who you are all right,' the man said. 'A shame on you, stealing like that in broad daylight.'

The child moved protectively towards his father. So this was stealing. It teased at him a moment: had he himself ever stolen? He sensed his father did not see this act as stealing. Neither did he. His father had never stolen.

'A lock of hay for an unfortunate horse.' Connaughton laughed it off. 'I'd walk into any field in the country for a lock of hay and nobody would say boo to me. And if I had it myself anyone was welcome to it.'

'Yes, but they'd have to ask for it.'

'And so I did. I asked Miss Jackson.'

'Miss Jackson,' the man scoffed. 'You know as well as I do Miss Jackson does not own this field. And even if she did,' he added, 'I doubt very much if she'd give it to you. No Jackson ever gave me anything.'

The man was sizing up before Connaughton, expanding his shoulders, lumping his fists. Suddenly he grabbed him by the shirt. 'Nor anyone else ever gave me hay either. Go back now where you came from.' He let go the shirt.

The child was already moving towards the car. He wished his father would follow. His father wasn't stealing, yet he didn't wish anyone to see him here, witness the embarrassment he found himself in.

'You're an unreasonable man,' Connaughton said, and wondered would he at least get away with the hay he already had in the car. 'A most unreasonable man. I had hay myself one time and if the likes of you asked for it, it was yours.'

'But you haven't it. And when you had I hadn't. And what you had you didn't know there were those without.'

'I beg your pardon.' Connaughton fumed. He did not know what to say next. Then, suddenly, he seemed to behold some vision. 'As God is my judge,' he shouted up at the sky and, crossing his arms, he went down on his knees. 'I gave hay when I had hay.'

Then he was on his feet again. He had paid all the homage he felt was required of him, would be necessary witness of his disdain for hay. He lifted an armful of it and threw it to the ground as though he hated it. The violence mounting in him scattered within its airy substance and settled at the man's feet.

'Ah, hay.' The man kicked it, he too hated it: derisory, contemptible stuff. 'I'm not talking about hay.'

'Jesus,' he continued, laughing, incredulous, 'you think everything is yours. Because you had it one time. You think you have a right to everything.' His laugh seemed to draw some of the anger out of him. Or hardened it: he became more controlled.

'When you had hay and gave it away as you say you did, you didn't need hay anyway. Am I right?' He waited for Connaughton to understand what he was referring to.

'You had a big farm of land. But times were bad. And as you'll agree, giving a lot of hay to cattle in those days wasn't going to do much for them. You couldn't get a price for them one way or the other. Am I right? Farmers gave cattle away almost.' The man shifted on his feet, began to stand at ease. He was warming to his task of dressing Connaughton down. 'So you sold your place. That's when I bought mine. And struggled, while you moved into town and continued to be a big shot.'

Connaughton stood back, studied this inquisitor to whom he could give neither Christian nor surname. Who seemed yet to know so much about him.

If his intention was to belittle him he instead achieved another effect. But only momentarily: Connaughton was gripped with regret for actions taken in his past. For having sold that farm . . . other actions. 'Come on,' he said to the boy. 'We're going. This man is haywire.'

The man stepped up to him in a last attempt to impress on him the magnitude of his misdemeanour. 'Would you like it if I walked down the street in town,' he said. 'And shouted to them all, "Come here and listen to my story, I caught Connaughton walking off with hay?" Would you like it if I told the civic guards? Or told your wife?' He paused, allowing his last question a moment's consideration. Then he turned and climbed up the hill. 'Take that arm of hay with you and never let me see you here again.'

The sun was yet high, but behind them now. It reflected, a

dusty gleam, off the red-lead petrol pumps. A hen pecking in the gravel round the pumps saw the oncoming car. She dropped, as though on starting blocks. She crouched, undecided, triggered, until the last moment. Connaughton braked and her all-important dash was a miraculous success. Then he turned to his son. The return journey, he decided, lacked levity. 'Why did the hen cross the road?' he asked.

Then he saw Miss Jackson.

She was at her gate, waving cows through. She had a hand on a cow's back and as she saw him she raised the hand in an unassured salute. He made to acknowledge her wave but he had passed her gate. She was out of sight.

As he looked forward, on the last empty stretch of road that led into town, cut off now from returning her salute, he was suddenly overcome with a sadness. A sadness for Miss Jackson, mingled with pity for himself at his recent treatment. His sentiment for her gained the upper hand. 'Sad creature' – he turned round to his son – 'in an uncaring world.'

The boy, not realising the confusion of emotion his father just now felt for humanity, thinking he was referring only to himself, said, 'Yes, Dada.'

He too thought the return trip lacked levity. He wondered would he remind his father of the question he had just put. Whose answer he had heard a million times.

There was no need.

'Why did the hen cross the road?' Connaughton brightened and lifted himself at the wheel. He had suddenly been visited by one of those rare, or as he called them himself, 'philosophical' moments. One of those moments that, as well as being pleased to relate, he always felt apologetic for. That saved him drowning in the sea of himself. His sea of endeavour and failure, self-pity and further opportunity.

    'I know, Dada. To get to the other side.'

    'No, to get a lock of hay.' He smiled.

WITHIN SIGHT OF THE ISLANDS

THEY TOOK TWO CARS. The children squabbled over which car they would travel in but it was three in the morning, and like squabbling that goes on in a dream it fizzled to nothing.

They slept through the small towns and were awakened over the wooden bridge of the wide river Shannon. Bridgeboards rattled beneath them, the sound going on for miles it seemed, slowly unravelling the dreams they had spun in. They sat up. A flash of river silver lifted like a fleeing heron away from them as they looked for the other car.

It was following. On its sidelights. The pale sheen of the windscreen formed a barrier they could not see through, but they knew the occupants were Barry the driver and Una. Una their favourite, Una, not Nurse who had to stay at home and mind the younger ones, not Mama who was asleep in their own car and was only going some of the way and then would be saying goodbye. Una had their holiday luggage, the buckets and spades and rugs, behind her on the back seat.

Blan Connaughton sat alongside her husband in the front car. The clapper bridge did not waken her. The baby she was expecting slept on within her. Connaughton too was asleep, or dreaming; drive-dreaming his way along the roads to the port. From time to time milk churns glimmered by, lighthouse signals at the end of long inland laneways. Like animals roving in the undergrowth, stray anxieties flitted across his field of vision. Worries approached out of the hedges forming in the early light and then dodged away. Connaughton smelled the sea while still on the flat inland country. He opened his window and the air felt warm, reminding him of childhood holidays.

The children dozed again. The pounding beneath them penetrated their minds with a strange, relentless voice. And then the mother stirred, just as the car came to a halt in the arm of the harbour. Barry's car slid like a shadow alongside.

The two-car idea had been Connaughton's. Barry was to take Blan home that evening in one. The other was to remain at the dock, in readiness for the return of the holiday-makers following the fortnight on the island. That was the idea; Blan would voyage out with them on the ship, she would say goodbye, and then she would return. In view of her condition it was safest. Barry would accompany her. That was the idea, but Connaughton did not think it was going to work and it worried him.

The line of cars waited in stillness, facing the shadowy hull of a ship which rose and lightly fell as the tide slurped and giggled between its side and the pier face.

A door opened in the ship and a square of light fell across the deck. Then a light was shone on it from a pole in the harbour and the loading began. Instructions were shouted and the winch creaked. A barrel clattered. Passengers emerged from cars. They pulled coats over their backs.

Barry wore his black Crombie, and hidden in the end of one long sleeve his fingers tonged the seed of a cigarette. He had never been on a dockside before, never seen a ship in real life, yet he managed to look at home in his surroundings; he might have been a shipping merchant overseeing a loading. A docker cursed softly beside him as he threw boxes of bacon onto the ship deck from a crumbling cardboard stack piled up there on the pier.

Barry was lost in fearful thought, scared of the position he had got himself into, wondering how he could have let it come about: that in a short time he should have to get into that iron thing. His biggest fear, however, was not of getting onto the ship, it was not even the outward journey. Already he was thinking of the return journey. For he thought he would have to brave that one alone. He suspected Connaughton's wife would step off with the others on the island, he suspected she would not be able to say goodbye to them; she would do that and leave him at the mercy of that sea on his own. The ship lurched slightly. The sudden strain of a rope against a bollard beside him brought him back to the present.

The ship sloped towards him, lifted suddenly on the swell. He seesawed with the swaying deck. His stomach somersaulted and quickly he turned to the man alongside him.

'Any chance of this ship tipping over, sir?' He pointed with seeming indifference towards it.

'The steamer,' the man corrected him. 'Hardly a chance.' With his foot he raked up rashers that had fallen from the boxes and stuck now to the slabstones. 'Hardly a chance. *Dun Aengus* is a dependable old tub.' Barry listened as the docker told him all about the ship: that because it sat so low in the water it was difficult to capsize, even in the worst storm; that the only danger, because of its low keel, was that of being beached on the sandbank off the smallest of the islands, the island they were headed for, when the tide was out.

'Hardly a chance' – on the strength of it Barry returned to Connaughton. 'Better get out the suitcases, boss, and get a move on. We don't want to be left on a sandbank.'

As they slipped away, with only a slight sensation of movement, from the brown land, the sun burst from behind the bar of cloud on the horizon. The children had already galloped a few times around the steamer's wooden gangplanks. And now the iron stairways, dripping with dew and sunburst, attracted them; one led up to the bridge, one down to the growling engine room.

In the moment of sunrise everything changed. Passengers watched the bulky, formless sea presence they floated free of become a harbour. Those black, rope-hauling outlines on its wall were men; the sun scorched along the lengths of their trousers. A wreck lay, half-sunken, in the harbour's mouth, its prow cocked upwards, a seagull balanced on it. And the steamer, which had been no more than a shape – in the sun it became a silver sea craft. A whispering huddle on its foredeck turned into a group of people dressed all in black. They had sat there patiently for hours though none of the passengers had noticed their presence. Now that the door to the steamer's hold was open they rose. The sun glinted off their suitcases. Together, as if bonded by some invisible chord, they went downstairs. Passengers shook heads, impressed with their fortitude. 'The island people.' And Barry was impressed with the ship. With the light of day his confidence grew. 'The *Dun Aengus* she's called,' he said. 'A dependable tub.'

Becoming fearful for the safety of her exploring children on the deck above, Blan Connaughton called Una. 'Get them down. We'll have breakfast, or supper,' she laughed, 'or something.' She looked through a steamed-up porthole at the waves below: 'The sea air sharpens the appetite.'

It was hot in the long lounge cabin. Through a tiny window at one end cups of tea emerged. People sat in groups throughout the low-ceilinged room. The room swayed with a slight grinding motion.

Blan arranged a picnic on their table: two large flasks of coffee, sandwiches on one serviette, scones on another, an open box of chocolates.

The children appeared; swinging out of Una.

'Sandwiches first,' Blan called as they sat, or stood, on the bench seat between Connaughton and Barry, 'a sweetie to finish.'

The engine thudded directly beneath. 'Dangerous smell of oil, boss,' Barry said, yet all the adults ate heartily.

The children ate nothing and raced between the high-backed seats with their chocolates. Once, as they ran past, Blan reached out and caught the boy close to her. 'Oh, we'll have a great time on our holidays.' He strove to pull free and she hugged him. Barry shook his head disapprovingly.

In spite of Blan's urgings Connaughton would not take a chocolate. As he watched her eat yet another an impulse passed through his mind: he wanted her to keep on eating; he wanted her to grow fat and unhappy on chocolates. He became aware of a sudden resentment towards her, but not of its reason. Somewhere else in his mind he was uneasy about a decision not yet settled. He did not associate the two.

'He'll kill you,' Barry reprimanded Blan. He had been watching her: two, three, four from the top layer, then delving for her favourites from the bottom layer.

'Who will, Barry?' she liked to poke fun with him.

'Didn't you tell me yourself?' he continued his oblique reference.

'Tell you what?'

'That he'd kill you if you ate as much as one chocolate.'

'Oh, Doc Kennedy.' Blan laughed. 'Don't mind him. Aren't I on holidays?'

'Doc Kennedy.' Barry nodded emphatically. 'Aren't I right, boss?' Connaughton laughed at how the ridiculous Barry could get away with the things he said to Blan, and though normally it gave him pleasure, he now wished with jealousy he had the same simple, fond approach as lay between them.

Blan pushed the chocolates away from her. 'Pass them round to those people, Una.' She pointed at a group of women. It was the group who had sat on the dark deck earlier. News of their condition and their business had been whispered around the cabin and by this time had reached Barry's ears. They were a party of emigrants, returning home from America to bury their mother. The elder ones sat sombrely, but the younger ones had bright American accents and sometimes when their talk became too excited they looked at the elder ones and stopped. When Barry relayed to Blan what he had heard she pushed more chocolates on them, cups of coffee. She spoke to them, and found out about the business of their husbands that would allow only the women to return. 'Poor women,' she said to Connaughton. 'Poor creatures, they were to come on holiday to see her later this year. They haven't been back to see her in ten years and now they never will again.'

Connaughton said he was going up on deck for fresh air. He did not like the morbid mood he had got into. As he left he saw Blan laugh and give comfort to the islanders. He was unhappy with himself, afraid he could not deal with the situation in her easy way. He was unhappy with her for being able to do so.

On his way up the children ran into him. 'Dada, Dada –' They struggled to a halt, entangled between his legs. 'We are going to bring Mama up to see everything . . . Look, Dada, look' – they had forgotten about Mama, Dada would do – 'look, a mountain.' They followed him up on deck.

To the left of them, rocky and clear, a headland slipped by.

Sheep clinging to its edges looked up and gazed at them, then returned to their grazing. One minute it seemed the headland was speaking to them: some final land communication across the gulf of sea. Then the ship swung away; they were out, on the uninterrupted roll of the deep.

The ship rattled now, and sighed out of all its iron joints. It was as if it had decided, once out of land-shot, that it need no longer contain its own natural noises.

Or else it was travelling faster. If that was so, the seagulls too travelled faster. And yet they didn't seem to move at all. They stood in the air, legs gingerly lowered as if to land, wings flattened out but not beating, feathers disarrayed by the slipsteam. Yet they held abreast the ship.

'Look at that big one,' the boy shrieked. He had seen its bloodied beak. It skimmed above the children's heads and then rejoined its complaining mates.

Connaughton did not look at the seagulls. His gaze was on the distant sky; his concern was the weather ahead. Then he looked at his children. 'These are companion seagulls.' His eyes softened, pleased with his phrase. 'You'll find a few of them will accompany us all the way.'

Suddenly the seagull cries became urgent, turned to a fury. A porthole opened out of the steamer's side. Without sign of any human activity, slops shot out of it, pocked into the sea. The birds threshed in the whirlpool. The ship drew away and for a while strove on its own. One of the children rushed downstairs – 'Mama, Mama' – to describe what she had seen. She returned instantly and this time she had Barry with her.

'You're not to let them fall over the side, sir,' he shouted from the shelter of an iron-framed doorway.

Then he teetered into the open. His coat opened in the wind and he flapped across the deck like a sheet of corrugated iron caught in a storm.

'Fierce wind, boss.' He collected himself on the rails and looked back in dread over his shoulder at the screaming wind-wail above the funnel. Below he had felt himself secure; now he clung on the rail, awaited the return of his equilibrium. 'Go up and see is the boss man all right, she told me. Tell him not to fall into the water with those children.'

The wind threw spray onto the deck. Barry found more to say. He battened his coat and backed himself to the spray and sun glare. 'That's a rough sea, boss.'

Connaughton took time to reply. 'Choppy.'

'That wind is travelling, boss.'

'Or is it the ship's movement, creating an illusion?'

Barry's bluster sagged a moment. 'Ah, it's the wind. Look at those waves.'

'Deceptive,' Connaughton said. 'Difficult to gauge.'

Barry read Connaughton's line of reasoning. 'So you think she'll be safe getting into one of those cowhide whatever you call thems you told me about?'

'Canvas.' Connaughton couldn't help laughing at Barry sometimes. 'Tar-coated canvas. Called currachs. Yes, maybe it will be calmer.' He shrugged. 'Safer water maybe off the beach.'

'I don't know, sir. The only safe water today is in holy water founts.' Barry spluttered and eyed the sea with his green land eye as though it were a coiling monster.

Now there were others on deck. They stood at the ship's prow.

Someone pointed forward. 'Look, you can barely see them.'

Connaughton's group moved forward. All strained to see the approaching islands.

Some saw them: a flat, lighter-coloured stain on the sea's edge. Others saw them, took them for another aberration of the horizon. Yet others imagined them. 'Which way?' Barry

shouted. His head swivelled from the white cliffs far away on
one side to the low, darker coastline on the other; to what
had earlier been the armpit of the bay but now was no
more than a reminder of something, of someplace safe. Water
streamed from his eye and flew away, loop-shaped, round the
ship funnel above.

'Straight ahead,' someone gave him directions, 'between here
and New York.'

Barry looked for something mountain-shaped, something
blue and tall on the horizon. He looked round for the children
to point out to them what he imagined.

But they had gone downstairs. Suddenly tired, they sulked
and burrowed sweets out of their mother's lap.

There were little groups now on the prow. With each moment that passed another group tracked down the islands'
whereabouts. Eventually everybody saw them. All sleep was
dispelled. Whispers from the crowd connected the steamer to
the faraway colony. From the distant specks, whispers seemed to return, to pulse a welcome. The specks drew nearer.
'That's the houses.' The elder women among the returning
funeral party lost their composure as soon as house clusters
became distinguishable. They named their villages, calling them
out in Irish.

'See it, that's where we're going.' They pointed out
excitedly to the younger ones the village they had once
left.

'Which, where, which is Grandmama's house?'

'I'm not sure which one, that's the village.'

'Gee whizz, Mum, you never told us there were no trees!'

Then the land was upon them. A great shining wall of sun
and sand, it moved towards them at great speed.

The steamer turned, sailed parallel to the land. Soon the
land became three. There were three islands. The steamer

headed first for the furthest, the largest one.

Everywhere there was turf. Stacked and stooked. Donkeys carried it on panniers. Some passengers disembarked, even some of those intended for the smaller islands. 'A half-hour or be left behind,' ship hands shouted at them.

Connaughton's children wandered. And discovered how far only when they heard the ship's siren. Loud and frightening. The ship stood above the pier and the cluster of houses. It was calling. Great, flapping swan, calling them. A woman waved at them. Again the ship siren blew, they ran to the waving woman. It was Una; she stood on the roadway halfway between them and the ship. They ran down the long brown corridor. It was the turf-stacked pier. Everybody seemed to be shouting at them. They saw Barry on deck. He was shaking his head. They were frightened but some of the onlookers, Una included, laughed. They boarded, breathless.

Connaughton and Blan were missing. The children found only the funeral party below decks. They stopped searching; something was going on above – they climbed on deck again, felt the lurch of the steamer as it buckled off the sea wall, listened to the last, shouted words between islandmen and ship's crew, listened to Barry knowingly explain the unmooring procedure to them.

Connaughton had scanned the weather all the way to the islands. He had looked in the distance hoping all the signs would be wrong and the sea would calm so that it would be safe for Blan to disembark, so that he would not have to stop her. If only conditions could be as they were in here, in the shelter. Off the smallest island there was no pier, only offshore shallows. Open seas where they would have to disembark into flimsy currachs – it could be impossible.

If his mind could only calm a little he could realise the squall was his ally. It would decide she would not go in the currach. The decision did not have to be his.

'Can we talk a minute . . . ?' He had brought her up on deck and they had stood behind the lifeboat in the stern where they had a view of the unloading but yet were cut off from sight.

'I'll be lonely without you all for the next two weeks,' she repeated. Her face was about to crease.

That was the moment when the siren blew and she saw her children gabble back like ducklings to the mother duck. She laughed at the sight but Connaughton's pained expression remained.

'So will I be lonely,' he almost accused. The engines throbbing up again knocked the words loudly out of him.

'How will you manage on your own?' she begged.

'We'll manage. The children like Una.' He faltered, realising she might find hurtful an admission that someone else could take care of her children.

Connaughton was forgetting that at home in the hotel Blan's children were in someone else's hands most of the time anyway. While she roamed, visited, helped at his business, enjoyed herself.

Blan was remembering that. But remembering too that in the hotel she could come to them if they wanted her.

Her hurt was defeating him. He gave up.

Blan felt his small hand about hers. It was something that always surprised her, the size of his hands. Suddenly discarding her own petulance, she drew him towards her. 'Yes, sweetheart, if you think I shouldn't.'

He buried his face in her coat so she could not see it crumple in release.

Then she went downstairs again, smiling to herself as she went. She had her children to think about, her husband, but there was also the life within her. There was that fear that sometimes gripped but that she always managed to shake off: that the birth was going to be touch and go. And besides, she mused as she descended into the darkness, there was his hotel to run. Her hotel to run. With all its characters; its faint, at times unsettling, atmosphere of debauch; its trace of decay that had not existed in the previous, sheltered life of her own up-bringing; its demands on her energies. The thought now jollied her. Connaughton stayed above, puzzled at her smile. Sometimes he wondered if he knew his own wife at all.

'At least,' he had been about to say, but did not for fear of exposing a thought that he had been hiding, even from himself. 'At least somebody will be at home to look after the business.'

A mile off the smallest island and suddenly the currachs surrounded the steamer. Like linseed-coated greyhounds they raced alongside. Almost all the passengers were on deck. They watched the manoeuvre as the currachs came together on the wind-sheltered side. They leaned over the railings to see. An oarsman out of the nearest currach stood up beneath them, grabbed the ship's belly. A line of bobbing boats formed, hand-held together by the oarsmen who shouted all the time to one another.

Boxes appeared from the side of the ship. Boxes, barrels, sacks; handed to the standing man in the first currach and passed side over side to the outer boats. Greetings were shouted between the boatmen and those in the hold, and sudden bursts of anxious speech whenever the boat chain threatened to come apart in the slopes of sea.

Then Connaughton, Una and the children were in the hold. A few others stood between them and the narrow exit but they could see they were at sea level. Wavelets dribbled through the door and across the iron floor of the hold. The currach chain had broken, was falling behind the steamer as it drifted fast across the bay in a wind. Voices rose. The boatmen took out their oars and rowed until once again they were upon the ship and fastened to its hull, a tail which stretched out to sea.

The funeral party was first to board the currachs. Shaking hands solemnly with each one of them, the boatmen conveyed sympathies.

It was the turn of Connaughton's group. The boatmen laughed as they were firmly handed, first Una, then the children one after another, then Connaughton, one boat to the next. The boatmen laughed shyly and openly by turns. Open amazement, then embarrassment of the outside world. Sudden seriousness, words of caution, of instruction, in mixed Irish and English – 'Aha, steady, steady' 'Step in the middle' 'Ní fédir snámh. I cannot swim, can you?' – followed by communal laughter.

Sea poured between the boats. Hands and arms steadied their movement outward to the boat that would carry them ashore.

'Bhfuil sibh ag dul teach Aindi?' a lean-faced man with massive teeth, nose and ears asked. 'Is mise Aindi.'

'Tá siad, tá siad. They are going to our house, Aindi,' another man answered impatiently, ashamed with Aindi for having questioned in Irish people who might not have a word of the language. This man had a postbag on his back. He had stepped across all of the boats to collect it from the ship.

Aindi's currach had a high, sloping prow. He tucked the children into it. In the centre of the boat, backs to them, Aindi and the postman worked sets of oars. In the stern, facing them, Connaughton and Una sat together. The children laughed from their haven seeing the others lashed with sea spray. Connaughton and Una laughed too; a reserve that had always existed between them momentarily melted. The oars grappled a few moments in the sea. Then both sets levered together and Aindi's currach broke free of the others, fought slowly around until it pointed to the island.

Blan had come up on deck. She stood alongside Barry. 'I won't look down till they're safe,' she said, looking into the distance. 'Are they all right, tell me?'

Barry too looked in the distance. He attempted to light a cigarette, wasting match after match. 'Oh, safe as a house,' he answered. 'Don't look down yet though. Not yet.'

'Why didn't you go yourself, Mam?' He didn't look at her; his stare remained in the distance.

'We talked it over,' she replied.

'Ah, that's what I knew you were at when the children were looking for you all over the place. I told them you were drowned.' He looked at her slyly to see if he was humouring her.

Blan did not laugh. 'So he wouldn't let you go,' Barry continued as soon as he had lit the cigarette. She looked at him. Her lips were rubbery with sorrow but she smiled.

He took a long pull from his cigarette. 'And he was right too not to,' he said gruffly.

But something was hardening within him, hardening in a ring round his throat, welling in his eyes. Something he wanted to say but could not. 'We better be on the move or be sat in the sandbank,' he was about to declare in his gruff tone. But he could bear her unhappiness no longer. His eyes hurt now, and words he had not intended blurted from him: 'I don't blame you feeling sorry for yourself.'

Blan smiled, pulling herself together. 'It's not myself I'm feeling sorry for, Barry. It's those people returning to the island for a funeral.' She pointed at the boat furthest off. 'You saw them. Happy and distraught they were at one and the same time. So happy you'd want to go with them. But so sad. Will they cry or laugh when they land?' she turned to Barry. 'Will they manage?'

'I know what you mean, Mam.' He thought and didn't know what else to say. He was glad when she told him the cigarettes were killing him. He was able to take his leave of her: 'I'll go downstairs so and die in peace.'

The children were overcome a few moments by the smells of tar and sea salt and fish scales on the floor of the currach. And – now they were free of the choppy waters round the ship – by the treacly roll of the waves underneath them and by the heavy fat drops dripping from the oars. The postman warned them not to budge. 'It's deep down there, stay put.'

They looked up just as the steamer's bow crossed before them. One solitary shape waved from its deck. A person saying something that was lost in the wind.

'Who is that?' The boy, the elder of the two pointed up.

'It's your Mama,' Una answered from the stern. 'Imagine, he doesn't know his own Mama!' She laughed. 'Wave good-bye to Mama.'

'Bye bye, Mama.' In response to Una's directive he waved at the squat figure on the foggy cliff-deck. Blithely he waved, then he turned about, raising himself above the currach's rim, feeling the wind lift his hair, watching the boat ahead of him rise above and lower below the creaking horizon.

Una's words echoed in Connaughton's mind: imagine, he doesn't know his own Mama.

Imagine, he doesn't even know his own Mama. And did he himself know her. His wife? The thought flashed that he might never see her again. It became a certainty: it was too late to learn to know her now because he would never see her again. Not ever. She would go home and it would happen. And who had sent her home? He had. Never see her again! His thought horrified him. A boatland of black-clad women, low in the water, sailed before the frame of his mind.

Directly on the heels of his thought, erupting behind it and pushing it aside, came a feeling of intense anxiety. Something else, something important he had forgotten. Stop, stop the boat: the shouts within his head tried to get out but could find no way. Overcome by a blind urge, his entire body sinewed in readiness. He grabbed the rim of the boat, about to vault over. He felt the splash of foam, the movement of Una's thigh next to his on the slippery seat, saw the island gulls crisscross before his eyes. It was in that same instant the flash of light rent the sky above the boats. A roar exploded above them, drowning out the shouts in Connaughton's head. He had a glimpse of his tightly gripping fingers lit white.

'The rocket, the coastguard rocket,' Aindi said quietly when it passed. 'Look, a fog coming.' He nodded towards the island. The rocket was to guide them to the island, Connaughton understood.

A silvery flicker sat a moment upon the sea surface, calming it, outlining the black boats. All other light had been sucked from the bay, all movement had come to a standstill in the silence left behind by the rocket bolt. Then the children set up a wail. 'Mama, the bang, where's Mama, I'm frightened.' They turned bare heads around but the steamer was gone.

Una comforted them. 'Hush, hush, it's all right: Mama is looking after us.'

Connaughton attempted to recover what had been going through his mind before the rocket went off. He remembered the important work detail that he had wanted to shout back across the water at Blan. The command he had wanted Blan to pass on to one of his staff back at home. He smiled to himself at the thought of his urgency of a moment previously. He

NOTICE BOX

HE HADN'T BEEN A GOOD BOY and he knew it. But now his mother was singing anyway, singing at the top of her voice. He felt bad. 'Let him go, let him tarry, let him sink or let him swim. He doesn't care for me and I don't care for him.' She sang gaily as she drove. Her window was open and the breeze played on her open shirt front.

She looked down at him on the bench seat beside her. 'Come on, sing along, what's got into you?' He frowned. 'Let him go and get another which I hope he will enjoy. For I'm going to marry a far nicer boy.' She looked at his pale face, his bare legs stiffened against the leatherette seat, and repeated the words slowly – 'He doesn't care for me . . .' – inviting him to join in. But there was no response. He frowned through the windscreen. The sun dived into a mantle of rushing clouds.

In the end he was stung into saying what was on his mind. 'I do care for you.' It came out sullenly and she wasn't sure what he had said. 'So it's not fair if you don't care for me!' There were tears in his eyes.

Then she understood. She took in a deep breath of the fresh morning air. 'My laddie.' She stopped the car and leaned over. 'My silly silly laddie, it's only a song. Your Mama loves you more than anything else in the wide wide world.' She grasped

him and held him with such desperation he thought he
would burst. He tried to look between her arms at the road.
He had been studying how the cloud shadows leaped across
it and wished to continue his studies. 'So sweet,' she said. He
squirmed away from her hugs.

'I'll sing so.' He took up again his stern stance by her side.
But after a while they were both laughing. 'Let him go and
get another which I hope he will enjoy. For I'm going to
marry a far nicer boy!'

Another day they were in the car. They were often in the
car together, roaming the countryside, visiting. This day she
told him to be especially good. She was visiting a doctor, a
very important doctor. 'The little boy of the house is a bit
odd so be especially nice to him.'

The place was surrounded by high walls. The iron gates
were so tall that as she opened them he thought, for the first
time in his life, that she looked small. The trees inside shut
out the sky. They drove, and reaching a clearing they saw the
massive block of a house. Clumps of tall grasses lined the
driveway up to the house. A small boy in a white shirt and
short-sleeved pullover like his own stood by the front steps
and held a toy scooter. 'There is David,' his mother said.
'Wave to David.' He waved but David did not wave back.
Instead he dropped his scooter and ran indoors.

'There's a good laddie, you'll stay out here and play with
David when he comes out.' She left him on his own.

He knew David was going to be like all the other children
his mother brought him to play with in the country. First
they ran away and when they did return they were unwilling
or unable to play any of his games, but instead climbed on
gates or farm buildings and looked down on him. But David
did not return. After a long time waiting he began to explore.

He entered a walled garden. At its distant end, too far away to investigate, glasshouses dazzled like fairytale castles. Along the straight rows that ended in a shimmer of light there stood gooseberry bushes, raspberry canes, strawberry plants. There were apple trees, plum trees, clumps of daffodils here and there beneath the trees, but nowhere was there any fruit. He broke and ate a stick of sour rhubarb.

By the time his mother left the house he had found the maze in the lawn.

'We have to go in here.' He pointed to a gap. 'And out here.' He ran excitedly about the hedge and showed her another gap. 'Come on.'

They abandoned themselves to the maze, and circling its first few beguiling outer rings they talked.

'Did you see David?'

'No. Quick, we have to try and escape, quick.'

'He's an odd boy. Spoiled by his mother. Thank God you're not like that.'

'Come on, Mama, or you're dead!'

'Oh, it's quiet here.'

Within a few minutes they were lost.

At first she laughed. 'We're lost.' She sat helplessly at the base of the tall hedge and her peals of laughter ran through the leafy corridors.

'We're lost, we're lost' – he had become frightened. And so she rose, keeping the good news she had been about to tell him until some other time.

'Silly laddie, of course we're not. This way, in a minute we'll be back in the garden.' A minute later the garden, anything, anything beyond the bound of the maze, they could not even envisage. 'What will we do?' she said.

He found the way out. Leading her through the opening, across the threshold of withered leaves. He felt like a hero in a storybook who has just led a helpless heroine through a wild wood. 'Oh what an intelligent man.' She smothered him with hugs. He shrugged her off.

Then something struck him. He realised why he had so easily, once he had put his mind to it, found a way out. It was because he had done it all before. And with his mother. It had been dark, and the branches overhanging. Yes, he had done it all before. But when? It had the memory now of a dream.

'He doesn't love his Mama.' She pouted her chubby lips. His mind, now he was free of the maze, had returned to the light of day, to his exposed position on the lawn that tumbled away on every side from them. Where they could be seen. 'I do, I do.' He raised his eyes heavenward, hoping she would get the hugging over with. It was not the first time such a declaration had been forced on him. He wondered why she still so much desired his affection. He was afraid he was too old for all that.

They were always out driving. Sometimes he enjoyed the drives, sometimes he did not. The place with the maze had been good. He had been allowed to wander on his own. But there was one house, the man kept breeding-horses and was enormous. He wanted his wife to become a Catholic like him and asked Mama to instruct her. 'Your Mama inspires me to faith,' this woman said. There he had to ride ponies with the boy of the house. There he did not enjoy.

And there they always wanted him to sing. 'Sing your little song for everybody, Lal,' Mama said, throwing up her head ready to accompany him, her curls falling back, exposing a high forehead. She prompted: 'She wears red feathers and a huly huly skirt . . . ' It was a song he had picked up from the hotel staff, that he liked. But they only wanted it sung so they could laugh when he came to the end. He knew that. He stared at the table, where little patties of butter melted in the sun, and sugar on top of the sponge cake glittered like broken glass. She sang the song in its entirety but could not prompt a word out of him. On the journey home she said she wished he would only realise what a sweet voice he had. 'You don't love me, you only want me to sing,' he said.

'I love you too.'

'You don't love me.'

'Don't sulk.'

'If you love me why do you leave me with Nurse all the time. I don't like Nurse.'

'Why don't you like Nurse?' From the way she asked he thought he detected that she was pleased to hear him say it.

'She has a big bottom and I have to do everything for her.'

'I'll speak to Nurse about her bottom.' She giggled.

'You're always going away somewhere. Why does she always give us baths now? The soap always goes in my eyes.'

'Mama loves you but you can't be her spoiled lump. Mamas have other things too to do.'

For a further five minutes he complained and she placated. He maddened her to the point almost where she lost control. 'Do you know what a notice box is?' she said.

But before they reached the petrol pumps at the town's edge they were singing together. 'She wears red feathers and a huly huly skirt . . . A rose in her hair, a gleam in her eye and love in her heart for me!'

'You're an ould cod,' she said.

Many clouds loomed on Lally's horizon, imagined and real. Nurse was a real cloud.

He was on a walk. A seemingly endless walk like all the others since his mother had stopped driving the car. They strode out along the straight road, the same road out of town they always took.

Nurse wheeled the pram and Una, one of the chamber-maids from his father's hotel, walked alongside her. They held his sister between them. He lolled behind. 'Nurse has fat fat legs and red red hair.' The fields and hedges passed them by; the hum went on in his head and would not stop. 'Nurse has fat fat legs and red red hair. But Una, her hair is black and her legs is skinny.'

The women held his sister's hands and the twins sat up-right in the pram, absorbing the view. Sometimes his sister walked, sometimes she was swung, 'one two three and up in the air', sometimes she was dragged. He trailed. 'I'm tired,' he whined. 'I'm thirsty.' He didn't think his feet would carry him any further. The road was hot, the birds were asleep. No cars passed. Unlike in town, out here nothing ever happened.

'Fred Diamond told me today he has already saved half the money for the house,' the red-headed cloud of his life was telling Una, oblivious to his complaints.

'Isn't Fred great?' Una said.

'Of course we won't have enough money to buy the house when we get married, but we'll live in his flat in Bank Street until we do.' Nurse nodded with certainty.

'Isn't he great, how did you get hold of such a gem?'

'Oh, that's a long story, but I'll tell you sometime.' They both laughed.

'Don't dawdle, Lally, slowcoach.' Nurse turned round to him and then because she was in good mood she teased. 'Wait till you see the present your Mama is going to bring you if you're good. Which would you prefer, Lally, a little baby brother or a girl?'

'A brother.' He glowered.

'What, not another little girl, who will chase you and hug you and kiss you!'

'Oh, soon enough he'll be doing the chasing himself!' said Una.

They had teased him like this before. That last comment always mortified him. He hated the overpowering thing there was about all the women who worked in the hotel, this subject they always discussed. He lingered on the dusty roadside and roughly pulled heads of grass while he waited for the conversation to turn to something else.

'Blood pressure.' Nurse nodded to her companion. 'She told me herself.' Nurse was privy to information other staff members did not receive. She made the most of her position. 'No driving, the doctor says, no chocolates and definitely no riding on horseback.'

'You'd pity her, she misses it.'

'She has to do it, no choice. And she won't give up the chocolates. Doesn't know how serious it is. Too many kids too quickly, she's had. You know she could haemorrhage.'

'Oh, haemorrhage.' Una pronounced the impressive word carefully. 'Still, you'd pity her.' They talked, dragging his sister, while he dropped further behind and daydreamed, one minute beneath a lofty cloud, the next beneath the flat sun. 'Look at him, lazybones,' Nurse said, 'and his Mama thinks he's an angel.'

'My feet are sore, Nurse.'

'So are mine. The sooner your mother is driving again the better for all of us.' She laughed with Una. 'Sore feet indeed.' She lowered her voice. 'Sore bottom if Mama let me have my way with him.'

Lally picked up songs about the hotel. All sorts of tunes drifted through the air. The wireless in the kitchen always played. It stood in the open window and could be tuned both by the kitchen staff and by the men whistling in the bottle plant outside. Sometimes, if there was an important race somewhere, Fanning came from the butcher shop next door, or the men came up from the coffin shed. They turned on a race commentary. A flurry of sharp sound bristled the air. The men bent rigid. Then the wireless went back to songs again.

The maids sang in the bedrooms, the waitresses each time they left the dining room. One waitress, returned from London, was most up to date: 'My old man's a dustman, he wears a dustman's hat.' She twanged in the accent she had picked up from her brief stay abroad. The kitchen staff ridiculed her: 'Cor Bloimey Trousers', they named her. Her songs seeped into his mind. Yet it was from his mother he picked up songs mostly.

But he did not have as much of his mother to himself nowadays. He would hear her voice, or echoes of her voice, through the corridors and staircases of the hotel. But when he reached the place where he thought he heard her there would be nothing but the ghostly presence of receding laughter on some other landing.

He would imagine he heard her in the kitchen. But when he reached the kitchen hers would not be one of the figures bustling about in its steamy heat. 'You'll knock somebody over,' the cook would shout. 'Out, out.' It worried him that the special dispensation he had enjoyed seemed no longer extended. He had had his mother's patronage. Her influence seemed to be waning.

He would run into the dining room. She will be sitting with diners, he imagined, regaling them with her stories as in the past. But in the dining room there would only sit solitary shapes amid polite sounds of cutlery. He would sample cold jam at one of the empty tables, drink a glass of the curiously flat and tasteless table water, and leave.

One day he was more sure than ever that he had heard her.

The laughter was coming from the top landing, where the linen wardrobe stood. When he got there he found there were two voices. But neither was his mother's; one belonged to Nurse, the other to Una the chambermaid.

'Thanks a lot for your help,' Una said. 'It's hard on your own.' He saw her stand on a chair, reach up and take down sheets from the wardrobe and place them on Nurse's outstretched arms. He withdrew quickly; Nurse would scold him if she saw him up here, miles away from the nursery, and he listened.

'Mama usually helped me with this job whenever she was about,' Una said, 'but since her confinement I have to do it on my own.'

'Any time you want me just ask,' Nurse said. 'Chance of a chat. I can just stick the kids in the nursery and come along. I suppose that's the one good thing about her confinement, forgive me saying it, is that I have a much freer hand with them. I'm a free woman.' She laughed.

'Not for long more.' Una laughed.

'Oh, Fred Diamond won't tie me down.'

'He will.'

'Well, I don't mind if he does. You know the song: "Diamonds Are A Girl's Best Friend". Will I tell you what Fred does?'

Lally heard the chair creak. Una was standing down on the floor in order to hear what Fred did.

'Come here to me, Fred says, and he sits me on his knee.'

'Ooh, ooh.'

'My bottom just fits nicely between his legs and then he kisses my neck. "Sittin' on the back seat akissin' and ahuggin' with Fred" – he sings that song and slaps me.'

'Where?'

'Oh, that's tellin',' Nurse laughed. 'In his flat.'

'You don't go to his flat!'

'Why not? It'll be our flat soon. Does it matter?'

'It's nice.'

'It was the children's mother got me Fred Diamond, you know.'

'Go on.'

'Yes. Mister Diamond came over here from England to work in the glass factory. He was busy by day, he's so skilled, teaching trainees and all, but at night . . . Nothing to do but every night sit in the bar. Would you like to meet a nice girl? Mama says to him one night. Up she comes to me in the nursery – I'll introduce you to a nice man. And that was the start of it. Me and my man.'

'Akissin' and ahuggin' with Fred.' Una laughed.

They both laughed. 'He's a devil.' Nurse laughed again.

'And Mama's an angel.'

Lally had already heard it said his mother was in confinement. That she had been ordered by the doctor to put her feet up. He wondered what confinement meant. There was one room he would not search. It was his parents' bedroom. Why he would not search that room he could not tell, but he began to suspect she spent her days there, behind the closed door.

There was a time and place, however, he knew he could always find her. Mama loved to serve drinks behind the bar in the evenings. There he would find her. There he got his chance to plague her. 'Mama, I'm thirsty. Mama, I'm not well.' Mama often grew tired with him then.

There was an evening like many others in the hotel: Mama was behind the bar, dunking glasses into the sudsy water of the sink. She wore an open-necked shirt, riding jodhpurs loosened round the waist and held with one of his father's ties. He sat on the bottom step of the stairs that led to the family quarters and which were behind the back door to the bar. The clink of glasses, the bar conversation, came through the door. Someone slowly crooned. 'There are some folks who say that I'm a dreamer. And I've no doubt there's truth in what they say.' Lally cried.

Now and then drinkers walked into the corridor before him and crossed to the Gents. Each time the Gents door flapped open he saw the green-streaked walls and heard the hiss of escaping water. It stank. One man gave him money. 'Time you should be in blanket street, laddie,' another said, 'and not be bothering your poor mother.'

The regulars liked to have his mother in the bar. His father was more serious; she laughed. Sometimes, because she enjoyed an audience, she sang. They raised their glasses in gratitude. 'What is life without a hearty woman?'

But now, with each time she popped her head round the door to her crying son, her heartiness was deserting her. 'No, no more lemonade.'

'Yes.' He kicked his feet on the floor.

In the end she relented. She bent to him, wiped his sodden eyes. 'You know what happens boys who cry all the time?'

'What?' he asked defiantly.

'Their eyes burn out of their heads. Like a sheet their face becomes, with two holes burned in it by the fairies from all the hot tears.' He was terrified and lifted the cooling glass to his face. 'Notice boxes, the fairies call such boys.'

Another day again they went on a walk. He, his sister, Nurse and Una. This day it began to rain and they didn't even leave the town but went into Harrington's ice-cream parlour, the Manhattan, a small dark room with armchair seats around three low round tables.

Nurse first stooped at the mirror in the tiny hallway and

took off her nurse bonnet, putting it in her bag and tidying her hair.

'Your hair is gorgeous,' Una said, ashamedly putting her hands to her own hair.

'Yours could be too. Would you like me to do it for you? I need all the practice I can get if I'm going to open the hairdressing shop.'

'Oh yes, the hairdressing shop.' Una looked at Nurse in wonder.

Una was impressed when Nurse asked Miss Harrington for four sundaes, two large and two small. But Miss Harrington just said, 'Four sundae, one size only', and walked away so slowly she was like a wind-up toy winding down.

Nurse said 'Oh', but quickly recovered and Lally, who was about to ask for a wafer, decided that a grown-up's sundae might be a better option. His sister did ask for a wafer. He thought how silly she was. She was told sundaes was all there was and that was what she was getting. They were set together at one table, given glasses of ice cream, long-handled spoons, and told not to mess.

Pop music played through a hatch in a corner. Miss Harrington put her head through once, thinking she heard the ring of the opening door, and then withdrew again.

'It's nice in here.' Una liked the tablecloths and the frilled curtains that cut the customers off from the street and the rain.

'Like it?' Nurse was pleased. 'Oh, you could meet anyone in here.' She touched up her hair.

'Like who?'

'Fred Diamond takes me in here and whispers things in my ear.' They both nearly fell out of their chairs laughing.

'I had to tell their Mama I'll be leaving when I get married,' Nurse said, growing suddenly serious.

'And what did she say?'

'Well, I told her about the hairdressing salon me and Fred Diamond are going to have in the flat and then she didn't mind. The idea of it is, I told her, that by the time we get our own house then the salon will be established.'

'What did she say?'

'She was delighted. I'll be your best customer, she said.'

Lally could hardly believe his ears he would be rid of Nurse. But when, he wondered. Soon? The sooner the better. He enjoyed his ice cream and told Nurse what a nice place it was.

Aunt arrived on one of her rare visits.

Aunt was one of his father's sisters. She was not the least like his mother. No crying and hugging reassurances with her; she was grown-up and fun and wanted him to treat her the same grown-up way she treated him. He liked her. She conversed knowledgeably about every corner of the earth and seemed to have been to most of them. Aunt loved his mother but disapproved of almost everything she did.

She disapproved too of Nurse. 'Their little minds need expanding' – she wagged her finger at Nurse one lunch hour she found all the children cluttered in the nursery, hopelessly mashing potato and cabbage into slimy moulds in an attempt to make it go away.

'Mama says I am in charge and I am to carry out her orders.'

'If Mama had her way you would simply be a valet to her children. You would see they were clean and well fed. But I ask you, is there not more to bringing up children? Is it sufficient to expand only their tummies?' She laughed uproariously, hoping Nurse would join her, hoping she could win her over.

'Come.' Her thin finger beckoned Lally from the nursery. Her flared nose drew him along the corridor. She led him to a window on the landing overlooking the street. 'You must explore the world.' She waved her arm dramatically and became helpless again with laughter. 'Look, you must start with your own huge Townhall Street.'

He followed her to her bedroom, along another corridor, passing on the way the closed door of his mother's room. She brought an atlas down from on top of a wardrobe. He felt on the brink of adventure.

Aunt left the hotel as abruptly as she had arrived. She always did everything by surprise. Nurse was once more in charge. Lally's world shrank again, though not to the measure it had done. 'I can't say your aunt and I see eye to eye,' Nurse said. 'Go on the street, but as long as Mama doesn't know.'

A time came when his mother's nightly appearances behind the bar were no more. He heard nothing of her now, not even the imagined echoes of her laughter roaming about the corridors and rooms. Finding company with the commercial travellers, the chambermaids and, increasingly, on the street, he grew accustomed to her absence.

But then one morning Nurse entered his room. He expected her, as usual, to straighten his clothes, comb his hair – pressing his head into her bosoms to hold it steady if it moved while she breathed heat down her nurse-collar bib onto his neck. Instead she smiled at him. 'Oh, such wonderful news!' There was relief in her voice. 'Wait till you see the little baby brother that your Mama is bringing you home. Your Dada is at the nursing home this very minute with them.'

His mother, it seemed, had been away ages. He had been bursting for some time with the need to tell her he was now going out on the street. 'Don't worry, Mama, it's all right,' he would have combated her concern. But now something inside his heart had turned him to independence of her. 'I don't care,' he said.

Yet as days went by and chatter of the new baby that was in the hospital filled the hotel, he found himself looking forward to her return.

He waited a few days. Then something happened. And gradually, as time passed, a dread entered the hotel, thickening its corridors with gloom. 'When is Mama coming home?' he asked.

'Soon,' they answered, 'soon.' But their faces were averted.

The atmosphere was at its strangest the day his baby brother returned. He was led up to a room in the hotel quarters, not the family quarters, which he thought odd, and shown a cot lying on a bed. He climbed onto the bed, looked into the cot and gazed on a shiny white head. It was asleep, eyes shut in total peace. 'Such a beautiful child, so healthy,' people nodded.

Nurse seemed to be in charge. People came. 'God bless the child,' they said to her and left while all the time he stayed, mesmerised by its gleaming presence. Every now and then someone shook a head, attempted to say something, and then there were shushes and whisperings and nudges in his direction.

That same afternoon he amused himself looking out the nursery window at the procession of cars on the street. The strange atmosphere had not yet gone but it seemed to be moving elsewhere from the hotel, to be within the cars that passed beneath him, to be crawling toward the distant ringing bell. It occurred to him as he looked how small was his nursery window, how small he was within.

'What are all the cars doing?' he asked Nurse.

'Oh, that's a funeral.'

He mused a little longer at the window and then wandered along the corridor to his parents' room. His parents' room was wide and high-ceilinged and somehow forbidding. It drew a lot of light in through its tall windows and he never went there unless accompanied by his mother.

The big bed was against the wall. She was sitting in it, giggling, delighted to see him. She held out her arms and he climbed into the warm bed. It was a happy meeting. She told him he was a good boy. He was reassured. And she told him she would always love him. They sang together: 'I belong to Glasgow, dear old Glasgow town.' They laughed, rolling their heads in mock drunkenness at the funny parts as they had done before. 'What's the matter with Glasgow for it's going round and round?'

Aunt and Nurse were together in the nursery when he returned. He was pleased to see Aunt. But she seemed taller, more angular and, with her quivering nose, more distant than before. Today she wore bright red lipstick and had powdered her face white as a sheet. She wore black leather gloves, a long black coat and looked more mysterious than ever. 'Aha,' she said, bestowing on him the faint smile that always signalled the beginning of a new story. 'Aha, sit down while I tell you something.' She sat on the sofa and patted the space alongside her. Nurse fidgeted with ornaments on the tiny mantelpiece, her face red from the glowing coal fire. 'The most ridiculous thing I ever heard.' Aunt looked around crossly at her. 'I don't blame his father because he is beside himself with grief, but somebody should have told him. Leaving it until the funeral is passing...'

She turned back to him. 'You know about the angels,' she said breezily. 'Your Mama is gone to heaven. She is gone to live up with God and his angels.'

'Oh,' he said. He looked out the window at the funeral that hadn't yet tailed off. The winter sunlight slanted off the cars' windows so he couldn't see the people within them. 'But Mama is in her room. She told me to be a good boy.'

'Dear oh dear.' Aunt shook her head from side to side. 'Some young man is making up stories.' She looked at Nurse, blaming her.

Lally was confused, suddenly, about time. 'But I was in the bed . . .' Had he not cuddled and sang beneath the bedclothes with Mama? It was just now, wasn't it? Or was it yesterday? Or when?

He looked at Nurse. Nurse would know he had been out of the room. Then he got that strange feeling. The one he had had the day he had led his mother from the maze. A certainty that it had happened before. His recent visit to his mother too had happened before. Or maybe it had happened only once. Maybe the time in the maze had happened only once. Maybe it all happened a long time ago. Oh had it happened or was it just about to happen? Whichever way, it was real. She had been real, well, laughing in the bed, looking like Mama always did. As she would be. Tomorrow, or soon.

He had no time to sort out his confusion because something else was going on in the room that demanded his attention. Why was the room seeming to shake? The afternoon sun shone in the window, reflecting off a mirror on the dressing table and dancing on the walls. Why was it dancing? The mirror was shaking, that was why.

Nurse stood alongside the dressing table, holding onto it. The sun shone on her blue cardigan and she shook too. Up and down she vibrated, the same unsteady motion as the room. 'Please, Nurse Sheehy,' Aunt said in a low voice, 'not in front of the boy. You may leave the room.'

'Sorry Miss Connaughton.' As Nurse brushed past them a drop splashed onto the little table at which they sat. 'Sorry, but if I could only believe it. If you had only seen how well she looked when she went. She was so good to me.'

During the night that followed, attention was lavished on Lally. He sat on the steps behind the bar and his father doled him out bottles of lemonade and orange. There were lots of people about, sagely wagging heads, whispering behind his back or squeezing money into his fist while telling him his mother was gone to heaven.

Later their dirges ebbed through the hotel: 'Landlord fill the flowing bowl until the wine flows over ... For tonight we'll merry merry be, and tomorrow we'll be sober.' When Nurse found him he was in the lounge. Her upright form took shape through the screen of cigarette smoke. 'I'm not tired, I'm not tired,' he repeated dreamily.

She steered him to his bedroom. 'Don't you know Mama does not allow you in the lounge.'

In the days that followed, the echoes of laughter he had imagined about the hotel during the period of his mother's confinement returned again, but now only faintly. They had become but vaguely outlined stirrings of the air. They appeared on deserted landings of the hotel, he felt them behind him as he mounted staircases. They no longer beckoned him; they terrified him, yet he would not wish them away.

Nurse did go away. She was dismissed and Aunt took charge of the children. She decided Lally should sleep with his father. 'You will be company for him,' she said. One night, just as he was climbing into the wide bed, he began, for no apparent reason, to cry. 'You mustn't,' Aunt said.

'I can't stop.'

Aunt reached across the bed for the glass ashtray his father used when smoking during the night. 'Here, see can your tears fill this.' He stopped. 'Isn't that clever?' She laughed, getting him to laugh too. 'It always stops them, that's how I stop mine. Not a thimbleful can one fill when one has to think about it.' Aunt was clever.

She stroked his hair. 'You must not cry again.' Her laughter had stopped and the sudden sadness it gave way to surprised him. He had never seen anything worry her before. 'If you do you will only upset your father.'

As he went off to sleep, his heat warming the bed for his father, the words 'notice box' occupied his mind. Someone, he couldn't remember who, had once told him he was one. He hated being a notice box.

Nurse Sheehy did not move far from the hotel but into an upstairs flat on the opposite side of Bank Street from the nursery. A spring afternoon arrived that awakened the street. Breaths of air warmed the concrete and corners lay in light. Lally had been looking out the nursery window, struck for the first time by his vantage point. He could see roofs to the very town's edge, fields beyond. On the other side of the road Nurse Sheehy too looked out. She had heard magpies screech outside and wanted to know what it was all about. Squabbling petulantly, they landed on the roof above the boy's window and it was then she saw his upturned head. He's looking for the magpies, she thought.

She looked behind her into the room. She admired again the glass partition Fred had built her for the hairdressing salon. The boy's upturned face returned to her mind and suddenly she thought of Mama, who had said she would be her 'best customer'. She looked again at her glass partition and a big hole, empty as the salon, opened inside her.

An impulse seized her. She opened her window and called across the street.

THE DAY OF THE LONG KNIVES

AUNT RACED ROUND THE TABLE, shoved the chairs beneath it again. She clapped hands, the piano started again. Then, 'a one two', erect as a stick, around the table again she led the children in a march. 'Keep going, I'm puffed.' She laughed at Kelleher the piano player and dropped out, holding her sides. She looked out the window, at the fair-day activity, at the stallholders trapped in the centre of a sway of cattle below, seeming in danger of being stampeded. She dismissed the tightness in her chest. It had bothered her before, but she dismissed it. The fair-day dinners took precedence; she would have to get down to the kitchens, supervise them. Yes, she would have to get down, but in due course. Right now she was attending to her first and foremost duty: the health and education of her widowed brother's children.

'Keeping time to music', that was the latest step in Aunt's education programme. The lounge on the second floor suited her designs in every way: it was the widest room in the hotel. And with three windows, the only room on any floor with three, it was the longest. A piano had long stood in one corner, wasted in its wax and silence. And 'left right left right', the children marched in single file about the centrally located mahogany table while Aunt marshalled and Kelleher played 'O'Donnell Abu' on the piano.

The music stopped. The boy at the head of the parade stopped. His sister behind him, a year younger than he, faltered and then stopped. But the two little ones, the twinnies, marched on. A confusion of shin bones and sandals ensued in the sunlight beneath the middle window until Kelleher resumed again: 'Proudly the note of the trumpet is sounding...' he sang as the troupe re-formed and scuffled around the far end of the table.

As they passed the sideboard it shook. The two porcelain swans with the coal-black beaks and heartless eyes glided a little closer together along its polished surface. The laughing Dresden man tilted his fat blue belly in fearful fairytale fashion as they passed beneath him and then they were at Aunt's side of the table again. As she had done on each of the previous rounds, she bent when the twinnies reached her and with a light ruler tapped on each of their left shins, 'left left left left', until they were in step once again.

Again there was a concertinaing of bodies, a commotion of feet. Again they took off, wheeling between the table and the wide bulk of the pianist at his tilted stool. The elder boy imagined himself marching out to battle. The girl behind him studied the motion of his posterior. The little ones lost direction and would have tangled with Kelleher's stool had not Aunt bundled them safely, 'left right left right', around the table again.

When they had twice marched through 'O'Donnell Abu' and marched through half 'A Nation Once Again' and the elder ones had been stirred by Kelleher's rendering – 'When boyhood's fire was in my blood I dreamt of ancient freemen...' – Aunt stooped to whisper Kelleher something and again the music stopped.

'Continue, children.' She looked up for a moment. 'Keep in time. Listen to pretend music. Show me how you can be soldiers.' Aunt's whisper in Kelleher's ear was the first real flutter of an indication. Something was amiss. They continued to march.

Now only the swish of rising and falling feet, the sandal fall on the carpet, punctuated the air. Between each step there was a tremble of silver on the sideboard, and though they had all been synchronised to the rousing tune, the feet were soon all out of step so that a continuous syncopation of contacts vibrated about the room.

Kelleher's huge head slowly nodded in agreement with whatever it was Aunt was saying. She turned round to the children. 'We'll take a little rest while I go and see if Auntie Dwyer can come and watch.' She stood stiff-backed a moment, eyes searching into the distance. Then, face set firmly forward as though in her mind a decision had just been made, she moved towards the door.

As her hand touched the white-pearl door handle she seemed suddenly to get a wonderful idea.

'Aha.' Her long nose twitched and her eyelids flickered. 'What does an army on the march need?' Slowly, with a deepening sense of mystery, she looked at all the children in turn. There was silence. An impatient sound, the tap atap tap of hooves on the road, hooves of a thousand head of cattle, entered the room.

'Mr Kelleher, do you know?'

He did. 'A full tummy.' She snorted with great pleasure at his reply. Mr Kelleher was one of Aunt's favourites; a good tease.

'Hot buttered scones and milk,' she elaborated, 'and Mr Kelleher is included.' She laid an almost accusing finger in his direction. 'And boy do we know how much Mr Kelleher enjoys scones.' Then, almost doubling up at the joke shared with the other grown-up, Aunt snorted out of the room.

As soon as she had left, Kelleher swapped his piano stool for one of the high-backed lounge armchairs. Its wooden arm-rests embraced him. He relaxed into its welled, wide seat and he would have slipped off to sleep almost instantly had not the children started.

'How is Austin? Is her cut from the barbed wire better?'

'And Polly? How many buckets of milk had she this morning?'

'And Moorpark?'

They knew the names of all his dairy cows. And though they had never seen them, Mr Kelleher kept them so well in-formed that the naming of them had become a game.

'I'm a lonely old returned Yank.' Kelleher himself had en-couraged the game on earlier visits to the hotel. 'No com-pany except for my Friesians.'

'Nonsense,' Aunt had chided him. 'You are the best judge of dairy cows around, I'm sure you can as easily judge the ladies!' But Aunt had adopted Kelleher. 'He has a travelled mind,' she once told her brother.

Aunt liked to, as she called it, 'develop the children's im-agination'. 'Kelleher and Gary Cooper' – she constructed the Kelleher legend – 'facing one another across the catwalk of a runaway train. Eye to eye, hands on holsters . . .' Aunt too had worked in the United States. She too had a legend.

She returned to the room with an elderly lady. The lady had a slightly bluish complexion. Bruised, reddish-blue about cheekbones and nose, powdered nose tip. A large woman, she wheezed into the room. 'My own auntie,' Aunt introduced her to Kelleher, 'the children's grand-aunt.' Auntie was slightly stooped. 'Salute Major Dwyer, soldiers. Major Dwyer will inspect the troops,' Aunt said. Auntie Dwyer, with the aid of her walking stick, stood almost as erect as Aunt and Aunt doubled up with laughter.

She whispered to Kelleher that Auntie Dwyer was a retired nurse. That she would be needed for the job in hand. The elder children looked at one another.

When Aunt set down the tray, first on the floor so she could cover a corner of the table with a cloth, and then on the table, the elder girl asked – as this was usual suppertime fare – why they were having supper in the day.

Aunt walked to the window. She stood there a moment, looking controlled, and in the sunlight the pale mask of her sharp face became paler than ever.

'Oh, silly Billy.' She pretended to be surprised at the child's ignorance. 'This is elevenses. This is the correct, the done thing' – she exaggerated her *th* sounds – 'among adult upper-crusts at home while you have playtime at school.' She laughed uproariously with the two grown-ups. Then she dished out the scones – 'just look at the lovely runny butter; mind it doesn't get on your clothes' – while she herself had black coffee, no scone, and Auntie Dwyer smoked the single cigarette she allowed herself each day.

'And now I'll tell you why you have no school today.' She smoothed a paper napkin over a tea trolley and wheeled it into a corner of the room by a window. 'It's because Doctor Brett is calling on us.' She beamed over her charges; the wax cherry-cluster brooch hanging from her slight breast gleamed poisonously. 'And if we don't dawdle we'll just about finish our scones before he arrives.'

The thumbs of the two youngest leaped to their mouths. 'Come, children,' Aunt said and leaned before them, gently prising out the thumbs, smoothing hair back from lowered eyes, facing them squarely. 'Remember what happened the last two times Doctor Brett visited? And you were so worried. What did he do?'

There was no reply.

She asked the eldest. She could always appeal to him; rely on him. In dealings with him her favoured method of child rearing was possible: adult-to-adult communication.

'What was it I said he would do?'

'You said he'd give us a little prod,' he answered directly, liking the way Aunt elevated him.

'And what was it he did?'

'He gave us a little prod.' He laughed.

'And did it hurt?'

'Oh no.'

'On either occasion?'

'No. It was only a little prod.'

'Well then,' she said, looking at the little ones.

'And what was it I told you the little prods were for?'

'To see if there is a little army inside in our blood that will protect us from . . . ' He couldn't remember the words. 'That's right,' she assisted him, 'from invasion by foreign bodies', and Auntie Dwyer, who was listening between silent expulsions of catarrh from her mouth to her handkerchief, nodded in agreement.

'Well, this time we will examine your arms where you got those little prods and we will know from looking whether the little army is in barracks.'

'Does the 'xamine hurt, Aunt?' one of the twins asked, but Aunt, because the bigger boy had asked her the sort of intelligent question she herself encouraged, first enlightened him and so the little one's terror lingered on.

'And what will he do if the little army isn't in barracks?' he had asked.

'Oh,' she sniffed dismissively, 'if it isn't he'll give you a bigger prod.'

'A bigger prod! Will it hurt?' the other children implored, while the elder boy took Aunt's straight answer bravely on the chin.

Aunt looked briskly at Auntie Dwyer.

'Just a little, would you say, Auntie?'

'The BCG can be ticklish.' Auntie Dwyer nodded professionally to Aunt. Turning to the children Auntie Dwyer told them it would be nonsense to worry because it would all be done with and forgotten in no time.

Then it was Kelleher's turn to reassure the children. To each of them he handed the same amount of money, a sixpenny piece, and then he backed out of the room.

There was a brief silence. Aunt bounded onto a chair and straightened the head of the stuffed deer above the mantelpiece. Then she looked at the stuffed fox above the door. 'We'll have to straighten you too,' she said, 'or you won't be able to talk to your pal when we've left you alone in the room.' None of the children laughed. The silence resumed. There was a creaking sound from the landing outside. The noise of scraping and beating in the street receded until it became a whisper.

Doctor Brett was a big man. He took off his topcoat. His waistcoat was held together by its two top buttons. 'And how are the patients today?' he asked once he was comfortably seated.

Aunt introduced him to Auntie Dwyer. 'A retired nurse, no less, to help you.'

'A retired matron, no less,' he answered. 'We know one another of old, Miss O'Dwyer and I.' He winked to the children. 'I bet you didn't know your grand-aunt and I stitched up manys the soldier together.'

Aunt winced at the doctor's reference to stitching up. It was insensitive in the circumstances. She was surprised too that he and Auntie were acquainted. And somehow a little disappointed. As she busied about behind the doctor she could not help but smile. 'Like a well-husbanded pig' – she remembered

how she had once described him to the amusement of her
brother. 'A garland of double chins about his neck any farmer
would be proud of.' Not that being overweight in itself was
a fault. Aunt knew that not everybody could be expected to
be slim. Just because she and all of her family were like that.
Spare as whippets.

Unlike Kelleher, or Doctor Piggott the hospital doctor, the
GP was not one of Aunt's favourites. Tiny sleek Piggott,
dogged but urbane: she swapped case histories with Piggott,
discussed treatments, gave advice. It had even occurred to her
recently how Piggott might be someone she could confide
in. Should she feel the need for such. Not since America had
she had a confidant. With this country doctor there could be
no exchanges of that nature. Nor would she have picked him
for this job had the choice been hers. For this job which she
feared would be, as Auntie Dwyer said, ticklish. Not that she
would admit such to anyone. Least of all to her brother, who
had enough troubles; who had to be protected.

But child rearing was a challenge in which one took the
rough with the smooth. Aunt moved deftly behind the doctor, checking last-second details. A challenge, particularly in
the circumstances. The circumstances ran through Aunt's head.
Her twinnies: they were so hopelessly lost, little mites. But
they would heal. The elder girl wasn't easy: those prying, all-
seeing eyes that affected Aunt's sense of purpose. She would
have to get on top of that. And the elder boy, the elder boy
particularly. His education was not going according to plan.
Things she had seen him get up to recently . . . And she would
not tell his father. He seemed too much in the company of
the hotel maids. 'No horseplay,' she had said to him one day
she had seen him mount a chair, jump onto the broad back
of the shrieking, delighted scullery maid. She had seen him
lift the apron of another, until the cream of her skin fleshed

through. She knew it was not horseplay. She thought it might be best he be sent to boarding school. Except she had no intention of doing that: that was admitting defeat. She had plans for him.

Ministered to by Auntie Dwyer, the doctor set up his little gas burner on the tea trolley on which the paper napkin had been laid. He filled a syringe with boiling water and with little chuckles of mirth he squirted his syringeful over the children. It was his way of lightening the operation, but they cowered away. Aunt sniffed in disapproval. Auntie Dwyer too disapproved, stiffening professionally on her chair. The doctor opened two flat boxes of surgical instruments, also a box with rows of bottles containing a creamy substance. He placed the box beside the burner. It had an invisible, but not inaudible, flame.

The children did not dwell on the glimmering battery of steel, symbol of the order and modernity that set this countryman alone and isolated from the people from whom he had sprung; they had retreated to the end window.

They looked down on the street. A huddle of cattle almost directly below swayed from roadway to footpath and back again. Bullocks rose onto the backs of one another, their tasselled underparts twitching idly. Every now and then one of them broke free and skidded into the open space between its group and the other groups. Two ragged men, custodians of the cattle lot, then charged after it with flailing sticks, returning it before the lot could break up in disorder.

Aunt's voice called. Left arms were bared to the shoulders and paraded in single file before Doctor Brett, who looked at each one for the raised bump that would indicate the presence of antibodies.

'Oh, there's a strong arm,' he admired the elder girl as she passed. 'Maybe we don't need another needle.'

The elder children exchanged looks when he made no further comment. But when Auntie Dwyer dabbed the freezing cotton wool on their arms and the ether evaporated almost immediately so too did any hope of avoiding the third prod.

The elder children were motioned out of the way, the little ones planted directly before the trolley. Brett sat behind it; the women stood on either side.

Four cold hands steadied the little boy's tensed faggot of an arm while the doctor held up a syringe. 'This time it will take a second longer.' He held his instrument before the child's eyes and squeezed lightly so that a globule welled onto the needle mouth and remained there. 'But you're a big soldier now.'

Then he jabbed. The little boy gave out a low moan. As the slow, deadening lead weighed into him his lips became blue. Auntie Dwyer dabbed him with cotton wool when the syringe had been withdrawn. Aunt carried him back to a chair.

The elder boy volunteered to go next. Aunt said it was better he wait until last. 'We may need your assistance, big guy,' she said.

The smaller girl snivelled in fear from the moment she saw her brother's deathly slump until she herself, a shivering bundle, was placed alongside him. She had kicked the doctor; not because of what he had done to her but because of what he had done to her brother. Auntie Dwyer ordered she be swaddled. Aunt found a heavy tablecloth from a drawer in the sideboard.

The elder girl corkscrewed out of Aunt's grip when it came to her turn, but Aunt capably pinned her down. 'Gee whiz,' Aunt tittered to Auntie Dwyer, 'you would think it was the Night of the Long Knives.'

'What do you mean, Long Knives?' Auntie Dwyer wheezed.

The bigger boy was not watching. He was looking out of

the middle window. Below him a wide creel of bonhams shone like eels in the sun. A man lifted them out. He caught each one by the hind leg, jerked it up in the air, handed it to a man standing above and alongside him in a small trailer. As each piglet, its trotters threshing in the air, was hoisted from the creel, it seemed to squeal in even greater agony than its fellows before it.

The girl again corkscrewed out of Aunt's grip, this time while the inoculant was flowing into her arm. The doctor examined his syringe; something had broken inside her.

'Dear, dear,' Auntie Dwyer clucked.

'Now for some fun,' the doctor said and waited, pincers at the ready, until Aunt had shaken the girl to a standstill.

'Now, Dorrie,' she said calmly as he plucked the steel out of the pulped arm, 'we're not a baby, nothing to be alarmed of.'

'You're cutting me,' the bigger boy whined when it came his turn. 'Get off.' This was not a prod; it was an excavation. 'Get off, Auntie Dwyer,' he bawled. 'Stopit cutting!'

He was in such a state when the end came he did not feel the cooling smear of antiseptic – the indication that it was all over. 'I'm going,' he shouted shamefully. He ran from the lounge, leaving the door open. He staggered up the linoleum stairway and into the light from the skylight on the staff quarters landing above.

Once the doctor's duties were done, Aunt was brusque. She would have seen him to the street. But Auntie Dwyer said she and he would stay in the lounge a while for a chat. Aunt said she would have tea and sandwiches sent up to them.

Kelleher was next on her list. Before she could go in search of him, however, she had her three charges delivered to the nursery. 'Her punctured balloons', as she decided she would call them when later relating the incident to her brother, humouring him. She would not mention his eldest son's retreat.

She headed then for the select bar. There, she knew, she would find Kelleher. It was his daily routine: a bottle of ale before dinner in the dining room.

She hoped she could count on Kelleher to come along to the laity reading she had planned in the Confraternity Hall. The local clergy she had little time for. 'The laity on the march', she knew it from her American experience. It was the only hope.

Kelleher was not in the select bar. It was crowded with the loud noises of men from the fair. Her next call was to the parlour behind the bar. There she found him, in the semi-dark. Nancy the barmaid had not yet raised the blinds. She stood behind a counter, smoking a cigarette, shining glasses, tinkling every now and then with laughter. Kelleher and Quinlan, a farmer and longtime resident of the parlour, sat at the other side. Aunt raised the blinds.

'I should have known where I'd find you,' she teased Kelleher, pulling him another bottle.

'Are they all right, the children?' He raised his eyes toward the room above him.

'Yes, taken it manfully,' she answered.

Then she teased Quinlan. 'You'll come to the meeting. Shock the clergy and maybe get to Paradise in spite of them!'

Quinlan raised himself from his glass. 'I would come to the meeting, Aunt, except it would make little difference. No reservations have been booked in Paradise for me. When I die, I'll knock on the window, and I'll say to you, Aunt, move over there a little for me and make yourself sparse.'

'Sparse.' In convulsions of laughter Aunt left the parlour.

Once in the back corridor she checked herself. The tiredness she had recently been noticing had suddenly caught up with her. She slumped a moment, knowing nobody could see her, and recovering went in search of the boy.

She climbed the stairs, one, two, three flights, and by the time she reached the top of the hotel she was winded again. And tight inside. She stood beneath the skylight. Nothing ever winded Aunt. She thought of the marching earlier, and rubbing her hand across her forehead tried to relieve the iron frown it had settled into. She held the banisters. A moment's rest was all she needed, she knew that.

As she stood there, sounds of the fair day filtered through the skylight. Shouting, and the hooves of cattle slithering around the corner of the hotel. There was a scraping sound. The street must be emptying, she thought. The shopkeepers are shovelling muck from the doors. Johnny Shortall's and Meagher Bros, on the far side of the street. Shovelling slush. In her mind's eye she saw it move in wavelets along the roadway. She saw them wipe spatters off windows, smelled the soiled sawdust they swept off shop floors. Its stench weakened her. She wondered how they had the enthusiasm to go on. She opened the door to the low-ceilinged attic in which the maids quartered.

Aunt was disappointed when she saw him. Settled in the damp bed linen on one of the trestle beds. One of a row of beds facing a tiny mantelpiece jammed beneath a sloping ceiling. He had a magazine at his knees.

He gave her a quick, hostile look and then stared at the weakly luminous holy water fount propped on the mantelpiece, letting her know that it and not the magazine was what he had been looking at all the time and that this was where he intended to stay. Aunt looked at it. She saw, clearly, immediately, the same object the boy had seen swim before his tear-filled eyes, seen swim into focus and blur again until in the end, to his enjoyment, he could blur or focus it at will. She saw a hideous piece of plastic.

But she was pleased he was dry-eyed, and that his sobbing

had stopped. Sometime, she noted, but not now, she would give him a lecture on idolatry.

She was pleased to see he had recovered, but she was disturbed at the nature and location of his recovery. So here was his sanctuary; it disturbed her. How many times had he slid in here before?

She was not, she said, disappointed with him. He, after all, was little more grown up yet than a child. It was the maids who disappointed her. No pride in themselves. The unmade beds ... Surprising that, people so good at making beds throughout the hotel every morning and yet couldn't make their own.

Sheets, bras and corsets, shoes, women's magazines with soft, greasy pages were jumbled between beds so that the floor was hardly visible. Quickly Aunt stooped between the beds, tidying. She gathered the combs, the brushes, the talcum, the lipsticks, the clumps of hair. Each removal created space into which more air, more light might enter; until she was satisfied the oily smell, the arousing, soothing dampness was gone.

She picked up the magazine that lay on his knees. She flicked the pages: page after page of handsome men who gazed into the eyes of women; eyes out of which little stars sprinkled, like salt from salt cellars.

Aunt was disappointed again. This time with him. Disappointed, she said, with his choice of reading material. She led him down the linoleum-covered steps, across the landing, down another stairs, up another stairs, away from hotel noises, into the quiet of the family's living quarters and into the even more cloistered atmosphere of her own small bedroom.

She sat him on the silk counterpane of her bed and drew a bundle of wide-paged magazines from beneath her dressing table. American magazines: *Saturday Evening Post*; *Life*. On their covers jacketed men stood beside jeeps. High up in pine forests they breathed mountain air.

'Should I tell your father where I found you or should I leave that to you?' Her tone was casual. 'You know your father has a wider hand than I, a better spanker.' She hold out a long hand for comparison.

'That is the reason for this little fat place, you know, but only on children.' She smacked him on the bottom, surprised at the force with which her hand met his rear, surprised at the desire, which she kept in check, to smack him again. 'What is far more important is the question of your reading. You'll like these' – she handed him the magazines, not looking at the face that had flared red as her cherry brooch. 'We'll share my mail-order from now on.' She was pleased, laughing in a sisterly way. 'And we'll see about getting you one of the classics. Let me see . . . ' She crooked her head sideways a few moments. 'What about *Little Women* . . . ? Or *Jo's Boys* . . . ? Or maybe *Good Wives* . . . ?' She pretended not to notice his look of shame 'Or what about . . . *Little Men*?' she relented. 'I think you should have graduated to *Little Men*.'

'Doctor Brett will not need to call again,' she went on casually. 'It seems a pity . . . ' the casual tone deserted her, became almost a sigh, wistful, almost exaggeratedly so '. . . a pity he could not have seen how brave you can be. How you can march . . . ' She looked out the window and over the house roofs at the distant mountain and sky. The boy could see only her straight silhouette. He could not see her hands. She held them before her, clasped to her front, her face set in what the twinnies called her 'poor Aunt sick' expression.

A magpie on an opposite rooftop captured her attention. It swooped down on a litter of straw at road level. Her eyes followed and settled on the street. There were spaces now between the cattle lots; parts of the road surface were visible again. Herds of cattle were wheeling away, driven down Bank

Street, clumping fearfully together, skidding along the road's centre to the station. The cattle trains would take them to the dockyards. They would cross the sea to Yorkshire, the fattening fields. Aunt watched a buyer stand astride the road and take one last look at his purchase. She watched him make a note on his chequebook. He took off the cattle dealer's calico that had protected his clothes and she admired his overcoat. Well-tailored, its velvet collar glistened damply. Kelleher passed at that same moment alongside him. On his way home. It seemed to Aunt he slouched. She watched shopowners on the far side of the street appear out of doors. Watched them blink in the sun and, suddenly industrious, take the protective barriers from their windows.

The stallholders were folding up canvas stalls, hastily piling them away in vans. Aunt smiled: the shopkeepers' reappearance was harrying them. She watched the departure; the cattle buyers, the hawkers, everything moving on. Her mind stilled. The tightness in her breast eased. As if something sharp had been removed from within her. She was travelling too. Not very far, yet, but on the start of something. To the city, the tumult of thought and progress, a taxi, her hotel, Jury's in Dame Street. She would slip through the revolving door. Joke with the elevator man. Thinking of the pleasure she would read on his face at seeing her again she smiled. George the elevator man, who would see she received her usual: her books and peace, her reservation for the opera, her black coffee and American cigarettes.

'Yes, how you can march, pardner.' She turned around to the boy, the sun's brightness pouring from her. He was reading her magazine.

'How you can march so like a soldier.' She clicked heels to attention. 'On the left foot, quick march.' Four airy strides brought her across her room. She sat then on her bed and with

CLOUDS OVER SUEZ

AUNT, HIS FATHER, BARRY WHO worked for his father, and himself. They were all cut off from the midnight Mass by a high brown partition. On his side there were only four pews and the people packed into them. He could hear chanting from the other side and he supposed this was the way churches were in monasteries.

Aunt rose and promptly fell to her knees again in the certainty that without her the congregation would not have known whether to sit, stand or kneel. Berry slept in a heap on the edge of a pew. He himself sat attentively, his ears peeled for the alleluia. 'The Christmas alleluia will inspire you,' Aunt had forewarned him. He denounced Barry, as would Aunt, but it was his kneeling father who caused him greatest concern.

His father knelt all the time. As he always did. On the Sundays, the weekdays, the confraternity Monday mornings on which he accompanied him to their local church. He did rise for hymns but then crumbled again on his knees, his face covered behind outstretched hands, lost to the world. He knew he had a lot to pray about; many tragedies had befallen him. He knew his focus was Jesus on the Cross. Even tonight, as the incense wafted with the rise and fall of the psalms into their part of the church – into the part, he decided, where the monks allowed ordinary people – even on this birthday night in Bethlehem, his father's vision was the outstretched figure on the Cross. He sensed that as his father's tragedies grew darker so too would the intensity of his devotion grow more severe.

His own trouble was that he could not create in himself the same devotion. Oh, he could pray for a minute or two. He could tell Jesus about his good daddy. He could ask Jesus to look after him. And look after his mama in heaven. And Aunt, well Aunt didn't need prayers. Oh, he could pray, deeply too, rightly or wrongly, for those things he wanted. Or at least for some of them. Of course he could not ask God if he might stop his father from teaching him to ride the pony. Learning to ride the pony was the most dreadful cross on his horizon. But he knew that God's designs and his father's were somehow the same. There were other things he wanted and could ask for. The hosanna rumbled over him. 'Dear God, please please, I want a rifle from Santa for Christmas.'

No, he could never pray like his father. He could not pray like him or ride a horse like him. He could not, when Communion time would arrive, walk round that partition and up to the marble altar rails with him. And find out what was going on. After a time, long before the offertory hymn and then the pause, the tinkle of bells, the awakening of communicants as they shuffled into the inner sanctum, like Barry, he was numbed into slumber.

The last rousing notes, pumped from the organ, came to rest among the high rafters. The last of the congregation were leaving the church. But he waited. He waited for his father and for Aunt; both of them were still praying. He wondered if the alleluia had been sung. He hadn't heard it. He felt bad about himself and wondered could he tell Aunt, if she asked him about it, that he had. She was not easily fooled. Then, seeing his father's posture, isolated at his bench from the rest of the world, he wondered what he could be feeling so bad about. A fleeting image of his father passed through his mind as he pondered: a whip in his hand, standing alongside the jump, coaxing the pony over it, while he himself clung terrified to its back. 'Dig in your heels, blast you!' the raucous roar. Now he wanted to put his arms round his slumped father. He was the best person in the world.

It was just as he smelled the extinguished candles. He heard a titter of laughter from the other side of the partition.

He walked from the church and into a night transformed by magic. 'Happy Christmas' – the greetings warmed the air. 'Happy Christmas, Lally,' someone called to him. The line of cars drove down the monastery drive, quickening once they turned into the road to town. The stars shone brighter now, stiller and deeper in space than ever, and below them the fields had become strangely shadowed.

'Great young lad for your age,' Barry said. 'I hope you said your prayers. And told that man above to keep an eye on Santy, whatever you want off him.'

He hoped Barry might ask him what he wanted. 'Oh, a rifle,' he would have said. 'Oh, the black rifle with the brown stock and the air sights, the one in Aunt's American catalogue.' Then his father and Aunt would be sure to remember; even if his recent suspicions regarding Santa held substance he would be safe. But Barry was already cocooned within a corner at the back of the car. His mind was already deaf to Aunt's rebuttal: 'Silly Paddy Barry, you don't ask Jesus for things like that.'

He woke. His father had stopped the car in the middle of the country and was pointing up through the windscreen and into the heavens. 'There he goes,' he said, 'between the stars. The reindeers, the sleigh: listen.'

'Where is he?' He looked through the windscreen; there was such a tremor in his father's voice.

'He drove over us, did you not hear?'

'Oh yes.' He heard distant music. He saw a light, it slid between stars, it was there an instant and then dropped out of the sky. 'But he's gone.'

'He's gone on his rounds.' His father turned to him, bestowed on him the most childlike smile he had ever seen.

'We better get quickly to bed then,' Aunt said drily.

'He has a long old journey.' Barry woke up and fell asleep again.

He thought deeply. 'What did he look like, Dada?'

'I couldn't see, but I heard him laughing.'

The years of growing doubt, the rumours, that disturbing titter he thought he had heard from behind the partition at the end of Mass, all fell away in that instant. The uncertainty of Santa and yet the promise, the distant echo of Santa's laugh, the light that moved through the sky, these became real, enwrapped in the psalm of the choir still vibrating in his ears.

First he heard the dog bark. Then, opening his eyes to bright light, he heard shrill voices. He jumped out of the bed he shared with his father and ran to the window. There, on the street, were the cowboys. The sun glinted from the roofs. In its light, the cowboys stood comparing guns, a dog yelping about their heels. Was he dreaming? He was weak with the sight. He rubbed his breath from the window.

He puzzled over the night before. Had he been awake or asleep? There had been noise from the bar-room below his bedroom. The usual noise: someone dredging a song, over and over again, 'The Wild Colonial Boy'. He imagined at one stage there was someone else in the bedroom. It would not have been his father. He would still have been in the bar cleaning the glasses after the drinkers. He imagined someone had moved across the room, there was a pinpoint glow of light. Like the cigarette glow every night when his father came to bed. Does Santa smoke cigarettes?

Suddenly he was in the present. He was awake. It was Christmas morning and he was standing at the window. In the silence of Santa's departure. His eyes darted across the expanse of empty bed, to its foot, to where a mound of parcels lay.

He threw aside a lightweight, fishnet stocking. It would be Ludo and Snakes and Ladders and some sweets, he received it every year. He tore at the parcel which, he could already see, was the wrong shape. He glimpsed something black and shiny through the wrapping paper. 'If it's not the rifle it must be a revolver.' It felt hard but did not have a revolver's shape. He pulled at it. It was the same as something of his father's, only smaller: a pair of binoculars.

It fell to the bed, tumbled onto the carpet. He did not pick it up. 'Oh Aunt,' he moaned, 'I asked for a rifle from Santy.' He had spent all last week looking at guns in the shop windows. In the light of day and under the streetlamps by night. Guns, revolvers, rifles; the rifle in the American catalogue he had pointed out to Aunt. In her *Saturday Evening Post*. 'We'll see,' she had said, 'we'll see.'

Then the door opened. His younger brother stood there, a holster on either hip, a gun in either hand. 'Oh look what I got from Santy.' The guns were so heavy, the barrels so long, he could hardly hold them straight. He had never seen such cool, blue barrels. 'You're too small, those guns are mine. Santy made a mistake. You're only five and I'm eight. Here, this is yours.' He picked up the binoculars and pushed them towards his younger brother. 'No.' His brother, armed to the teeth as he was, beginning already to feel outmanoeuvred, backed from the room. 'No, he gave them to me, they're mine.' He raised his voice; if Aunt was about, she would come to his assistance.

'Here, take this.' He decided on an approach. 'You're better on ponies than I am. I don't like ponies. You and Dada do. This is for you to watch the races with.'

It was a costly admission he was making. His father, he had often heard it said, was a fine horseman. He had ridden point-to-points, was now a prominent huntsman. His father tried to make horsemen of both his brother and he. He so much wanted to be like him but he stiffened in dread whenever he was seated on a pony, whilst his brother already loved them. And last summer . . . last summer his father had schooled him over low fences. 'I can't, I can't,' he had pleaded, with such conviction that his first reaction to every future task would be 'I can't', and he had fallen off even before reaching the fences. Last summer had been a painful business. 'Here, take these binoculars and you can go instead of me to the races. Santy made a mistake.'

But then Aunt was at the door. 'Oh my, my,' she said. He could tell her tone indicated disappointment. He knew she had witnessed everything that had taken place. 'Tears, and on such a happy morning.'

Then her eyes lit up. 'Oh Lally, show me what you got. My my, a pair of binoculars. Your father will be so pleased.' Her eyes passed over his face, over his misery. 'I want you both to come downstairs and show him what Santa Claus, good good Santa Claus, brought you.'

He knew then, even before he said it, that what he was about to say next was untrue. That Aunt knew otherwise. 'It's a mistake,' he said sullenly. 'The guns are mine. The binoculars are for him.'

'Why is it a mistake?' she asked calmly.

'I didn't ask for binoculars.'

'Oh poor Santa. Fancy Santa making a mistake. But you must remember Santa is having a very difficult time this year. You do know about the Suez blockade don't you?' She had a way of making him look at her, of raising his eyes to hers.

'Yes.'

She had shown him a picture in the newspaper: a line of enormous ships whose prows reared above the banks of a narrow cutting of water while far below on the ground stood a camel. 'Only the camel budges,' she had said. 'And camels I'll have you know, Lal, are not noted budgers!'

'Yes.'

'Well, Santa wrote to me some time ago and explained how, because of the Suez blockade, he could only bring certain toys this year. Do your best, I wrote back to him. If you can't carry guns across the canal, I added, knowing guns would be a particular problem, my eldest nephew would be delighted with binoculars. Then when he goes racing with his father he can show them off.'

'Did you tell all that to Santa?' The younger boy was impressed.

'I did tell all that to Santa, and told him too what a spoilsport old Anthony Eden is.' She giggled.

Aunt scrutinised the listening children, looking pleased with herself. Lally squinted up at her: her story sounded plausible, he wanted to believe it, but was she making it up? She told so many stories: about all the parts of the world she had visited. Stories about herself, involved in all sorts of adventures. While she worked in Boston, before she had come home to look after himself, his brother and sisters. Aunt had been housekeeper to a houseful of young Catholic priests. They had sounded great fun: 'my big pets', she still called them. 'And I was their high priestess.' She had been receptive to ideas in America.

'Children must be treated just like adults.' America had taught her that. 'Truthfully, openly. But remember too that imaginations must not be neglected.' Right now he didn't feel like having his imagination cultivated. 'Why did he get guns then and I didn't?' he asked.

Aunt was becoming annoyed because the older boy refused to be sidetracked by her elaborations. But she remained calm.

'Come, come,' she shivered. 'It's cold. Have you forgotten your posh new clothes. Christmas Day and still in your bare feet and pyjamas, what will your father say?

'Lally, you won't disappoint him, will you? You know he is taking you racing tomorrow. Oh, I can picture you two tomorrow. You and your father in the parade ring, as sharply turned out as two buttons.' She made a bouquet of her hand and blew it an admiring kiss, 'My two handsome men. It will be his first day back since your mama . . .' The hand she lightly laid on his shoulder weighed down on him heavily.

'Now let's see what nice clothes we will put on you today.' She took the smaller boy to his room and when she returned she again laid her hand on the bigger boy's shoulder. She stooped to his level and looked into his eyes. He could see in hers the reflection of his long face and of the binoculars where she had hung them over his neck. He held her eyes a moment, surprised at their pale blueness. As he looked they diminished in size so that his own reflection became lost. 'It does one good not to get what one wants,' she said. The black points of her eyes flickered away from him and focused somewhere away in the distance. He fought not to understand what she was saying, and at the same time wondered what it was her eyes were looking for.

The hotel was quieter than on any other morning of the year. This morning the only two guests on the register were the two permanent ones, middle-aged Miss Carroll and old Miss Dwyer.

As the two boys, now fully clad, walked down the stairs that led from the family quarters, Miss Dwyer was also making her way down the wider hotel stairs. All were headed towards the dining room, where Aunt and the boys' father were already seated over breakfast. They met beneath the arch in the dark, Christmas-decorated foyer.

'And look who Santa has come to,' Miss Dwyer wheezed. 'Look at his big guns and his lovely new clothes.' She admired the bigger boy. 'And what did you get?' The smaller boy was holding a pair of binoculars.

'Look through this, Auntie Dwyer,' the smaller boy said, 'and see.' As soon as Aunt had left them to dress the bigger boy had allowed his younger brother to look through the binoculars at the straggle of cowboys who had reappeared at the far end of the street. But only on condition he held the guns. The little boy had become infatuated with what he could see.

'Dear me.' Miss Dwyer looked through the wrong ends. The balloons she beheld on the foyer wall were distant cherries. 'Dear, dear me.'

'Santa made a mistake, Auntie Dwyer,' the bigger boy was sticking to his story. 'It was the Suez Canal. It was old Anthony Eden's fault.'

He would stick to his story too when they presented themselves to his father. He could already picture him. He and Aunt would be the only ones in the long dining room. They would be seated at its far end, in the weak sunlight, beneath the paper globe that decorated it each Christmas and which each Christmas seemed a little smaller than it had the year before. His father, this one morning, would have no mail to go through, would be the essence of gaiety. Eager to appraise whatever it was Santa had brought his children.

Aunt would be furious, but she would say nothing.

His brother pushed open the dining room door. 'Look, Dada, look what I got' – he waved his binoculars – 'Santa made a 'istake.'

Suddenly he knew who would be the horseman in his family. He knew who would be the apple of his father's eye. He was appalled. But it was too late.

He knew too that this Christmas, on which he had celebrated his first midnight Mass, was the Christmas of his last real Santa Claus.

Bitterly, he wondered how he could have clung for so long to such a foolish notion. And yet . . . He hung back at the doorway, hands frozen to the revolver handles, a gunfighter in stasis. And yet . . . What other notion could there have been . . ? The notion of the remote figure of his father, parcel-laden at the foot of his bed . . ? His father . . ? Oh no. Ever since its first dawning in his mind that notion had seemed the most far-fetched of all.

As he struggled with his revelation of a world without Santa another revelation, somehow connected but even more far-fetched than the first, rushed at him. It blinded him as it too fought for consideration. It came between him and the sight of his younger brother, standing in the middle of the dining room, peering at him through the binoculars. 'Dada look, Lally got guns.'

It was something that had struck him once before. Once, when he had asked Aunt something about God and she had told him about her nervous breakdown in America. 'There are pitiable people,' she had said, 'who don't believe in God. Faith in Christ lost.'

'There aren't, Aunt?'

'Yes there are! Like me. When I lost my faith. And had my terrible crisis. My terrible emptiness.' As she had said it she had looked across her shoulder and shuddered as if a cloud hung over her. 'But for my dear Boston boys. They nursed me through.'

And now Aunt believed in midnight Mass again . . . Did she? In midnight Mass. His father certainly did.

And he did.

Even though he had not got what he asked for. The guns, oh the guns, he tried to walk like a sheriff. But as he skirted between the empty tables to that table at the far end of the dining room the guns hanging at his waist weighed him down heavily.

SPRING FLOWERS

L ALLY'S FATHER TOOK HIS EYES off the laneway ahead of
him. Through a gap in the hazel hedgerow he had seen
a tractor. It bounced across a meadow, making slow headway
yet defiantly holding the cutter bar of its mowing machine
in the up position. Lally too caught sight of it. It was too stuffy,
though, in the car to pay it attention. Smothered in grass, it
barely reached the surface of his mind.

He toppled about in his seat. It seemed to him the bumpy
laneway would never end. Inward it burrowed, into the world,
inward, downward, until his head began to nod and he thought
they passed down valleys of trees and fields into the fresh well
of the earth. His father hammered his feet on the brakes and
he opened his eyes. A yard lay spread out before them. They
slid and skidded and slammed to rest on a mound of yellow
weeds. He would have hit the dashboard had not his father
thrown an arm in front of him.

He got out on the solid ground, vibrated in the warm air
awhile, out of the hot leather. His stomach settled down.

Something seemed about to happen in the engine, which
was releasing and rending as though it would crack apart. But
then it too settled down.

His father whistled softly to himself, forced wind through

his teeth rather, as he looked for a sign of life about the yard. A collie, black and white, stood up and slowly straightened itself.

His father lit a cigarette and strode towards the sheds. The yard was in silence. It was bound on two of its sides by low-slung sheds. Collapsed iron gates and bits of rusting machinery bounded its third. The gable end of a house completed the enclosure.

A pigeon lifted off from the shade of a sycamore tree and startled the silence. Then everything was still again and Lally was standing in the centre of this area and it was more than just a receptacle for animals and buckets. It had an existence of its own, spread out before him, that he could not name.

He looked into a puddle, wondering if he stirred its muddy bottom would the oily slick that coloured its surface disappear. It looked deep.

A door in the gable of the house scraped open and a big man, deep-jowled, big head, cap reaching only across part of it, emerged from within. Tugging at the cap, he banged the door behind him. He grabbed a stick that stood propped against the wall. Then he drew a hand across nose and mouth, flicked something, food or spit, onto the ground.

'I was eatin' the bite of dinner,' the big man called. 'It was only the luck of God ye got me at home. I have a meadow to cut down there but ye might never find me if I was below and she's kind of heedless.' He nodded his head back towards the house. 'She might send ye anywhere lookin' for me.'

The man's name was Billy Burke, 'Ructions' Burke as he was sometimes called, and Lally knew him; he often bought meat at his father's butcher shop. He also visited his father's lounge bar.

On the occasions his father had time to tell him stories, usually while they drove about the countryside, he sometimes told him about Billy Burke. His father would have been a good storyteller if it wasn't that as he got closer to the funny part he laughed more and more himself so that his listeners never enjoyed the humour as it was meant to be enjoyed; they laughed as much at his spluttering as at his stories. He wasn't a professional storyteller; his heart was too much in the telling.

His stories were about 'characters', as he called them, and Lally always enjoyed them. Billy Burke, however, was a different sort of 'character'. He'd seen his father having to push Burke out of the bar one night late. Both of them were shouting at the tops of their voices. Both of them with clenched jaws. Burke had caught his hand in the side of the door and wouldn't let go, so that the door could not be closed on him.

'Great day, Billy,' his father greeted him now.

'Do you think it's settled, Connaughton?'

'I do. Are the heifers in?'

Burke did not answer the question immediately. Instead he enquired about his man Egan. Egan, he said, had gone into town on the tractor yesterday and hadn't come home.

'I'm worried this good weather will break. Every winter and spring he's here and he won't stir out of the place. Won't come to race meeting, point-to-point, a drink, nothing. As soon as good weather, and hay to be saved ... and he has to shag off to a public house.'

This, he explained, was the real reason they had caught him at home. He was waiting for Egan. He thought they might have seen him. Then he answered Connaughton's question.

'They are in.' Attempting to step over a puddle he sent a spray up his inside trouser-leg.

With surprising agility he sprang onto dry ground. 'Bloody Egan,' he cursed. 'I told him to sweep the yard too, but no, he wouldn't.'

Lally, who had puzzled at some difference in Billy's

appearance, now realised what the puzzle was. He wore shoes.
He had never before seen him wear anything other than wellingtons. In the shoes he looked lighter, more tame. Almost
tame enough to tell him about the tractor he had seen in the
field. Except he wasn't sure if he had really seen it. Especially
when his father didn't mention anything about it. It mustn't
have been Egan.

'They are in,' Billy said again and headed towards the shed.
It was so dark within its shade that nothing of its interior was
visible. 'And a good job too they are in. The fly is so bad out
there today it would run them wild around the field. They'd
lose weight.

'We don't want them losing condition,' he winked at the
boy scrambling across the puddles in his wake, 'to have your
father tell us they're not good enough.' Seeing Billy's bleary
eye close and slowly reopen, Lally's first inclination was to
wince. But he smiled. He smiled at Billy, then at his father.

'What do you think of them, victualler?' The men stood
by the wide entrance to the shed, adjusting their eyes to its
darkness. There was a wide gate across it, and two heifers lay
chewing in its shadow, staring at the glare of the day outside.
One flicked a fly with continuous slight movements of an ear.

'Hup.' Burke found a clod of hard dung and lobbed it on
the back of one of the beasts. They both rose.

'Well?' he enquired again as they stiffened, making bone-
groaning sounds. 'What did I tell you, I told you last night
they were quality.'

Quality. Lally knew what quality meant. It meant fleshy
neck flaps that hung from beneath the jaw to beneath the
forelegs. These two had it. They were certainly fat as any heifers
he'd seen on previous buying expeditions. But they were dirty.
Heavy knuckles of dung scaled from their tails so that every
time one of them moved there was a noise like the rattle of

rosary beads. Along their bellies, necks and faces they were streaked with muck. The stench of stagnant water lifted off them. It had a cooling effect.

His father shi-shi-shiddled. That was the way Lally described his sound of broken but regularly occurring outbreaths through slightly parted teeth. Not a whistling sound. Rather the expression of a rhythm from somewhere within him. It went along with the look of pleasure he always wore when he judged cattle.

'But they are very small.' He seemed to be talking to himself.

'Too fat.' He was still addressing himself; he climbed over the gate for a closer inspection.

'Nice, Billy, nice on the surface.' He shook his head in disappointment at Burke. 'Nice but no substance, too much fat, won't kill out. Too much waste.'

'Jesus, Connaughton.' Burke in turn climbed over the gate. Lally saw the beginnings of a wink in his direction and this time avoided it. 'I never yet seen you satisfied.

'Too much fat.' He mimicked Connaughton's condemnation. 'Too much waste, won't kill out . . . If I tell you I gave them heifers the best of treatment over the winter, victualler . . . If I tell you I let them out in the bite of grass I saved for them as early as April . . . If, if I tell you I watched them every day until they were just right before callin' you out here . . .' Burke lost the thread of his counterattack and regained it again: ' . . . to have you tell me there's too much waste on them, well that's, that's . . .' he looked up towards the rickety support beams for inspiration ' . . . well that's the bloody limit!' He looked hurt.

Connaughton drew a cigarette from his box. He tapped the cigarette end against the box, packing its tobacco. Sliding it through his fingers he tapped its other end. At the same time he walked behind one of the heifers with a sheaf of straw bedding, shushing her before him. He scowled intently.

'Connaughton.' The shout suddenly broke out of Burke, recalling both men from silent thought. 'How much are you offering me for them?' His great golfclub-shaped stick thumped the ground and spatters leaped out of the litter.

Connaughton laughed. There was a challenge in the laugh, but it had the effect on the boy of relief. He drew on his cigarette. 'Oh, you name your price,' he said. 'That's your privilege.'

Burke scraped dung from the side of his shoes with the stick. For a time he became so intent on this exercise that the boy also became involved. He itched to point out to the farmer places that he hadn't scraped. He wanted to prise a big clump that clung between the shoe's heel and sole.

'Well, I'll be honest with you,' Billy said, and became absorbed again in his shoes. 'I won't beat about the bush, take them or leave them, I want forty pounds a head for them.'

The boy looked at the men. Burke seemed in despair; his father seemed furious. 'Billy,' he said, 'you're wasting my time dragging me out here. We both have better to be doing. Go and cut your hay.

'And you get into that car, Lally.'

As they backed the car out of the yard Burke splashed round to the boy's door and grabbed the handle. With a great show of patience Connaughton drew back the handbrake and let the engine idle.

'Hould on,' Burke said. 'What's your hurry?' The sleeves of Connaughton's shirt had fallen loose; he rolled them over the elbows again. It was hot in the car.

'Young fella' – Burke's purple-skinned head filled the open window – 'do you like apples?'

Lally did like apples. Apples, white soda bread, age-stained seedcake, damp Marietta biscuits: anything that came his way on these trips he ate, while his father haggled over prices. And he wished now he could leave the car; the smell of petrol was overpowering. Yet he looked towards his father for approval.

'Don't mind your ould father. I'll show you where to get Beauty of Baths that if you close your eyes you'll swear you're eatin' sugar.

'Go through the house,' he said. 'She'll give you a bag. When you're full yourself fill up the bag and take it home to your brothers and sisters.' He winked at Connaughton who took out another cigarette.

'Go on,' his father said, drumming it against the pack. 'I won't delay long here. Don't go too far.'

As the boy walked towards the side door he could hear Burke: 'The poor little divils, I always brang their mother the bag of apples. Every fifteenth of August, God rest her.' Then he let out a fierce shout at the dog; it rose from its position at the door and Lally stepped through.

The cool tunnel of a long corridor reached before him. At its end there was light; there seemed to be a door leading off. He drew a finger along the shiny, bumpy wallpaper. Beads of water fell off at his touch; the smell of cooked cabbage clung to him. He turned into the room and he was suddenly in light again. It shone from tall yellow walls, tall blue kitchen dressers. In its silence he had time to look around. From three levels the light met his eyes: from a high table in the centre of the floor, from a lower table by the window on which stood a bread bin, and, at an in-between level, from a still layer of flour dust that stretched from wall to wall. Then he saw the woman.

She was kneeling beneath the kitchen sink, her head down, her thin behind poking outwards. She seemed intent on something, he couldn't see what it was. As he wondered whether he would announce himself or slip out again into the corridor he heard a sharp *snap*! She leaped backwards onto her heels and toppling sideways she saw him. He saw with surprise a flash of pale thin face and leg. Quickly she covered the leg with the navy crossover pinafore that stretched almost the length of her body. Then, as surprised as he, she looked up at him. 'Oh you gave me a fright.'

He saw a mousetrap. It was what had made the noise. He wondered why she did not mention it, lying now inert and sprung, and instead told him how he didn't know who she was and how he couldn't be expected to because on the last occasion he'd seen her he was in the pram. 'But I know who you are. Oh that wasn't all that long ago.'

'And know your mother too,' she added, lifting herself off the floor. 'Lovely lady.' She loved to watch his mother every Sunday, she said, going up to the altar rails. 'Such a little angel.' The layer of flour dust swirled now all around her and she stooped before him so that their faces were at about the same level. A mass of orange-coloured hair flecked with flour, almost a fleece, grew from her cheeks and beneath her chin. 'Sometimes I think she's going to fly away altogether from us.' She bent even closer to him. 'Because your mother ...' She became suddenly grave as she considered, then she went on with a flourish ' ... she's a flower of spring!'

She stood over him then and studied him.

'You're very like her, you know.'

'I am not. I'm like my father.'

'Ooh.' She laughed, it was almost mocking, but came from some depth within her. She stood back from him, reappraising. 'Ooh there's only one of your father. Him and Billy Burke out there, they'll be around a long time. Him and Billy Burke and me. God help us. For only the good die young.'

There was a commotion in the corridor and Burke was in the kitchen. 'Is she jawing again?' he said to the boy. 'Don't mind her, she has a mouth so wide she can hold ten clothes pins in it when she hangs washing.' She stopped talking. 'The money jar,' he said. She took it from one of the dressers. 'The luck-penny,' he muttered and turning away from her he withdrew some money. She held out her hand for the jar's return but he replaced it in the dresser.

'Can't you see the young lad wants an apple.' He turned to her as he left the kitchen. 'Stop annoying him and give him a bag. He's to take home some to his sisters. They're only fallin' off the tree out there. And clean the muck off them for him.

'God be good to the little children.' His voice tunnelled back up the corridor as he returned to the yard.

It was a brown sugar bag. She brought a bowl from the dresser and decanted sugar from the bag until it piled high. She brought down a cup and decanted the little that was left into it. 'Lord save us,' she said as she noticed the tip of the boy's head at about the same level as her elbow, his eyes peering into the puffed-up sugar, assaying its depth. 'Would you look at the size of him.' Her lips trembled with amazement. Then she spoke to herself. 'I wonder would his mother still remember Lizzie Burke? She would not. She'd be too busy. All her childer to look after now. And him.

'Those are baking apples.' She pointed at them when she had pulled open a heavy dark door in the hallway and he found himself at the front of the house. The grass was high, almost touching the door. It reached up the apple trees. A clothes line sagged into it. He could tell straightaway which was the eating apple tree. The other trees looked densely green while it stood apart, slight and light-leafed, its fruit a fiery red in the sunlight. 'Tell your mother Burke will drop her in a bag of bakers too when they're ready.'

He picked a few apples off the ground. Their undersides were soft. He searched into the grass tangle but could find no more. He knew one should take only windfalls: his father had told him so. Waiting until she had withdrawn to the house he reached into the tree for the lower apples.

The pigs alarmed him as suddenly they burst through a gap. Their good-humoured grappling sounded to him testy and ill-tempered. Pigs in orchards he had seen before: their job was to mop up windfalls. But never before had he been there the same time as they; he climbed into the heart of the tree.

The long bodies undulated beneath him. Every now and then he reached for an apple that bit too far and almost toppled over and then they squealed up at him, blinking, short-sighted, into the tree. The rims of their noses quivered; steel rings sown into them shrapnelled light up at him.

As he sat, hoping they would go away, he thought about Lizzie Burke. He was puzzled by what she had said about his mother. How could she not know? Her appearance, too, puzzled him. One minute she looked all right, the next minute a little frightening, or wild. She was . . . oh he didn't know what she was. His father's word came to him. She was 'cracked'.

The pigs continued to circle beneath him and he wondered would he be left in the tree for ever. He wondered which would be worst – to shout for assistance and be found or not to shout and be found – when suddenly, as at a signal, though he neither heard nor saw it, the whole herd raised heads. Each one held itself poised, the same length of time, as though listening, then all together they wheeled about for the gap and in high spirits, making flesh-rubbing noises with the insides of their legs, they were gone.

Now, he thought. He held the bag to his chest so that it wouldn't burst and he jumped to the ground. He hadn't much time. He didn't want to return to the house. Not with his bagful of apples. She would want to clean them. She would see they were not windfalls. But the door was ajar; he might get through without being noticed. She might be setting the mousetrap again. The only other way was over the wall and it was too high.

Then he heard the two of them. 'Shut up, you're useless. You will not give Connaughton a cup of tea. And make a bloody show of yourself. He's all right, stay where you are.' She wheedled some reply Lally could not hear. 'What makes you that sure his wife will thank you for it?' Burke again. 'You made enough show of yourself when you worked for them in the hotel. Did she thank you then? Did she stop him dumping you back out here on me with your suitcase in your paws? To stay here ever since, roosting. If you were fit to come out itself and get him to split the difference on the price of those heifers I'd say OK, come out. But you wouldn't do that for me.' Lally heard a door slam and Lizzie's voice start up. In earnest conversation with herself: 'And what makes you so sure it was him turned me out of the hotel? Huh? And so sure it was not her?' There was silence a moment, then he heard something ring, not the mousetrap, more like a lid going on a tin. ''Course Burke thinks he knows everything. Everything that goes on. Well Burke might be surprised. Burke knows nothing.'

A squeal turned him sharply around. The pigs; they would be upon him. There was the wall. With one quick glance everything flashed through his mind: the timeless light on the orchard; the dark wall that trapped it. He didn't think. It was high. And crumbling. He scrambled over it.

The car was hotter than ever. He eased his bare legs onto the seat leather; it grafted itself to the backs of his thighs. He nibbled through an apple, tracing the lipstick tint that rippled through the flesh of Beauty of Baths. But the noises from the shed were growing louder. And the movements, though he tried not to look, were growing wilder.

'You insult me with that kind of offer.' Burke looked hurt. Now bareheaded, his cap lay limp on a bar of the gate. 'You insult my name as a decent man.' He waved his stick before Connaughton as though about to strike him.

'I don't insult anyone, Billy.' Connaughton's voice was equally heated. 'But by God you're no decent man.'

'And you're no angel, victualler. Thirty-five quid a head, take them or leave them. Else you have no interest in doing business!'

'Is it codding me you are!' Lally winced. He hated it whenever he heard his father rasp out those words, the anger in him. 'Is it codding me you are, Billy . . . As it is you're losing me money bringing me out here. You want me to close down the stall altogether?'

'I didn't ask you out, there's other buyers.'

'Take your heifers elsewhere then.'

Connaughton waved at the boy in the car. Fixing his eyes on the wall in front of him the boy pretended not to notice. He could not keep up his pretence for long. 'Lally, come here.' He peeled himself from his seat.

'Hould out that hand,' Burke was shouting, 'hould out your hand.' He tussled with Connaughton, attempted to grab his hand and slap his own on top of it. 'And don't leave this house without doing business. By God if you do,' he wheezed, 'don't ever drive in here again.'

The first time Lally had witnessed these antics he had been frightened; he thought his father would be hurt. He had since deduced what it all meant: the hand slap settled a deal, or the imminence of one. Once it was done there was no way back. Tangler's word of honour.

Connaughton wrenched free, and having rounded the heifers, by now staring over the gate oblivious to the men within wrestling over their fates, he called the boy to him and whispered over the gate's bars: 'Will you do something for me for God's sake.'

'Do what for you?' The boy knew what. He had seen others do it for his father. Grown-ups he sometimes brought along with him. Tanglers.

'You know what.'

'But I'm only, I'm only . . . I'm not old enough. Get her in there to do it!' His father was asking him to be go-between. The tangler. To split the difference. If possible in his father's favour! No! He was panic-stricken.

He stood in the yard and watched a small bird balance on the gate of the shed. From the straw-dunged heights within, the men looked down at him. He studied the straw and wondered how deep it was. He wondered why Burke didn't dig it out; soon it would reach the ceiling. He studied the heifers and wondered what might happen were he to say nothing.

'Why,' he mumbled at length, it was something he had heard others say, 'why don't you split the difference?'

'Is it codding me you are?' his father shouted. His chin quivered and he shot fingers into his hair, tossing it. 'Do you even know what the difference is?'

Suddenly he was close to tears: 'I don't know,' he answered in a voice even more unsure than on his first interception. 'Just split it anyway.' He looked away.

'What?' Connaughton shouted. 'What are you saying? Do you want me ruined? Look at me, I'm giving him thirty-two pound a head.' He climbed over the gate, making for Lally. 'My last offer and I want a pound a head luck-penny.'

He is offering thirty-one pounds a head – Lally recovered again as he did some quick mental arithmetic – and Burke wants thirty-five. Thirty-three would be in the middle.

'Thirty-four pound a head's my limit,' Burke roared down

at him, 'and no luck-penny. Nothing could bring him luck.'
At the same time, pushing out the gate before him, he ran
to Connaughton's car and grabbed the chequebook from on
top of the dashboard.

'Here,' he said, 'this is for yourself.' He stuck a pound note
deep in Lally's pocket. 'Give your father that chequebook. Tell
L.W. Connaughton to sign a cheque for sixty-eight quid to
Billy Burke.' He swaggered.

'Here, give him back that pound. Give it back to him.'
Connaughton caught one of Lally's arms.

'Never let it be said . . .' Burke shouted, catching his other
arm. 'Never let it be said a Burke wasn't over-generous.' He
stuffed another pound in the boy's pocket. 'Put that in your
money box.'

He could feel his arm sockets loosen as the men tugged him
in different directions. Then Connaughton became suddenly
resigned. 'Hold out your hand,' he commanded and looking
Burke directly in the eyes he brought his hand down sharply
on the other man's. He wrote a cheque on top of the boiling
hood of the car. 'You shouldn't have,' he said, handing it to
the big man.

'Get into your car now.' Burke held Lally's arm. His hold
this time was gentle, almost a caress. 'That's the young lad's
money now mind,' he shouted into the car at Connaughton
who was already seated. 'I was fond of his mother.' Then, as
if suddenly reminded, he shouted, 'If you see Egan in town
tell him Burke wants him.'

As they climbed up the long laneway, past fields it seemed
were becoming drier and less green, Lally wondered what his
father meant: 'You shouldn't have.' He always said this when
adults pressed money on him. Telling him he shouldn't have
taken it. Was that what it was? Or was it Burke he was talking

to? And what could he have done about it anyway? Could he have stopped it? Could he keep it now?

Branches from the dusty hazel trees rattled against the car's roof. There was no talk within, just that sound and the sound of the wheels as they followed the course of the tractor tracks, skewing one way and then the other. The driver, deep in thought, was letting the car take its own course home.

'Here, would you like an apple?' The boy held up the bag. He felt sorry for his father. He thought, from the scowl on his face, that he had been cheated. 'They are not windfalls,' he wanted to say. 'They are the best apples on the tree.' But he could not say it. If his father could only know the best apples on the tree were in his bag then he might think the bargain had swung a little his way. But he couldn't risk saying it for fear he'd disapprove. One only took windfalls.

The luck-penny too worried him. If he kept it his father most certainly would not count the bargain as having swung his way. Apple gain or not. But could he possibly keep it? It was unimaginable wealth.

Connaughton looked at the apples and then smiled at him. 'I'll try one,' he said. 'See if I can manage with these false teeth. So you met Lizzie. Poor Lizzie is an old wallflower now.' Lally liked the way he said it: sometimes he could say a thing like this, 'an old wallflower now', gently, casually. He continued in the same tone. 'Poor Lizzie, a long time ago Billy and Lizzie and I used to walk home from school together. Lizzie used to wear a short dress, she liked to show off her nice legs. Oh a swell she was.' Connaughton lost himself in thought for a moment. Then he brought himself back to the present. 'By the way, you might give me the two pounds. Just in case it gets lost.'

They drew out on the wide road leading to town. His father had begun his shi-shi-shiddle sound again: he was thinking.

Pleased with his sale. 'Watch out for Egan on the tractor.' He suddenly laughed, knowing Egan had not gone to ground but was in the fields cutting hay. 'Watch out for him or he'll be so drunk coming home he'll knock us down and kill us stone dead!' He spluttered with laughter.

When he saw the boy's intent look as it peeled round the bends in the hedgerow for the sight of a runaway tractor the devilishness went out of him. 'Don't mind,' he said softly, but then thinking of Burke's strategies his spluttering started up again. 'Oh Billy, Billy. You make up a story about Egan as a pretext for staying put about the yard. In case I should think it is eagerness to sell the heifers is staying you. Our casual Billy! But then you have to leave yourself without your middleman. Oh what a blunder. Oh Billy, Billy.' He laughed, shaking his head.

'You made a great middleman yourself.' He looked down at the boy. 'Well done.' Not quite understanding the reason for his father's merriment Lally flushed with pride. Manfully he flexed his arms and shoulders. They still ached from the stretching that had almost split him from side to side.

'Do you know,' Connaughton continued, he felt happy now, 'this apple reminds me of the last time I ate an apple . . . It was in your grandmother's orchard. I'll tell you the story . . .

'Your grandmother, you know, she was the best gardener I ever knew.' The boy stared out the window, eyebrows knitted, listening, but too embarrassed to look at his father.

'My grandmother,' he wanted to ask, 'that would be your mother?' He did not say it.

He just knew the word *mother* was not mentioned. And would not be. That was an unstruck bargain. Something they had arrived at, at a time that would remain unspoken.

Right now, in any event, it was Burke's housekeeper-wife-mother-sister, or Egan's wife, or whatever she was, that whetted his curiosity: she had never heard his mother was dead. Imagine that. When had she last been out of the house? And why hadn't she been? And why hadn't Billy told her? He wondered would his father have among his collection of stories a story about Lizzie Burke.

No, he would ask no questions about Lizzie Burke. About once upon a time in the hotel. He listened. 'Your grandmother was a wizard: the feasts she could concoct from the produce of that garden and that orchard. Well, there was a special treat she baked out of apples, and God forgive me whatever was in it I couldn't get enough of it . . . ' Enthralled, he watched the old images as they flickered onto the screen of his father's inward-looking eye. The listener, the teller. Intent. Bushes sprang out of the roadside, grasped at them, missed. And slipped away in the car's slipstream as lightly as phantoms slip into the summer wildflower shade.

THE SPOILS OF WAR

THE BOYS WERE GATHERED in an anxious knot at the foot of the hotel garden. The time had arrived at last. The strike on Jack Day's orchard.

Dick Kane was from Lacy Estate, the council housing at the town's edge. Though more daring than the other three, even he was nervous. 'Ssh, Kelly, listen,' he said.

Jimmy Kelly, Townhall Street, was repeating the first two lines of a refrain:

D-Day,
What do you say?

He had the jitters and was giving them to the others. 'Ssh,' Dick told him. 'He'll hear us, ssh.'

They were waiting. Waiting until they heard the same refrain Jimmy muttered, but until they heard it coming from the street. It was to be a decoy – Masterminded by Dick, the other half of whose ragabag of comrades were under orders to congregate outside Jack Day's front door and taunt so the foraging party could go about their harvest at the back.

Toddy Black, also Lacy Estate, was the third member of the party. And Lally the fourth. They stood now in his father's hotel garden, overlooking Jack Day's orchard. 'Hey La', these boys called him. He loved to be called La.

Lally was surprised at the company he nowadays found himself in. Surprised and excited.

What used his mother tell him? 'Don't let me see you play with that Jimmy Kelly. Good little laddies like you don't play with corner boys like him. A naughty boy.'

What Lally could not understand was that Jimmy's father, Peter Kelly, owned the biggest shop in town, a hardware store. Its front took up as much street as the front of his own father's hotel. And if his mother only knew it, it would be he, rather than the more careful Jimmy, who would most likely get into trouble.

Instead of allowing him to play with the boys around town, his mother drove him out the country to her friends' houses. All of his mother's friends had one thing in common. All of them belonged to the world of hunting and horses. So that wherever he went, whoever he played with – and he always had to teach them the games, games he had learned from the town boys – the business of pony riding invariably arose. Then he lost interest completely and his mother scolded him on the way home in the car. 'If you could only see yourself in the saddle, you have a nicer seat than any of them. Such a little man on a pony.' Useless they were at games. They didn't know any of them: Cowboys and Indians, Gangs, anything.

Other aspects of those visits with his mother he preferred to forget. Occasions when she dropped him and drove on somewhere else. Long days in the country wilderness. Then he cried on the way home in the car and upset her and felt shameful for having done so.

Though sometimes his wonderful Mama sang, and then he joined in. In the front seat beside her. Looking through a windscreen off which raindrops ran. Or were they tears? Or did the tears happen only once? Those days, the happiness and the tantrums. As far into his past as he could remember, they were indistinguishable.

Nowadays Aunt was in charge.

Aunt carried out his mother's separatist policies for some time. Until one day, she suddenly decided he was grown up and allowed him the run of the street. She didn't believe in 'precious' children. Sooner or later everybody had to face the world. The sooner the better. There had been problems with her own upbringing. Brought up like 'little ladies', she and her sisters had been. And Lally's father, brought up with funny ideas. She had been entrusted the care of her nieces and nephews, and she was not going to repeat mistakes. 'We learn from history.'

When Lally first went to school, at four, his mother accompanied him. She held his hand. She walked up the street with him. Sometimes she would not let go his hand. Sometimes she turned round and walked him home again before even reaching the school. She did that until she got an assurance from Sister Annunciata that he would be given a seat on his own at the head of the class. She could be happier then, a little happier: the stern Annunciata would treat him more gently than the others. He wasn't happier; he could then know his school companions only from a distance, and the frightening Sister Annunciata only from up close. 'Sister Annunciata, the big fat tomato,' they rhymed from the rear of the room each time she waddled out on the corridor. He knew he was first in the firing line should she swoop back in surprise. He could not join in. One day he did, in a whisper, and got a quick clout for his troubles. Companions, if companions he had, were remote.

Now he was eight and the most popular boy on the street.

Hordes of children played with him in the yard his father was transforming into a cattle mart at the back of the hotel. It was due to him the boys could play there. With its pens, chutes, rings, stand, it was a Cowboys and Indians world. Dangerous old crumbling buildings coming down, new buildings of rough-edged concrete going up. Ideal. 'Bang, La, you're dead.' 'No I'm not.' 'Bang, you are.'

The boys joined him in the yard: he joined them on the street. He had the run of the store behind Jimmy Kelly's hardware shop. Barrels of soft putty stood open beside barrels of nails. He belonged to a gang up in Richmond at the far end of town, a junior member, who had been warned nevertheless: 'Even you, La, if the Parkview gang catch you, they'll tie you to the dead tree and let the pissmires sting your arse off.' Access to the haunts of so many friends. Man about town. He'd never had such freedom, and he loved it.

It was only recently, however, he'd begun to stray down Bank Street.

Bank Street, the side street off Townhall Street, ended abruptly at the crossroads where Lacy Estate began. Townhall Street spilled on one end into Church Street, which continued into Parkview, and on the other into River Street, which extended into Richmond. It was the town's main thoroughfare. Bank Street had been the town's sleepy siding, once upon a time, but since Lacy Estate was built the clatter of footsteps on its footpath had increased. It was a street of tall railinged houses. Most of the more eccentric and retiring of the town's citizenry lived there. The hotel's side entrance, the archway, led into it and one day Lally, instead of heading up the long run of main streets as he normally did, wandered into Bank Street.

He strayed to its very end ... But he was not sure of the Lacy Estate boys. Aunt might be a lot more liberal than his mother but he doubted even she approved of the Lacy Estate boys. At last, however, he let himself be contaminated: he joined the refrain the Lacy Estate boys took up in passing Jack Day's house.

Nobody knew how it had started. Nobody could say who, or whose father, had made it up. Jack Day was just one of those people who invited taunts. He was a short, broad-shouldered man in a hat and pullover, never a coat, who kept to himself by day and gave vent to his irascibility by night, propped at the counters of the pubs. He was esteemed at every pub he drank in, good entertainment.

He had a history. He had fought in the war in Burma, receiving a head injury which, townspeople said, was responsible for his humours. 'They had to rivet a metal plate onto his brain box to fix him.'

'The Yellow Peril', he called the residents of Lacy Estate. They trampled over his street, hordes of them, he imagined, knocked in his dustbin. He took it upon himself, on behalf of the street residents, to protect his and their properties.

> D-Day,
> What do you say?
> You killed a Jew
> In World War Two.

They would line up outside his house and chant it. Imagining him fuming behind his drawn curtains they would wait a few minutes and then complete the refrain:

> D-Day,
> What do you say?
> Go to bed
> And mend your head.

When he burst, threatening, out the door – 'little fuckin' twerps' – they would scatter, laughing and fearful, only to regroup again and chant again as soon as he had returned to the house.

It was a sultry day. In here, at the foot of the garden, below the cattle mart yard, there was hardly a sound. Lally wished he too could be at peace. As the trees that swayed above the gooseberry bushes. As the birds, startled from time to time into dreamy twitter, unseen somewhere, in the hazy air. A faint crackle now and then of drying twigs was the only indication that there might be movement in the greenery. He wished things in the garden could be again as once they were: when he could look into Jack Day's orchard without intent, his imagination at full rein. Back in the dawdling infinity of his beginnings.

'A good job you have us for friends, La,' Toddy Black, the second Lacy Estate boy told him. 'A good job you told us D-Day has his orchard at the back of your garden. You'd never rob it without us.'

Toddy was repeating what Dick had already said. As Lally had led his three co-conspirators beneath the hotel archway, through the cattle mart, skirting an apron of fresh concrete where workmen laid down an extension to the yard, Dick had said: 'You'd never do it without us you know. Wait till all the boys in the front start singin' day-day to D-Day. He'll go mad, and we'll just walk in and fill up. Lucky you told us before all the apples are ate.' It was barely August, the apples as yet green balls.

The chorus on the road had not yet begun. 'I told them to count to three hundred,' Dick said, 'and then start singin'. They must be gone past that now. They must be at five hundred by now.'

'They must be at a million or something by now,' Toddy Black said.

'No, they couldn't count that far, they're not at three hundred yet.' Jimmy tried to delay time.

'They can't fuckin' count, that's their problem,' Dick said, and spat on the ground. 'We'll give them one more minute.'

'Can't fuckin' count, you're right, Dick.' Toddy too spat on the ground and looked accusingly at Jimmy.

Only for a second did Lally query the company he was in. Only for a second did he remember what had happened a few days previously. The same boys he now stood beside had drowned a litter of the hotel kittens in a barrel of water while he had watched and joined in the laughter. The bag of kittens had taken an age to sink. 'Place is crawlin' with bloody cats, that'll cut them back': one of the yardhands had given them pennies for the job he normally did himself.

Lally looked at the back of Jack Day's house, blank apart from a sky-glazed window. It had never seemed as forbidding. He looked at his helpers. In the minds of the Lacy Estate boys there was only one direction. Forward. He could see it in their tightly screwed eyes. Whereas Jimmy Kelly, Jimmy, his first true friend . . . Who he had asked along for that reason. Now he couldn't but feel disdain for him. Because Jimmy Kelly's wide open eyes already looked backward.

'Look, that's where we go through,' Dick said. It was a gap made by the town's dog patrols. 'I'll go first, then Toddy, then you, La, then Kelly.'

At last they heard the wail. It was faint, rising over Jack Day's roof, descending again, drifting over the trees of green apples to where they stood:

> D-Day,
> What do you say?
> You killed a Jew
> In World War Two . . .

There was a moment's silence and then a little louder:

> D-Day,
> What do you say?
> Go to bed
> And mend your head...

'Will we go now?' Lally attempted to take charge. He wished to retrieve at least some authority; it was his back garden. He looked at his friends, the bold-faced boys from Lacy Estate, the increasingly more nervous Jimmy Kelly.

'No – wait.' Dick cocked his ear. He was suspicious of the signals he was receiving. He had not yet heard the roars – 'Little fuckin' twerps' – and then his hired chorus disperse, nor the regrouping, the louder, repeated, more joyous rendering.

They waited. The chorus did start up again, but not with the triumphant air of a choir that feels it is effecting something.

'Come on,' Dick said, 'he's not there.'

'Are you sure?' Lally said as he followed Toddy.

'Of course I'm sure. Just run if you see him.'

'I'm not going in,' Jimmy Kelly said. They left him, standing on the gap.

Jack Day's orchard was like a jungle. The Lacy Estate boys crashed into long, hollow-stemmed, bamboo-like weed through which earthen pathways crisscrossed. In a moment they had shimmied up the apple trees.

'Yauck, this one is a cooker,' Toddy called out, expelling suddy spits into the air. 'What's yours like Dick?'

'Smashin' apples Toddy.' Toddy swung off his tree and onto Dick's. 'Feck off Toddy, this is my tree,' Dick said.

'Ah Dick let me taste.'

Dick had unzipped the top of his tunic and was stuffing the hard apples into it. Lally hadn't got any apples yet. From where he stood he could see the monkey-figures on the tree. He too wanted to go to their tree, loath to move away from them and pick on his own.

The volume of noise from the street was becoming louder, more desperate: 'What did you do? You killed a Jew. When did you kill it? In World War Two.' He looked up, checking the position of his exit. He could see where Jimmy's head poked up, standing in the ditch, his body cut off by weeds. 'Hey Jimmy, I'm over here,' he whispered.

Jimmy's white hands pushed through. 'Lally get us one, get us an apple.'

'Come in yourself.' More whispers. 'There's no one here.'

He saw Jimmy's face, a big moon, the same instant it twisted up in terror. He heard a crazed crackling in the undergrowth, saw an arm reach up and Jimmy come flying into the orchard.

'Little fuckin' twerps' – he heard Jack Day's whoops. 'Thought I wasn't here. Thought I was after the other little fuckin' twerps on the street.'

'Let me go,' Jimmy screamed.

'Always check your rearguard first before you go into action. Company command, you hear. And now I'll tan yours. First yours by God,' he sounded serious, 'and then all the others'.'

Lally looked up in the trees. Dick and Toddy had already slid silently down. They pounded now along the earthen pathways. Lally followed them but when he saw where they were going he stopped. 'Through his house,' Dick said urgently, 'through his back door.' Lally was not going in there.

He doubled around. Up one pathway, down another, seeing nothing. 'The door is locked' – he heard Dick. The voice seemed to be miles away now.

Then he saw Dick again: scrambling up the side of a high roof.

'How didja get up there?' Toddy howled.

'Here, over here.'

He saw them both against the skyline. Apples were bobbing out of their clothes, Toddy hanging on to the sleeve of
Dick's tunic. 'I'm slippin' Dick, I'm slippin', look where we
are!'

'I can't look. Let me go. I'll fuckin' fall.'

Then they were gone, the sound of apples hopping off roof
and gutters.

'Look what you've done to me you little pisser!' It was a
tone of disgust. It came from the end of the orchard. 'Little
twerp funks it, afraid to go over the top, wets his pants on
me. Get to blazes outa here and never let me see you again.'

Lally could hear Jimmy's sobbings. Jack Day must have
released him because they were moving farther and farther into
the distance. 'I'll tell my mother, I'll tell my mother...'

He himself was like a trapped rabbit. He scuttled about in
the undergrowth, beneath the heavy, glinting sky, his legs and
face burned with nettle and briar. Every now and then he stopped, looked up but could see no sign of the terror he knew
must now be stalking him and him alone. He grew so frightened he gave up, stood, and awaited the pounce. When the lunge
did come, the hat and crazed face crashing into his vision, he
startled away again.

But the grip knocked all the life out of him. He found
himself swept on a powerful wave across the orchard's length.
Head down, he found himself smelling the bruised and battered vegetation. Then he was in a cement yard, looking into
a drain. His captor held him in one arm, searched for a key
and unlocked a door with the other.

He was in a room. Jack Day stood at a window, looking
out, his back to him, seeming to tremble.

When he came towards him the room filled with light but
his face beneath the hat burned darkly with an anger that was
real and frightening. It was the first sustained anger Lally had

seen in his life. His father's, by comparison, was like a match lighting and going out again.

'I'd beat the livin' daylights outa you,' he said, unclenching his fists, 'except for one thing.'

For a moment Lally thought the 'one thing' was because he was who he was – the son of Lally Connaughton – and he felt both relief and shame. 'You're the only one who stood your ground. You have prisoner's rights.'

Jack Day drew closer, his eyes slitting mercilessly in spite of the reprieve he seemed to be offering.

'I've been watching you, you little fuckin' twerp. Hard to believe and your mother such a good woman, but you're no damned different now to the rest of them. Gone to the bad since she died.' He looked at him for a moment, walking around him, as if deciding something. 'Nice fat little arse you have too for slapping.' Then he nodded in the direction of the door. 'Get out of me sight and tell your father to give you a good hammering.'

He burned with shame. He walked through the orchard and over the gap. It was only as he walked through the cattle mart yard he could allow his behind parts to relax. He had not been able to look behind him, had feared the slap might yet arrive on those unguarded regions.

There was nobody in the yard. The cement workers had gone. He cried. But then he saw the clump of boys. Beneath the hotel archway, awaiting news of his capture and release. They would not come any further. Dick was there, and Toddy. Jimmy Kelly was not. Gone home to his mother, he thought, then realised they were looking at him as at a hero.

He dried his tears and a sudden impulse overcame him. He would display his bravado . . . The apron of wet cement, he would run right across, leave his footprints on it as he had seen others do in devilment. 'Look,' he shouted to the boys.

Halfway across he was seized. He felt the life shake out of him, a rough hand come down on him. Then he felt hot, his legs and trousers, hot and stinging. He was being carried at speed, water squirting out the legs of his short trousers and onto the pavement. 'Aw Jesus,' the cement foreman shouted. 'He ruins me yard, he pisses all over me!'

The man released him. He slumped away. The man had dumped him in sight of his friends and admirers. His former friends and admirers. 'You want to get a good hidin' from your father.'

He escaped to the outhouse the hotel cats lived and bred in. Crates of empty ale bottles loomed in tumbling stacks all around him. He pulled the door behind him and stood in total darkness.

After a long time he noticed little shafts of light. They were coming from holes in the slates. Little by little the wall of black receded. Bottles began to glint. He heard a movement and saw the points of a cat's eyes. From the same direction he heard scraping and guessed it was one of the litter of kittens he had seen a few days previously. Nausea wretched through him at the memory of their blind squirming. He clenched his teeth against the faint but grating cries.

He studied the silver specks that danced within the light beams. It seemed there was no order in their movement. Slowly they wandered into the light, tossed about with great liveliness once within it, and then slowly wandered out.

Eventually it became so quiet out in the yard that he opened the door to find out what was going on. He could hear no sound of his friends. He looked for them beneath the archway. The daylight dazzled him; he cupped his eyes protectingly.

THE HORSEBOX

CONNAUGHTON DROVE DOWN BANK STREET and pulled up the car where the boy was playing with his pals. They had been selecting teams for Cowboys and he was already selected. 'Come on, I'm in a hurry,' Connaughton said, holding open the door, and the boy jumped in alongside him.

He did not complain; he did not even hesitate. It would not have occurred to him that things could be any different. If his father said come, he went. Only once, long ago, he had complained, and then Aunt had told him he had upset his father because he was lonely and needed company. So that was the end of that.

And for Connaughton's part, had the boy said no, he probably would not have been disappointed. Surprised maybe, but not disappointed; he took it for granted his son went on these excursions with him, enjoyed them.

And so the big black car and its two occupants once again pulled out of the town on the edge of the hills. The clouds drifted across it as they left, shunting away the soft light it had bathed in all morning and shrinking the tall commercial houses whose windows only moments earlier had sparkled in the sun.

Maybe that was the reason for the boy's moment of anxiety: the change of light. It happened just as they passed the council estate: the mortar on its terraced houses became suddenly mud-coloured, its squat box hedges turned poisonously dark, and the iron bars of its clamped-shut gates made him shiver. He took one last look at his town and for that moment was unable to reassure himself that it would still be there on his return, that the game he had been taken away from would still be in progress.

His father did not look back. His future lay in the direction in which he drove.

They drove past the tinker camp on the edge of town. Plumes of smoke, narrow as the stovepipes they arose from, stood in single line above the caravans. The caravans were closely parked, six or so of them back to back, yet each seemed self-sufficient, absorbed in its own existence. The boy was struck by that: each caravan its own habitation, a gap between each for wind and air to blow around, so different to the look of the joined houses on the street.

He wondered what it was like within the caravans. Sometimes when passing he saw the camp children at play; they pushed a wobbly iron-wheeled contraption or ran about with sticks, trousers sliding loosely off their bottoms. They were not about today. He tried to see into the caravans but it was too dim. The thought of his own living quarters back in the high-ceilinged rooms of the hotel rushed unbidden to his mind.

But the camp horses were about; they stood on the grass verge as always, stock still and sullen-eyed. And the boy leaned back into his car seat as always, expecting his father's abrupt stop and his quick study of the horses – something that embarrassed him, though it didn't seem to worry his father – for a head nearly always poked out of a caravan door to see what was going on.

Connaughton, the keen judge of horses, today did not stop, did not even slow down. His mind was too much on what lay before him.

Connaughton's mind, to be more correct, was in a state of unease. It darted back and forward. Backward to doubt, forward to the one clear path and the great hope, backward again to something someone had only hours earlier said to him.

Fanning, one of his employees, his butcher, had a way of saying one thing whose true intent was something else. He had said it to him earlier as together they hooked sheep carcases in the window of the stall, displaying them in the morning light. Right now Fanning's words were uppermost in Connaughton's mind.

Attempting to find a way back to happier thoughts he looked down at the boy beside him but saw only the same grave expression he himself wore. Sometimes he laughed at the way his son copied him, but not this time. He drove on, along the stretch of road that passed the station, his driving erratic, fast one moment, slow the next, when without any apparent reason his mind again cleared. A flash of delight passed through him, a train of images. He looked down at the boy – think of the future, that's the idea – and he decided to forget Fanning's comment. Based on suspicion it was, mere suspicion.

'And what age are you now?' he asked kindly, his spirits further lifted as they whizzed up the slope of the railway bridge. The boy always readied himself for his single glimpse of the line. There was a gap in the ivy where the wall was broken. This time, however, surprised at his father's sudden interest in him, he looked up instead.

'Eight,' he said as his stomach jolted over the hump.

'There, can you see the field?' – Connaughton pointed, suddenly excited – 'Quick, look, in the sunshine. The sun is on it.'

A crack of light had split the clouds and spilled across a hill in the distance. The boy looked just in time to see it race across the patchwork of fields on the hill's brow and then fly away, as if jumping off a shadow and onto nowhere.

The fields and lands behind them belonged to Connaughton's cousin Timmy. That was where they were now headed. Connaughton's horse was out there. Since its last breakdown on the racecourse it had been stabled with Timmy. Now it was recovering again, exercising again, in Timmy's secluded fields, away from prying eyes. It was to be the object of a gamble again.

'Timmy is silent as the grave,' Connaughton had assured Fanning and the few others from the town who shared the knowledge of the horse's recovery. Today he would decide if it was ready for the racetrack.

Connaughton looked down at the boy again, remembering he had been about to flatter him. 'Eight, I'd never have thought it, sure you're a man already. Eight, oh my, oh my.' And while the boy arranged his feelings – pleasure at his father's sudden interest in him, but amazement because he did not even know his age – Connaughton thought out his next question.

He hummed to himself a few moment before coming out with it. He pulled out his box of cigarettes. 'How would you like to live in the country?' He sounded casual.

'Whereabouts?'

'In a big house.'

'As big as our hotel?'

'As big as.'

'Whereabouts?'

'Does it matter whereabouts?' Connaughton laughed in sudden impatience. 'In the country. In a big house in the country.'

'And not in the hotel?'

'We'd be able to have our own stables.' Connaughton laughed again, an uneasy laugh which began a silence.

'You know what I'm going to get,' he announced before the silence could become noticeable. 'I'm going to get a car telephone.'

'A car telephone!' The awkward moment had passed. 'But how would you drive, you'd crash!' The boy was relieved and confused, both in the same instant.

'Why would I crash, silly?' Connaughton was amused. 'And please God, all going well over the next few weeks, I'll buy a horsebox too.'

'And can I go in the back of it next time we go to the races?'

Connaughton stepped across a ploughed field, the boy struggling through the heavy clay in his wake.

He rounded the elbow of hedge that shut off the horse's gallop from the view of the road and then stopped and looked in admiration.

A man held a rein while a horse turned him round and round. The man crouched low to the ground and inclined his body backwards; the horse seemed intent on yanking him off his feet.

'Whoa, whoa,' he said and, catching sight of Connaughton, 'he's fresh in himself, Lally.'

'Shush the boy.' Connaughton looked up at the forehead with the white blaze across it, took the rein, a brief smile lighting his face. 'Shush the boy, shush the New Hope.' The horse snorted. 'Good morning, Timmy,' Connaughton said.

Timmy tightened a peaked cap round his head. It had come askew with his exertions. 'He looks topping,' he said by way of reply.

Timmy was red-cheeked, Connaughton was sallow, and yet they resembled one another. There was a wariness about the eyes and mouths of both men, though Timmy had a wider jaw and a slackness about him which made him appear more easygoing.

'First time we'll have had the saddle on him since his

breakdown in Fairyhouse,' Connaughton said tersely.

'You brought the little man along, I see.' Timmy looked down at the boy. 'Will you pop on his back for a canter, you're just the right weight for a jock. Maybe we'd make a better one out of you than we did out of your ould father!' He laughed, attempting to lighten the atmosphere; he had sensed Connaughton's anxiety. He too was anxious about the forthcoming trial.

Connaughton took out a cigarette and Timmy gulped an apple he had pulled from his pocket. 'Did you get the Lad Egan?' he asked.

'Fanning is driving him out.' Connaughton took his eyes off the horse. 'Or I hope he is.'

'Uhu, what's wrong?' Timmy asked. The expression of concern Connaughton had worn earlier had returned to his face.

'Bloody bad mood Fanning's in this morning, whatever it is. Extraordinary genius, he can change his moods like a weathervane.'

'Did you say something to him?'

'Nothing.'

'Did he say something to you?'

'He thinks I'm moving too fast with New Hope. "Do you not think you should wait a bit longer?" he said to me this morning.'

'That remains to be seen. But New Hope looks ready now, even if Fanning isn't.'

They both looked up at the eager head, and the horse rewarded its admirers with a little backstep shuffle, swayed its haunches like a flaunting dancer. 'You're a character.' A new smile brightened Connaughton's face and he shook his head at the horse.

Two men, one tall, one short, rounded the hedge. The tall

one was Fanning, Fanning in his butcher's white coat, his white oilskin apron, his butcher's knife stuck deep in its scabbard. He flapped through the wet grass. The Lad Egan, at his elbow, grappled with the heavy saddle and the racing bridle.

'Like dawn in winter,' Timmy whispered to Connaughton, 'late but no use complaining about it.'

No words were passed, no greetings, until the horse was saddled and Lad Egan mounted, his riding crop locked beneath his shoulder.

Then Connaughton slapped the horse's neck. The drizzle had become heavier so that an imprint of his hand remained on the neck. 'The ground might be slippery, Lad,' he said. 'Don't turn him too sharply on the corners. I'm walking now to the far end of the gallop' – he gave Lad Egan his instructions – 'I want you to gallop wide behind where I'll be standing. No short cuts. I don't want him damaging himself.' As he spoke he rose the stirrup irons so that Lad Egan's knees were almost in his mouth, so that it looked as though the horse's slightest movement would topple him. 'The rain will keep us private.' He looked up at the low clouds as he set off from the group about the horse.

Walking quickly, Connaughton began to cross the field. The boy ran to keep abreast of him. 'You stay with Timmy' – he was sent back.

'Come here and stay with me, young lad.' Timmy held out a hand. 'The boss doesn't want the young lad listening to him cursing at you, Egan,' he joked once he was sure Connaughton was out of earshot.

They watched Connaughton go through a wide gap and then climb a long hill in the next field, the field on which the sun had shone earlier. The boy felt a sadness as he watched, sensing how the tension that seemed to be easing out of the company was due to his father.

When Timmy spoke, a new, superior tone in his voice, he brought the jockey sliding down the horse's saddle to his level. 'You know your course, Lad,' his mouth tightened. 'Around this field once, through that gap, up the hill where the boss is gone, down into the hollow at the other side where he'll be standing, around the boss twice, back again and around this field. That's a good test.'

Connaughton stood on top of the hill, removed from them but yet in command, like a starter on a faraway rostrum. They saw him raise an arm. 'Are you right, Lad?' Timmy called. 'Don't spare him, let him out.'

The horse's hooves slammed backwards in the turf. They heard the girth round its belly take the stress. A white hand-kerchief flashed. 'Go.' Lad Egan lumbered all the weight that was beneath him into one forward thrust. Timmy shouted to Fanning, who had remained quiet all along. 'We'll let him out, only way we can be sure of what's in him.'

Galloping round the field's perimeter the horse quickened, let out its neck. The men watched it. The boy screwed his eyes until it became a flickering blur against a changing background of light and trees.

'Not a snort out of him.' Timmy murmured at first to himself and then to the others. 'Not a sound of breathing, a good sign.'

New Hope wheeled round the far corner of the field and the ground sprang as he turned towards them again. Now they could hear his breathing. 'Light and even,' Timmy said, a strain in his voice. 'I don't think he'll blow up today.' He looked to Fanning for reassurance.

'That quarter is holding up too,' Fanning said.

The horse drew past them. Spatters of mud dashed against their clothing. Timmy clenched his fists. 'Keep him going,' he shouted after Lad Egan until he had ridden through the gap and over the brow of the hill.

Once the horse was gone and could no longer occupy attention, Timmy gave expression to doubts about Connaughton that had been forming in his head. He felt that in addition to worry over the outcome of New Hope's trial something else also bothered his cousin. 'You're off colour, Fanning, are you in disagreement with us?' he began on Fanning.

'I'm not in disagreement with you.' Fanning had wide shoulders, a neck not much less wide, a strength at odds with the impression of misery his face conveyed. It was the posture, harried and anxious, he wore when he and Timmy laid the money for Connaughton at race meetings. It had become the permanent expression of his face. 'I'm wasting my time out here though, I have work to do back in the stall.'

'You're in disagreement with the boss then; he tells me you think it's too early to try out the horse.'

'Too early, that's rich.' Fanning sniffed. Drizzle was greasing down his apron; it formed rivulets between the clots of lard. 'Too early yes, but it wasn't New Hope I was talking about.'

'New Hopes looks fine?'

'He does. But wait till we see how he is when he comes in off the gallop.'

'He'll be all right.' Timmy tried to sound certain. 'With a bit of schooling he'll be ready. We might pull off the gamble.'

'And with a bit of luck.' Fanning turned his back to the mist that had now changed into rain and was slanting towards them. 'And that fool Egan doesn't open his mouth and bring down his price. Yes, we could win money.'

'So you're not worried?'

'I am. Not about New Hope. It's what the boss wants to do with his winnings that worries me.'

'And what's that?' Timmy laughed, humoured at Fanning's expression of his misgivings, relieved also, sensing an explanation concerning his cousin's mood.

Fanning looked at Timmy and remembering the boy nodded in his direction. At the same moment, as if accommodating the men, the boy moved back a few yards to the ditch, and breaking a hazel switch from it, swished the wet ears off stalks of grass. But he kept within earshot.

Fanning waited until he thought the boy far enough away before answering Timmy's question. 'He wants to take his girlfriend to Killarney on a honeymoon. And then he wants to pay off the death duties on her farm.'

Timmy laughed, as though Fanning had taken leave of his senses. 'Girlfriend? But Blan, Blan hardly . . . God rest her . . . dead?'

'A widow from the hills, Timmy, from over the county border. I'm surprised you don't know. You don't hear much do you? Everybody in town does. Even though he thinks himself it's a secret.'

Timmy was a straightforward person, not given to curiosity; this time, however, his natural wariness demanded it. 'Do I know her?'

Suddenly they heard shouts through the rain. They both looked up. The boy stopped his furious swishing at the grass. Then, not wanting to draw attention to himself, he started up again.

'He's putting the Lad through his paces,' Timmy said, attempting to dismiss growing doubts about the horse. 'Will he give the Lad the mount in Galway?'

'Lad Egan?'

'Yes, it would keep the plan to ourselves?'

'No he won't, he'll have a good jock up.'

'Do I know her?' Timmy asked again.

'She's broke.' Fanning announced what he considered the most relevant detail. 'Death duties and an understocked farm.

He's walking himself into trouble going up there.'

'Isn't that the way he likes it?' Timmy said. 'A handsome woman I'd bet,' he said a moment later.

'A fine woman,' Fanning conceded. 'You may have seen her at cattle marts. Big woman. She wears the hair up in brown plaits. But it's too early, Timmy, too early after Blan. Not right,' he appealed. Because they were cousins, and Timmy the elder of the two, Fanning had always considered him an influence on Connaughton.

'And would he go and live up there?' Timmy knew that while Connaughton might agonise over what others thought, in the end neither he nor anybody else influenced him.

The men looked at the boy. Having run out of grass heads he was drawing closer to them with his flailing stick. 'He never thought the hotel was the place to bring up a family.' Fanning lowered his voice. 'Yes he would go. And make a big mistake.'

Timmy considered: 'He likes new pastures. And they'd have a mother. Maybe he should go.'

'Maybe he shouldn't.' Fanning shook his head vigorously.

Suddenly Timmy's concerned expression changed. A look of cunning came over him. He eyed Fanning with the beginnings of a look of disbelief. 'He needs a good gamble under his belt so he can get married, is that what you're telling me?' he said.

'That's it,' Fanning answered. Had he looked at Timmy he might have been warned of the trap which Timmy was laying for him and which sooner or later he would fall into.

The boy had begun to look towards the further fields. He didn't believe the story he was hearing. He wondered why his father was taking so long.

'But the man would gamble anyway,' Timmy went on. 'He feels life owes him. Always has – once you're born with the silver spoon, even if you have it taken away from you, you think it's your right always to have everything. Especially since he gave up the other.' He threw his cupped hand to his mouth, indicating the raising of a glass.

Fanning did not wish to discuss the nature of Connaughton's gambling. 'He wants to take her to the Lakes of Killarney is what I heard this morning. That's why I blew a fuse. That's why I couldn't keep my feelings to myself any longer. What the hell is keeping him in that field anyway?' He looked up the rainswept hill.

'Ssh,' Timmy said, nodding towards the boy whose impression of looking in the opposite direction did not convince him. 'Ssh,' he lowered his voice. 'So the honeymoon is the final straw with you, Fanning?' His tone had changed. It had hardened. 'A man going on honeymoon is the straw that has upset you.' Fanning gave him a look of incomprehension and he went on: 'Nonsense Fanning. What's wrong with you has nothing to do with a honeymoon. Your problem is you are afraid. You are afraid because this time his need to win is not just for you and for me and for the gamble as it always used to be but so he can marry the mountain woman, take her to Killarney and settle her.'

'I'm not afraid. What am I afraid of?'

Timmy walked up to Fanning until their faces almost touched. 'Afraid, because this time he has so much to lose. Afraid, because he'll be so keen to win that he'll lose all sense of judgement entirely, and things will go worse than ever wrong.'

The boy, who was watching, could make little sense of what was being said. He could not understand why Timmy accused Fanning of fear when he himself looked the more afraid. He wondered how his father could be responsible.

Something, he sensed, was changing in his life. He was

filled with apprehension, as were the men. It excited him. It was all about him, like the drizzle.

'What's he doing in that dip? How many times has he put the horse around it? How are we to know but it mightn't be worth tuppence by the time he's finished down there? Why wouldn't he let us watch?' In an attempt to escape Timmy's terrorising Fanning stood on his toes as if looking over the hill.

'Not at all, Fanning, you have nothing any more than the usual to be feared of. I told you already. He's a gambler because he's a gambler. Nothing to do with a woman. What's a flutter to you and me is a matter of life and death to the boss.'

'I don't know why you're arguing with me. Do you want us together in this thing or not? I'm not sure if I'd call it just a flutter either. How do you know how much money he's putting on? How do you know how much money he has spent on her already? Every weekend away nowadays. And impressing her. Why else did he buy the big car? And talks now about a horsebox. To move his house and home in. I don't know why you're arguing with me. You're wasting my time both of you, I should be back in the stall.'

Timmy shook his head, putting an end to Fanning's complaining tone. 'I'm not arguing with you,' he said as though speaking to a child.

And Timmy was not arguing. Timmy was preparing his betting partner for the big day: schooling him over the gamble on the racecourse. He didn't want to have him lose nerve at the very moment he held the money in his hand to the bookmakers. He was steeling Fanning and he was steeling himself. For while he may not have been as apprehensive of Connaughton's ambitions as was his partner, he had to find a way for himself to fall in with them. His next remark ended Fanning's complaining. It made Fanning so stop, stand and gape that the boy wished he understood what it had meant.

'Wouldn't it be good for Connaughton to go and show himself with a woman again at the races?' Timmy had said and then paused. 'It would change all our lives, mind. Know that. This bet could be our last. Best make it work.'

Fanning had stood, gaped and gone silent. Whether he was considering what Timmy had said, or whether he realised further discussion was pointless, he had stopped talking.

The boy listened on, hoping some more might be said. A rhythmic sound hung in the air. It could have been the sound of hoof beats. It could have been in his head. He looked at the men, anxiously staring, now that conversation was done, at the gap in the hedge. Their faces flickered as an anxiety raged within them, now one way, now the other: will Connaughton's horse come home right or will it not? He got no nearer understanding Timmy's remark beyond the fact that it was of importance.

They saw the shape take form through the mist.

They looked for a slackening of its pace, they looked for the fault in its stride. 'Pull him up,' Fanning shouted, 'You're killing him Egan, pull him up.'

Connaughton appeared. They looked for a sign. They could not tell his reaction. As he drew closer they saw his face glisten with beads of mist. He patted the horse and lifted a leg, feeling in it for heat. 'Get him in and dry him off quick,' he said to the jockey. He reassured them. 'He's genuine,' he said. They didn't appear convinced. 'Galway in July,' he said.

'Has he a chance?'

'Ever notice in July, Timmy, how remote are the clouds, how untroubled is the sky!'

Connaughton looked flushed, his moment of affirmation seemed to strain him. He looked like a child attempting a bold face, attempting to convince adults. 'Are you sure?' Timmy said, but did not look at him.

An awkward moment followed. Nobody would look at anybody else. The question died on Timmy's lips. Then all of them watched the horse, led away to its stable by Egan. It seemed to have recovered quickly. Its hind quarters swaggered as when it had been fresh and eager for its gallop so that only by looking at it closely could anyone say with conviction that it sagged slightly on one side. Nobody seemed to want to look closely. The boy moved to a new patch of the field and guillotined heads of grass again with his stick.

Beaten by Connaughton's burst of youthfulness Timmy looked at Fanning. 'We'll enter him so for the Plate,' he said. Fanning did not have to look back. He nodded in agreement.

The drizzle had stopped but raindrops clung onto Connaughton's windscreen as he drove back towards the hotel. He had forgotten to turn on his windscreen wipers; he was deep in thought. The boy had squinted his eyes into tight slits. At first he could see only a mass of grey, formless countryside. A solid pinnacle began to take shape. It was the spire of the distant church. They were nearing the town.

Then he made out the form of the railway bridge. Lost in vague imaginings of a new life, a life somewhere up in the hills, the slishing noise that the wheels made through the puddles on the road barely intruded into his mind.

They crossed the bridge. The railway line passed beneath. The boy did not look down, yet it seared through his mind, a double line crossing it, racing towards some distant destination.

Passing the tinker camp Connaughton stopped and pointed out a chestnut mare that he said he had not noticed on the outward journey. 'Make a good ladies' hunter,' he said, 'what do you think?' The boy did not respond.

'You're sopping wet.' Connaughton looked down at him. 'You're like something the cat brought in.' Again the boy did not respond.

'Penny for your thoughts,' Connaughton tried again, 'tuppence if they're good. What age did you tell me you were?'

'Eight.'

'Eight, when I was your age I used to think a lot too. I had a philosopher's bent, I used to be told. Things didn't work out that way for me though. I became more inclined towards action. Ever hear the expression' – he had become reflective – 'look before you leap? Maybe it's you will be the philosopher.

'And maybe New Hope will look before he leaps.' He tried once more to humour the boy. 'And we'll all win the Galway Plate.'

There was no further talk, though with every corner of the road they rounded, with every landmark they passed on the run into town, the need grew stronger: Connaughton wanted to ask the boy what he thought was the problem with Fanning. Even though he knew the answer.

'Fanning is not opposed,' he wanted to say. 'Fanning is for it. Don't you think so?' He wanted reassurance. 'And you will be too.' He wanted to tell him about his new mother. The wife he had married and taken to the Lakes of Killarney on honeymoon the weekend just gone by. He wanted to tell him that he too would be brought to Killarney. He too would ride in the little rowing boat. And unlike his new mother he would not almost overturn the boat when he stepped into it. He wanted to tell him about her embarrassed laugh when the boat had rocked in the shallow water. About his Lady of the Lamplight. Yes, his Lady of the Lamplight, he had called her. Lamplight. Why had he said that? Oh yes, he remembered. That night. The soft glow through their window. His Lady of the Lamplight. Imagine him saying a thing like that!

'She wants to meet you,' he wanted to say.

He forgot about Fanning, drove up to his hotel – the premises on which he was about to gamble his horse's chances. He dismissed the small worry he had about it. He parked, steering into a narrow gap between cars, without even looking where he was going.

And the boy too wanted to say something. As they had driven up Bank Street, the sun shining familiarly on it again, sending its pebbledash walls to sleep, his father had opened the window; a warm breeze had blown in, and a butterfly. He had watched it flutter on the dashboard, flutter out again. He too wanted to say something, to shout something. A voice shouted so loud inside him it hurt his head. 'Fanning is opposed,' it was saying. 'Is. Is. Is. And Fanning is right. And when I grow up I don't don't don't want to be a philosopher!'

But the shouting in his head stopped. Even before they got out of the car and stood on the white pavement and he ran to resume the game with his friends. And began to hear the new, quieter voice. 'What does a philosopher do, Dada?' this voice was saying. 'What's it like where we have to go up the hills in the horsebox?'

THE FINGER STUMP

MANY TIMES LALLY HAD WATCHED his father take down the shotgun from its place on the high dressing table and then walk up the Deerpark resting it on his arm.

He had watched his brother, his stepbrother, pull it down too. He did not walk up the field with it but pouched it beside him in the cab of the tractor so that if a rabbit or pheasant rose on his travels he could pot it. Everywhere his brother went the tractor went. 'Lazy as a lump of shit,' the workman, Dickie Cobbett, said he was. His father preferred to walk, and so did Lally. The tractor did not appeal to him. And Dickie's assessment of his brother pleased him.

It will be back in its place before they get home, he thought to himself. I'll clean the barrels with the pull-through, they won't even know it's been out of the house.

He stood on the chair. Both the others could reach the gun without it. He was about to lean into the dresser and tear some cubes off the jelly block, but today's business was more important; his hand reached higher. Today he could have taken the jelly, a spoon of Golden Syrup, anything, there was no one about but himself and old Dancie. The creak of the floorboards above him was only her making the beds. Yet today its sound, like all the other sounds he could hear or imagine about the big house, made him jumpy.

He helped himself to the gun. It was more solid than he had expected. Quickly he ran his hands along its smooth, wooden stock, liking its shine, the straight length of its barrels and wondering why Dickie Cobbett called it a bastard of a gun.

The gun was heavy. He would have to carry it correctly, as he saw his father do, otherwise it would be too cumbersome. Through the kitchen he grappled with it, through the carpeted hall. He would return it in three hours: it would be that at least before they returned from the funeral.

Passing the coatstand mirror he caught a glimpse of himself and delayed a moment for inspection. One hour to walk to Farpark, half an hour to count the sheep – the reason he, and he alone, had been allowed to stay at home from school – one hour to walk back, half an hour to spare. Quick march soldier, he swung the gun through the front door.

Outdoors he noticed the same sort of watchful silence as was in the house. Passing alongside the clothesline he smelled washing powder from the limply hanging clothes. When he kicked a stone ahead of himself, attempting to muster some life into the day, draw from it some response to his important event, the stone came to a stop without hardly rattling.

'Where is Wild Bill Hickock off to?' Dickie Cobbett stood at the Deerpark gate and eyed him mockingly.

'To herd the sheep. Daddy said to bring the gun in case there might be any scaldcrows.'

'Make sure you don't shoot yourself.'

'I will.'

'You haven't it loaded?'

'No.'

'You're sure? Give us a look.'

Dickie took the gun and nestled it comfortably into his shoulder. He squinted down the barrel, looking for something to aim at. A squawking magpie jigged on an ash tree from which twigs dislodged. A cat on one of the branches crept towards it. Dickie held the cat in his sights and when it sprang onto a neighbouring branch his gun barrel jerked upwards. 'Bang, gotcha,' he said. 'Dead-eye Dick.

'Did y'ever shoot outa this?' he asked.

'No, but in the shooting gallery I shot.'

'That was only a popgun. Put up a tin on the wall and I'll show you.'

Dickie had shot tins off the wall before, he and Lally's brother, smashing them backwards into eternity and laughing at the blast's effect. Lally knew he would have to be on his own before he could find courage to pull the trigger.

'No. Dancie would hear.'

'Shag oul Dancie, grey-haired, deaf and blind badger. She wouldn't hear if both barrels went off up her hole.'

'Here.' Lally gave Dickie the cigarettes he had stolen from Dancie's box while she was upstairs.

'Watch that bastard, it has a wicked kick,' Dickie advised him, satisfied with his parley. 'For Christ's sake don't hold it in front of your face before you shoot. Make sure you get it into your shoulders. If you come back here spittin' teeth, don't cry to me.'

He walked the length of the Deerpark, leaving the house and farmyard a long way behind and cut off by the rise over which he had climbed. 'Make sure you get it into your shoulder,' he said to himself. 'Bastard of a gun.' It was growing so heavy he could hardly carry it. He wondered what the kickback was going to be like. 'Like a sledgehammer,' his brother had said. 'For every forward action there must be a backward and equal reaction, that'll tell you what it's like.' A sledgehammer... was there a way, other than raising the gun to his arm, of shooting?

He stopped and drank from a stream that divided Deerpark and Rampark. It was softened by rain and smelled of the weeds clinging from the bank and brushed out like hair by the slow-running water. As his ear lowered to the grass he heard the permanent rustle of breeze that blew across those hills. He sensed something. A smell, faint on the breeze, of carrion lying somewhere up above, of death. A fever penetrated into his bone, weakened him. He was about to give up his idea of shooting the gun when he thought of how Dickie Cobbett would greet his return if he found the gun barrels clean. And another thought spurred him: if he did shoot something . . . he might even display it for his father's appraisal. Surprise his brother.

Standing on the tip of the Rampark he saw the house again, barely distinguishable now from its surround of trees and walls, its influence over him waning. The sky was overhung with cloud. Above him it drifted, high it seemed, and light, but it sagged darkly on the horizon limiting his vision. The breeze had dropped.

He strode down the far side of the hill towards the sheep. 'Pay heed to how they look when you first see them,' his father always said. 'If the sheep are restless something is up.' They were restless. They paced, heads raised, high-stepping, about the field. But he did not pay heed. With each step he was becoming more agitated, the job in hand shutting everything else out of his mind.

It was time to enter Farpark: sloping into a valley, damp cobwebs clung to its gorse and sedge-grass. He broke the gun before creeping through the barbed wire, but did not load it. The lesson of his father's finger was not lost on him, even now. Once upon a time, when his father was seventeen, he had crossed a ditch, his finger placed into the barrel of his shotgun, steadying himself. One cartridge sat in that barrel and waited for the cock-off. He had forgotten it was there until the stock thudded into the ditch he had been crossing. 'The faithful old dog whined at heel all the way home and for a whole week slunk outside my door while I lay in fever in my bed.' His father could never adequately convey in his retellings of this story the pain and fear that had dragged him home across the fields that day. But he could show the smooth-topped stump where his longest finger had once been. Lally would never cross a ditch with a loaded gun.

At first he thought the rabbits were cobwebs. He had only to walk a few yards into the field, however, when he saw them for what they were. They were grazing, a family of them. His target would be one of them. Not a crow, not a pheasant, not a tin can, not a plump big rabbit but one of these baby rabbit things; the sight of them brought him to his senses.

His step slowed. He anticipated the bang and the kick of the gun. Right up against his ear his brother had shot off the gun one day he splattered a crow. He saw the blue flame blast and then the fallen crow make circles in the road's dust with its wing.

Carefully he inserted the two cartridges and locked the breech. There was a stream he had to cross. He was tempted to splash, warn the rabbits. Instead he looked down, picking his way carefully over the stepping stones. Davy Doheny's old cottage stood by the stream. Davy was his father's other workman. He knew he would not be within the house. His father had loaned him these past few days to the Miss Butlers who farmed down the valley. He was thinning their mangels.

Nevertheless he looked in Davy's window. He was such an odd fellow, he thought, never seen except when called upon to mend dogs' broken limbs, or at music festivals, preferably many miles distant, where he played a three-button accordion.

He could make out nothing within the window's darkness and when he looked about again the rabbits had disappeared.

He was now nearing the field's end. The sheep clumped ahead of him into an ever-tightening knot, their callings to one another crisscrossing beneath the cover of cloud.

To his right was the rabbit bank; it was there they had found sanctuary when they sensed fear in their midst. Imagining them in the burrow mouths, listening, gauging the pitch of any sound, he retreated a little so the sheep, given space to spread out, might settle down again in the drizzle.

A rabbit scampered onto the grass and the air seemed suddenly sucked of movement. It stood stock still a few moments, then looked up, sitting on its haunches. He stared at his quarry, certain it was looking at him. He wondered why it did not move. Too young, he figured, to run from danger.

'Make sure you get the gun into your shoulder.' He raised it to eye level, the beating in his chest quickened and still the rabbit did not move. In the instant he knew he should not kill it he felt the trigger. Its touch gave him a fright. His whole body had been tensed for the explosion; his body, it was, forced him to get it over with. Quick. He pulled, there was no shot.

After a few moments in which he noticed the silence about him had not shattered, he saw the rabbit was still in the same position, still looking at him. He lowered the gun from where it had become wedged in his shoulder and as he did so he noticed the closed safety catch.

A little rush of something passed through him then: the rabbit remained before him, something had to be done about it. Dickie Cobbett would laugh at this, so would his brother. They would ridicule the soft-hearted dithering into which he had fallen. Smoothly, calmer, he slid the safety catch across and again raised the gun.

Then, in quick succession, the rabbit moved, the gun went

off, something hit him in the chest and the gun went off again. Above his head the sky seemed to have suddenly rent open. He saw the bolt of blue and above it the hedge and field passing upside down and a sheep staggering crazily towards the ditch.

Seconds passed while his breath would not return. It seemed an eternity. He thought he had shot himself and knew, horrified, that if the air did not soon return to his lungs he would die.

The muscles in his chest seemed to have seized. Briefly he wondered if maybe he was supposed to die. 'Oh Jesus don't let me'; he was surprised at his helplessness in face of such an event. But then something loosened within him and slowly his breath returned. He knew he was lying on the grass. There was no sight anywhere of the rabbit at which he had aimed, and the sheep had all scarpered to the upper end of the field and were bleating anew. A trace of gunpowder hung in the air and in his nostrils.

He realised then it was the stock of the gun had hit him, and not once, but twice in quick succession. Lifting the damp woollen pullover from his chest he found two pressure points, the shapes of two small white eggs, on either side, just below his collarbone. He sat there a few moments. A whole range of feelings had passed through his mind. First there had been fright, then vague stirrings about life and its sudden inevitable ending for him. Now he began to feel about himself a sense of achievement. He hadn't shot a rabbit. But he had pulled a gun trigger. And not once but twice, in rapid succession. He walked up through the limp grass and counted the sheep.

Three times he counted the sheep, following them down the field, then up, then down again. He was one short. His father had said seventy-nine. No matter what way he counted he could only arrive at seventy-eight. He counted a fourth time but this time could only find seventy-seven.

Then he broke out in a sweat. It ran into the drizzle that rolled from his hair down over his face, trickled saltily into his mouth. He remembered what he had seen, or thought he had seen, the moment he thought he had shot himself ... The bolt of blue, the white of a sheep staggering towards the ditch. Seventy-seven, seventy-eight, seventy-nine, the second shot, the one that had gone off accidentally ... He couldn't have. He panicked and ran to count the sheep again but now he had disturbed them to such an extent they packed in a solid mass, like wool loaded into a yarn sack, and would not be counted.

It was getting late and the gun had to be returned; he was in ragged retreat. As he passed Davy's cottage on his way out of the field something caught his eye which stopped him abruptly. There, outside the cottage, in a little fenced-off garden, lay a motionless sheep. It did not occur to him to wonder how the sheep might have got in there and lay now amid the stacks of firewood and tall wet dandelions of Davy's garden. The uppermost thought in his mind was how he must get her out, dispose of her. He knew already he was going to drag her down the field to a part where the stagnant ditch was deepest and throw her in where the weed covered her over. If she was still alive he was first going to give her the third cartridge he had in his pocket. The truth must never be let out.

But would he have the strength? There were streams and narrow passages of briar through which he would have to haul her. An even more trigger-happy thought came to his mind. He looked at the longest finger of his left hand and at the opening of the gun barrel. Do it. Then they will have to feel sorry for me. Distract them, that's it. The thought was so close he almost fainted.

He saw a movement within the small window of Davy's house, a sudden glint of something white within the darkness. The raising of a cup, he thought, the lifting of a cup of tea to someone's lips. It whipped his mind to even greater confusion, put an end to his consideration of how the ewe could have staggered, of all places, into Davy's haggard. He retraced his steps, wondering if Davy had already seen him.

Lally struggled across the one-hundred-acre Deerpark. By the time he was near the house his knees hurt from the banging of the gun stock and he pitied himself and everything about his situation. But his sobbing had subsided and his mind was working on a way of retrieving a situation from which, only a few minutes before, hopelessness had stared.

The sight of Dickie Cobbett, again at the Deerpark gate, helped him pull himself together.

'Haha, Wild Bill Hickock, and what's for the dinner,' Dickie sneered, 'a buffalo or a big fat lamb?'

He looked at Dickie in alarm, wondering how could he have been so close to the mark.

'What did you shoot?'

'A crow.'

'How many shots to put the mighty vulture down?'

'Dickie . . .' He faltered.

'What?'

'Dickie, sure you won't say I took the gun out if you're asked?'

'Why so, did you murder someone?'

'I did not.'

'Who's up there to murder anyway,' Dickie giggled, 'unless you got Lily Butler's mad daughter Easie with her knickers down pissing behind the ditch?'

'I didn't.'

'Or Davy, did you slug Davy?'

'No, sure Davy is thinning the Butlers' mangels.' Here was a chance to verify if maybe it was Davy he had seen through the window.

'Maybe he is, maybe he's not. Maybe he shagged home for a cup of tea. Did you see the dog and you up there, 'cause if you did you can rest assured Davy was up there too.'

'I didn't.' He hadn't seen the dog. That, at least, he felt, was something.

'Go on, lave in that gun before they come back. And clane out the barrels with the pull-through. I'll say nothin'.'

'Thanks, Dickie.'

'Thanks me arse, get me a few of Dancie's fags if you get the chance.'

'Thanks, Dickie.' He walked to the kitchen smiling to himself: the long-standing feud between Dickie and Dancie, who after all were related, nephew and aunt, always cheered him. Any closeness between them, he understood, must not be seen by him or his family. It must remain hidden behind a comical open war.

'Give me a hand with this,' his father shouted when he returned from the funeral. Still dressed in his good clothes he had been attempting to drag the trailer across to where the tractor stood. He held its hitch. It was awkward and heavy and swung him wildly as it waved back and forth. He looked distraught. Lally had seen him like this before. 'I'm an unfortunate man,' he spluttered. 'God help me, do I deserve these crosses in my path? Did you go up and look at the sheep like you were asked?'

Lally stared blankly at the ineffectual black-suited figure dancing in agony before him and did not reply. 'Did you count the sheep? You fool, you didn't,' his father answered his own question. 'You should be horsewhipped. Get in that trailer before I lose my temper.' He himself jumped on the tractor seat. 'Depend on them to do something for me?' He threw his eyes heavenward and fumbled with the gear stick. 'Oh have pity on me.'

As they drove up the laneway Lally shuddered about in the trailer and cried. He jumped obligingly out at the Deerpark gate. A row of rain droplets the length of the gate fell to the ground as he opened it.

His father drove recklessly across the humpy Deerpark field; Lally hunched on his heels attempting to save his rear end as it banged on the trailer floor. He clung to the tailgate wondering if he let himself fall out would it save him from the doom he was quickly driving towards. The ground churned by beneath him. The thought that he would be killed if he fell comforted him but his hands would not let go.

When his father halted the tractor outside Farpark it occurred to Lally he was still crying. He had been crying all the way down and now all the way up again. The brave soldier who had earlier set out . . . he considered how babyish he must be.

'What are you crying for?' The voice sounded unreal in the silence left behind by the suddenly switched-off tractor engine.

'Nothing.'

'It must be something.'

'Nothing.'

'Nothing.' His father lost his temper with exasperation. 'Couldn't be less. Stop crying for nothing.'

The shout had the effect of reducing the cry to a whimper, but the whimper, like the drip from a tap that needs a new washer, would not stop.

'Stop it.'

'Yes Daddy.'

'Now.'

'I can't Daddy.'

'Why can't you?'

'I'm afraid.'

'Afraid of what?' Scum and rage bubbled from the corners of his mouth. 'Stop it!'

The cloud had broken over Farpark and now the evening sun shone through. It lit the dark-stained wetness of the field until the grass was a dazzling sheen, he felt it burn his salty eyes.

'I'll try, Daddy,' he choked.

Suddenly something softened within his father. His temper subsided as quickly as it had flared. 'Dry up your tears like a good man. I'm not going to hurt you.'

'I know Daddy, I know you're not going to hurt me.' More tears burst from him at the thought he could have the idea the man before him whom he idolised could hurt him.

His father rubbed the scum from his lips. 'Come on.' His voice had softened completely. 'You remind me of someone once upon a time. Come on, we have a job to do.'

They found the ewe stretched out in Davy's shed, dry mud and litter sticking to its swollen stomach, a dark-red stain tightening the wool beneath its neck.

'Lally, Lally.' His father spoke softly now. 'If only you could have looked at them like you were told I wouldn't have this misfortune on me now.' His censure was no longer conducted through anger, he wanted pity. Lally felt infinitely sorry for him.

He opened the ewe's delicately freckled lips and examined its teeth. They were perfect, straight, without a chip. 'Only a young hogget, what a shame.' He shook his head. 'I met Davy at Butlers' mangels on our way home. He was up here, he thinks it might be dogs. If only you could have been here you might have frightened them away.'

The memory of the restless flock that time earlier when he had entered the field flooded like a slow light across Lally's mind. But what time had Davy been here? What time had Davy found out? The question that burned to be asked would have to remain on his lips. 'Come on, Lally.' He anchored himself to his father's voice. He was sliding helplessly back into the confusion from which that morning, when he had lifted the gun to his shoulder, he had attempted to emerge. 'Come on, Lally.' His father was pointing at a lamb, adrift from the rest of the flock and bleating. 'We'll have to catch it and raise it on the bottle. It'll have to be a pet lamb.'

That night he saw his father leave the house with the gun. He pictured him roaming the shadowy fields, the dark glint in his eyes looking out for the lights of a blood-loving dog, the joint of his amputated finger twitching, its baldness a shiny mute moon. He wondered would he find something to pull the trigger on. A hare, a fox perhaps, looming suddenly before him, the stock walloping back into his shoulders, as he hoped his father had downed the dog. The dog that so far as Lally knew did not exist, though he could now no longer be sure.

And Davy's story . . . Had Davy seen him up there? Was he attempting to protect him? Surely Davy would not make up a story like that, he who abhorred all needless killing? Such a story would put even his own dog at risk should it come within the sights of his employer's mad gun. Lally did not know.

He only knew his father's quest disturbed him. He turned over and over in his bed. 'Count sheep,' his father had once advised when he had complained of not getting off to sleep. He did not count sheep. Slowly he drifted into uncertain terrain where he stumbled a few times before responsibility fell away from him.

He awoke from a dream and didn't know where he was. He

heard sounds from downstairs that after a few moments became the voices of his parents. They drifted up the shallow-stepped stairs with the crack of light from the open kitchen door.

He heard his father's rubber boots flop, first one and then the other, to the floor. He heard the teapot lid fall on the enamel of the sink.

'Drew a blank,' he heard his father complain. 'Say a prayer the killer doesn't strike again tonight. Tomorrow we'll have to move the flock down. Oh, I should never have put them up there in the first place. Too far from the house. I'm unfortunate.'

'I could have told you that. I thought you'd shoot yourself walking around in those hills in the pitch-dark.' His stepmother's reply was sharp.

It jolted him wide awake. He had been dreaming and now he remembered the dream. He had been counting, not sheep, but fingers. His finger had been stuck up the barrel of a shotgun. 'Daddy, Daddy, no, no, you can't,' he had shouted in disbelief. His father had pulled the trigger, a shot went off, and then there was a gap where the finger should have been.

He sat upright in his bed. The conversation downstairs was ended now. Over and over again he counted his fingers; they were sticky but all of them were there.

'WHISKEY WHEN YOU'RE SICK MAKES YOU WELL…'

DID I REALISE WHAT I HAD BEEN DOING? I hardly think so. 'Sitting at the kitchen table like all the others,' I would have said had I been asked. Until Mam had suddenly borne down on me: 'Do you realise what you are doing? Filthy, furtive habit. Take those hands from your pockets.' And the whole crowd of them about the table stared at me. 'Look at the strips he has torn off his pocket insides,' she said. 'I'll sew them up. Then he won't be able to claw holes in them. Put your hands on the table. God is watching you. And your own mother.' (Mam is not my real mother.) 'Shame.'

Oh God, furtive. I hated the way she said that. I pretended not to know what she was talking about.

So it was for good reason I could have cheered when Daddy clanked, a bucket hanging from either arm, into the kitchen. It was hot in the kitchen: the skin of cold morning lifted like fog from the buckets' enamel. They had been witnesses, all of them. Of my hands bare and uncomforted on the table top. I had borne their looks. Now it would end.

Not that now I could return my hands to where they had been. No. Nor would I ever again.

But would the embarrassment end? That was my next worry. Relief deserted me as soon, almost, as it had arisen.

Fear displaced it. Would she tell Daddy? I feared she would. She had got the others to guffaw at me, yes. But that didn't mean she herself thought it funny. No, on the contrary. You see sometimes I think I know Mam. She looks brave; oh, able for anything and everything – when in fact she is afraid. I had seen the look she gave me when she pounced: she was frightened. So yes, she would tell him. Then she wouldn't have to worry about my rush into filthy ways, he could worry. She would love too to belittle me in Daddy's eyes. Whenever I seek escape, my heart darts into narrowing dark regions ahead of me. It did then.

Daddy walked with a flourish into the kitchen. He drew down one of the empty ale bottles from the shelf above the sink. It is one of the few things he does with a flourish, and why he should do so always puzzles me – or did until the events of this very day. After all, the appearance of the ale bottle always means trouble.

So I could have sang then, contradictory as it might seem. Because I knew his routine, what he was about to say next. I was saved. My own unhappy incident (which I don't want to talk about any further) would not now be related: there was more important business.

'Whiskey when you're sick makes you well.' Daddy recited it as he filled the bottle under the tap, shook it, emptied it, rinsed it again. 'Whiskey makes you sick when you're well. Repeat that axiom.' He smiled sublimely, as though he had said something of deep spiritual import.

He had recited clearly as always, slowly as always; we had hung, waiting on his words as always, and yet not one of us could repeat it.

There were ten of us children about the table. Some are Daddy's children by an earlier marriage. Some are Mam's by an earlier marriage. Some belong to the marriage of Daddy

and Mam. 'As if they didn't have children enough,' is what
I have heard people say. So, there were ten of us children at
the table, there was Mam also and there were the workmen.
The usual Saturday morning eleven o'clock crowd, listening
to whatever jawing was going on between Mam and Thomas.
Hoping an opportunity would arise for laughter: any diversion rather than be singled out for attention.

Neither Thomas or the other workmen, Dickie (who is
Thomas's nephew) or Davy, would have attempted to repeat
Daddy's conundrum, or axiom as he calls it. It would not have
been, they would have felt, their place to do so. While they
will laugh with Mam, they are always on guard with Daddy.
And Mam would not have bothered to repeat it. Why? In case
she got it wrong? In any event she was in one of her winking,
joking moods with the workmen. And as for Dancie, our
housekeeper, hovering about behind the table, making sure
we were not fighting – when Daddy becomes eloquent, as
sometimes he does when he draws down the ale bottle, his
words fly beyond Dancie's reach. She listens only when he
gives orders or when an animal dies and he complains. Then
she pities him. 'Unfortunate man,' she says, 'killing himself
working.'

So it was left to us children to repeat the axiom. I came
nearest. Some of the others could not repeat even the first half
of it. Of if they did, as soon as they got to the second half
it confused them so that they then went back and got the first
part wrong also.

'Whiskey when you're sick makes you well; whiskey when
you're well makes you sick,' they blabbered. 'No, I'll try again.
When you're well whiskey makes you sick; and ... when
you're sick whiskey makes you well. That's it, that's it!'

But it wasn't. I sat there a long time thinking. And suddenly, like a light shining down a tunnel of jumbled words,

it came together. 'Whiskey when you're sick makes you well, whiskey...' But Richie saw that I had it. He kicked me on the ankle beneath the table's cover and at the same time he warned me, his fingers to his lips, not to cry out. I didn't cry out but I lost my picture of words and couldn't recover it again for Daddy.

Richie can't bear it if I get things right.

I'd say Mam heard him kick me, and my knee jerk against the table. But she didn't, for the sake of peace, say anything.

I'll say this in Mam's favour: if it was Richie got the kick, and kept his mouth shut about it, she'd ignore it just the same. Even though he is her own eldest son. She doesn't have favourites. But of course he wouldn't keep his mouth shut. He'd bawl. Probably kill whoever kicked him.

No, Mam doesn't like to excite Daddy over these squabbling incidents. It is important to her he thinks everybody in the house is happy. She just went on cracking the pile of monkey nuts she had before her on the table. She went on smoking her cigarette and eating the nuts and joking with the workmen.

It is rare that Daddy comes into the kitchen at morning-tea time. As soon as he leaves the house after breakfast it is generally for the day's duration. We don't see him again. He is gone to the auctioneer job at his cattle mart or to value land or to buy cattle or greyhounds. I hate when this happens. I like him to be around. Except when Mam too goes with him. That is good. Then we children can get on with killing one another. Whenever he comes into the house during the day it is either to make a phone call, in which case he loses his temper with the telephone operator, shouts at her down the line and then comes into the kitchen complaining of her stupidity, or else it is to get the ale bottle. Then he carries in with him his flourish, his axiom and, barely lurking beneath that, his anxiety.

Daddy's anxiety follows him like the gun dog that is always about his heels. Sometimes, when he is out in the yard, or up in the field, hesitating over something, coming to some decision or other, he stands still. It is rare for Daddy to stand still. He stands still, straddles his feet and the gun dog man-oeuvres its long, faithful body between them. Then, when Daddy turns to go again, decision made, unaware, due to his anxiety, of the gun dog's presence, he trips across its body. He falls to the ground, usually with a clatter of the buckets he is carrying and roars at the dog, 'You fool, you simple fool.' The dog runs to the coalhouse, head in paws, and yelps long and loud and everybody laughs behind Daddy's back. But it is not long before the dog takes up its vigil again at his heels. Daddy's anxiety is like the dog. It never deserts him long.

Except sometimes, when he is getting the ale bottle, then it does. Sometimes. It did then because he laughed when one of the girls, Marguerite, asked him to 'say it again, ah please'. But he didn't say it again. He beat the egg, added the milk to it and lumped the mix into the bottle until it was half full. Then he went out to the sitting room and when he returned, the bottle was full. It's always the same: half-full when he goes out, full when he returns. The second half is whiskey.

'Not a sick sheep again,' said Mam, 'and we have that ap-pointment.' Though neither of them had told us, we children knew there was something the matter with Mam and the ap-pointment was with the hospital. (Maybe that was the reason too, now I come to think of it, she was in such jokey mood – trying to put her mind off things.)

'Yes, a sick sheep,' Daddy said, and his mournful expres-sion – 'gun dog expression' Mam calls it – returned. 'Afraid so. I found a young ewe in the Deerpark, staggering badly. I lifted her but she went down again. A chill maybe, and I think the whiskey might help.'

Thomas, as I have said, is one of our workmen. It is he who jokes with Mam during mealtimes. He's the brother of Dancie, our housekeeper. They are enemies. 'Pity I couldn't stagger a bit,' Thomas said. 'And maybe I'd get some whiskey.' Davy, Dickie, Mam, even Daddy, they all laughed at this. It had been an attempt to dispel Daddy's anxiety. So that they didn't have to feel they had to leave the table: an attempt to prolong tea break. And it worked. Dancie is Thomas's fiercest adversary. 'And indeed you have staggered,' she said. 'Many a time. When you stagger it's not for want of whiskey. It's because you've had too much of it. Drunken disgrace!'

Mam gave a shorter laugh this time and told Daddy he would have to forget the ewe or else they could forget about the appointment.

Daddy offered cigarettes to Mam and to the men. He didn't offer Dancie one because he knew she wouldn't take it. 'I only smoke my own,' she says.

In front of everybody else then, while the men were shuffling in their chairs, awkward in Daddy's presence, he asked me to dose the sick ewe.

I looked down at the table as soon as he said it. I could not look at anyone. At the workmen, my brothers, especially Richie. If our kitchen didn't have that window that faces the sun it would be a closed box. Right now, window or no window, it was a box, and I was enclosed. I knew they were all looking at me. And Thomas and Dickie and Mam and Richie were laughing.

'I'm busy,' Daddy said. 'You've watched me enough times dose sheep to know how to do it.'

'But how will he catch her,' Mam said, 'when he can't even catch that harmless fool of a dog?'

'Easy catch her,' Daddy said, 'she's on the ground.'

Mam is a handsome woman. I've heard many of the men

say that. 'Handsome,' they say, 'handsome rather than pretty'. Lots of men. They travel from miles around to see her. They usually have errands – to borrow a trailer, to help with the cattle skulling – and all of them have a laugh with her. 'She's a great woman, Mrs Connell, I don't know how she manages.' They go away half-happy. While at the same time Daddy runs around the farm intent on his work.

Half-happy yes, at least they've known her longer than he. I think they are trying to say that to him. But Daddy lives here now and he does the jobs they once did. He holds the calves' testicles while she squeezes. He holds the bullocks' horns while she saws.

Yes, there is no doubt she can work hard – handsome or not, with that thick black hair, plaited in photos of her widowed days but shorn shortly after she married Daddy. She is strong. There is a ring of muscle round the calves of her legs that wellington boots cling against whenever she wears them. It is very attractive. But I can't look at Mam and at these things about her. And it is not simply because if I did, or if I said anything true to her, she would deride me. It is, I think, because she sees a bit of Daddy in me. It does make sense, does it not? He, behind whose back she laughs, all of us having to laugh at him too – because we know what's good for us. He, who she fears, while at the same time deeply loves. It is in the very same spirit she laughs at me. What is she afraid of in me?

I didn't listen attentively while Daddy instructed me about dosing the ewe. I watched the kitchen table. I followed the grains in the wood. I prefer our table when it is not covered by the oilcloth. When there is only the bare wood and the sun can shine on it like it did now, it means it is not an occasion and table manners is not something we have got to be as careful of.

He instructed me again when we got out in the yard.

Morning is always the nicest time in our yard because then the sun warms the front wall of the house, turning it into a sleepy, quiet place that smiles even while all of us children are quarrelling.

Now we were on our own I could listen to Daddy. I notice that when he talks to you and you are one of a group it is to the group he is talking. Mam is the same, but not to the same extent. 'No favourites,' she says. 'I treat all equally. I won't make fish of one and flesh of another.' It must be hard on her to lower her own children to everybody else's level. Sometimes I think it's as if we were all away at school somewhere. 'Just don't let it grind the bottle,' Daddy said. 'That's a good lad. Dose it slowly. And if it starts coughing, for God's sake stop.'

Ever since the day I came to live in this house with Daddy and with Mam and the other children there have been many things I have not liked. But there are things I have liked. Some things in Mam for example. Some other feeling beneath our attitudes to one another. And the fields. I like them all. I like the Deerpark for its size and for the rocky streams that flow, almost hidden, beneath steep grassy banks.

I bucked about on the tractor's mudguard as Thomas drove over the ruts and hollows on the track that leads to the Deerpark. One of Daddy's other workmen, Mam's other workmen I should say because they were here before Daddy, sat on the other mudguard. We didn't balance one another, because he is far heavier than I. It didn't matter, however; the tractor was that heavy. And yet it reared over hillocks as if it were a lunging horse. With every lunge I held tightly to the mudguard. Clods of dirt from the wheel lugs flew over my head and into the air like birds, and Thomas laughed at me.

'Harmless man your ould fellow,' he teased. 'That he'd pour whiskey into a half-dead sheep and wouldn't drink a drop himself.'

'It's true, Davy, isn't it?' he said.

'True,' Davy said, 'even a bottle of ale itself. Then life might run a bit simpler for him.'

Thomas's next remark was not intended for my ears. But I heard it, even above the tractor's chopping whine. 'Maybe it's that he can't drink it,' he said. 'They say he was a fish on it one time. Fightin' and crashin' cars.'

'I heard that,' Davy said. 'Drank a farm out, I heard. Now he has to leave it alone altogether. One drop and he's on his way to drinkin' out another farm.'

I know where the drink is kept. In a sort of tabernacle sideboard in the sitting room. It never comes out except for visitors. Mam doesn't touch it either. She has already told me to avoid it. 'Smoke when you grow up,' she said. 'Then people won't think you're too odd. A person who doesn't either smoke or drink is mean. But don't ever drink.'

When Thomas stopped the tractor and let me off I was unsteady on my feet. A few moments passed before the ground became still. 'The sick ewe is over there.' Thomas pointed. I could see her on her back, alone, on marshy ground through which no tractor could pass. The flock had bolted from the tractor, she kicked in the air but could not move. 'Looks like she'll need it all,' he said. 'Make sure you don't dose any of it into yourself.' Then he grew serious. Whatever else can be said of Thomas he takes his work seriously. 'If she is not on her feet when we come back we'll collect.'

They left me. After a few minutes the tractor was hardly audible, the sound of seeping water rose from the ground. I was alone in that place. I like it up there. It's on top of the world. Where sounds of distant dogs and tractors drift and ebb and the silence of all the farms in the plain below, only interrupted now and then by clanging milk churns, is a presence that can be felt.

Daddy brought his children to live here a while ago. We crossed the county, ourselves and our belongings, in a large horsebox. Sometimes I am very unsure about what he thinks of me. I suppose he loves me. But I am not sure. He never says, instead he does things. Like the things he did when he came to live here. One of the first things he did was fill the Deerpark with sheep. Blackfaced mountain sheep, bought off Slievenamon. They can't be fenced in; they go through anything, wander for miles, and everybody around laughed watching Daddy rebuild fallen stone walls about a hundred acres. But he did it. And then he bought six premium rams.

I lifted the sheep to her feet before I took the bottle from my pocket. She would not stand and I had to lie her on the ground again so I could get it out and uncork it. I like the smell of sheep: oily and warm, especially when they are close-packed in a shed. But I love the smell of whiskey.

It makes me feel warm. When I was two years old I drank a bottle of whiskey. Daddy told me the story once when we were driving in the car. I was teething and it was his prescription: 'Whiskey when you're sick makes you well; whiskey makes you sick when you're well.' That's it. I've got it, his axiom. He believes in his axiom. Yes, what happened it seems is I was teething. I had been given a spoonful of whiskey and the bottle had been left by my cot.

I lifted the ewe again and smelled the whiskey. For one thing I was pleased: she had no maggots. The first time I saw maggots on a sheep's back I was horrified. I could have run. Being a town boy I wasn't used to such sights. I was with Daddy. I noticed nothing at first and then I saw its back, where the wool had fallen off. It was moving. A seething, screaming mass. Daddy simply washed them off with disinfectant. He scraped them off with his bare hands and they fell like snow to the grass. Some fell down inside my wellington boots. I said nothing, just loosened my hold on the sheep until Daddy roared at me to tighten my grip.

'You polished off the bottle,' Daddy said, 'and when your mother came up you were crowing in the cot like a bar-room singer!' That is about the only reference he ever made to my mother. He never talks about her unless it is about something funny and he can quickly get off the subject. I never discuss her of course. I cried once, you see, but he looked so miserable when I did that I dried up – and I've remained dry.

Once the notion rushed to my head that I might taste the whiskey nothing could stop me. That spot, at the back of the Deerpark, is the most isolated spot on earth. There is nothing up there. Not even the swish of trees. Curlews with their lonely cries, that is all.

I need not have worried about maggots on the sheep's back. It was late October: a dampness in the hollows, and water cobwebs on the grass, even though the sun shone clearly. Summer is the maggot season.

I drank a little of the bottle first and then I gulped it halfway down. I drank it quickly because of the terrible taste but stopped because I thought of the ewe who needed it.

The whiskey itself had been a vague but gentle sensation. There had been a taste too of lemonade. That puzzled me. It was the egg, not the whiskey, which had been so sickening.

The ewe loved it. Her black-pudding tongue funnelled about the bottle neck and she sucked. When she had finished, her teeth ground the bottle neck. I realised after a few minutes why she had taken so familiarly to the bottle: I recognised the speckles beneath her eyes – she had been our bottle-reared pet lamb.

I hugged that sheep for a moment. It was like regaining a long-lost friend. She had been my pet of the previous summer, following me about like the gun dog follows Daddy, bumping into my legs whenever I stopped walking. Now she had horns.

I was amazed I could have forgotten her. I remembered again the day on which she had been turned out with the rest of the flock. 'She'll have to harden up,' Daddy had said. She had returned a few times, bleated at the gate. Against orders I had brought her a bottle of milk. In the end she had drifted farther and farther, lost herself among the flock.

Even as I drank the medicine I felt bad, knowing I was depriving the ewe. Now, knowing it was the old pet, I felt even worse. I was likely to receive one of two punishments. 'Whiskey makes you sick when you're well' – being well I would take ill. Or – 'Whiskey when you're sick makes you well' – the pet lamb hadn't had enough and would die. I already felt sick.

As I descended the humps and hummocks of the Deerpark my nausea grew. It was the egg, my stomach told me, had done it. Clots of egg heaved off the walls of my stomach.

Whiskey when you're sick makes you well – I knew two things: one, I would have to get some for myself if I wanted to get better; two, I would have to get some for the pet lamb if it wasn't to die. I would have to, somehow, get into the sitting room, our house's holy of holies, walk across the vast carpet, and ... tabernacle drink cupboard, open it.

I have not eaten raw egg since and I never will. I vomited just as I reached the yard. I was so weak I could only cling to the gate and watch as the gun dog lapped it up. Dancie saw me through the kitchen window. She made me come inside and sit down. The quietness of the kitchen at that time of day must have calmed my stomach. There was a bubble of something from the cooker and the sound overhead of the girls laying out the linen. I began to think again of the mission I had set myself.

A few moments passed before I would accept the coast was clear. Dancie had gone upstairs, the girls too were upstairs, the boys outside at their jobs. The car was not in the yard, which meant Daddy and Mam hadn't yet returned from the doctor. It is not often Mam has something the matter with her. Never before in fact since I've met her, apart from having babies, that is, and as I wondered what could be her complaint I thought also of my good luck. God, I thought, must be giving me a second chance. I made a promise: if he allows me to rob the whiskey I will see the pet lamb receives it first.

I rinsed the bottle, half filled it with milk, omitted the egg, took off my boots – it is a sin to enter the sitting room in mucky boots – tiptoed across the hall. The sound of the kitchen clock, the sun rays from the rose window above the hall door, followed me.

If it was quiet in the hall, the sitting room was quieter: silent as a chapel, and as dark; the curtains pulled across, the armchairs as if shrouded. This is forbidden territory. There were no forbidden places in my, in Daddy's, previous home. I was about to turn back but I heard the crows outside. They are on the chimney, I thought, fighting over twigs, because the sound was coming down the fireplace. They calmed me. Then, very faintly, I heard the sound of a jet plane, high, crossing the heavens, and I opened the tabernacle door.

The bottles stood waiting. Three bottles: a whiskey bottle, a bottle of lemonade and a sherry, A Winter's Tale.

Quickly I transferred some whiskey to the milk. My mind was frozen but my hand shook. Whiskey spilled on my fingers and I licked them. Either my eyes had closed or I was looking down the black tunnel where only fear and nothingness live; I put the whiskey to my mouth and gulped deeply once and then again.

The first impression was of burning heat inside me. My eyes watered and my ears seemed to burst. After a while I got better.

I was about to return the bottle when the car rolled into the yard. Mam and Daddy were back; peace was fled and I panicked. The girls were already filing down the stairs. The curious girls, wanting to know about Mam's ailment. 'Of course it's not another baby,' I heard Marguerite say.

By the time I had corked the bottle and returned it, clinking it against its companions, it was too late; the hall door scraped open. I heard voices, but only for an instant. Everybody, I decided, must have gone into the kitchen. Out the door as quick as you can, I thought, thanking God for a further reprieve, but then the voices returned.

I stood in the centre of the room, unable to decide which way to move. At the last moment – I actually saw the door handle turn – I leaped across the length of the carpet to the corner where the grand piano stood and hid behind it.

The door opened. Light shot in. I faced the wall, sure I was exposed, huddled against it, behind the piano. I was in shadow. The moment I made the decision to hide I knew it was binding. I would be in trouble if whoever was now entering the room caught me. I could not give myself away, walk out and say, 'It's only me', much as I felt compelled to. I could not move, could not look.

Voices followed the light coming from the hall. 'Did anyone see young Lally?' (Young Lally, that's me, I am Lally, second name William, third name John. Mam called me Bill when I came to live here first. 'To avoid confusion,' she said. But the name didn't catch on.) Nobody had seen young Lally. 'Well wherever he is, his wellingtons are a disgraceful puddle of muck in the middle of the kitchen.' It was Mam's voice. Then the sitting room door closed and I was in gloom again, except that this time somebody else was in the room with me.

I heard the sideboard open. Then the faint pop of the whiskey cork. A sigh then and the sound of a drink pouring. I had to look.

It was Daddy. Standing with another ale bottle in hand. Maybe it was the dimness of the light, but I had never seen Daddy look so thin, so worried before.

He had poured a measure into the little pewter cup. He lifted it to his lips – looking at him from behind like that he reminded me of the priest at Holy Communion – and quickly he swallowed it. The ale bottle was the usual half-fill of milk. He poured some whiskey into the milk, but only a few drops; he filled it with lemonade. Another sick sheep, I thought.

Suddenly Daddy was on his knees, his face cupped in his hands. 'I made a pledge to you, dear Lord,' he moaned loudly. 'Have I broken it? Do you begrudge these dribbles out of the medicine of sick beasts? Forgive me if I do it this way.'

This is the sort of thing Daddy does. Once he knelt because one of the boys would not go to school. He was giving it up, he said. 'I fall on my knees to you,' Daddy pleaded. 'Go, for the sake of our Heavenly Mother, go to school.' But he didn't go. Had it been me I certainly would have gone. For Daddy's sake.

He stiffened then in a sort of murmured prayer whose words I could not make out. I tried to understand what I had seen and heard: what was the purpose of the lemonade? Surely there was nothing medicinal about lemonade? While clarity would not enter my mind, my stomach again swirled with nausea. I felt like vomiting yet could not give myself away. My position had changed. Now I was the witness, not the thief – I had forgotten that a few moments before it had been my turn to drink the whiskey. I could not have him know I had seen him.

The mumbled prayer stopped and he looked up. 'Why do you send these crosses down upon me?' he shouted angrily. For a moment I thought he was talking to me, that he knew I was behind the piano. I didn't know what to answer. But he didn't give me time. 'Not my will dear Lord but thine.' He calmed a bit. 'From this day forward only lemonade will pass my lips. Into the milk will go only the whiskey. Please let her recover.'

Let who recover, I wondered, the sheep or Mam?

Daddy replaced the bottle and stooped from the room, clutched the medicine preparation as though he were an altar boy with the cruet.

I hardly had time to think things out – why the lemonade? why Daddy's flourish before each visit to the sitting room? – when again I heard the door handle turn.

He is returning for more, I thought. I tightened myself into the shadow of the piano.

But this time the footfall was different. Heavier. It was Mam.

I can't tell which scared me most, having to watch Daddy or Mam. Mam lifted the whiskey bottle. But she didn't drink from it. She lifted it to eye level. She did the same thing with the lemonade. Then she smiled, grimly, sort of disappointed, and shook her head from side to side. 'Give us strength,' she said. 'Give him strength.'

Oh, she was so close. Surely she had found me out. She was studying the whiskey level. She knew I had drank from it. She would walk across to the piano and find me. She had to know I was there. But then Mam too left the room.

I waited a long time. When I could hear outside again all the sounds of day, the warring crows, an argument between some of the younger children, I knew I would have to leave the room. I wondered how I would do it. How I would pass unnoticed, in my stockinged feet, to the other side? Who I would most likely be seen by?

I had a quick swig of the whiskey while I was preparing my excuses ... 'The lamb hadn't enough medicine. I'm getting her more ...' A quick swig of the whiskey and a long swig of the sherry. It was the one drink, I decided, I could drink as much of as I liked.

Nobody was levelling the detective's eye on the sherry.

And all sorts of words passed through my head. The words Daddy recites when he is in good form: 'Whiskey when you're sick ...' and so on. And other words he recites when he comes out of the sitting room: 'Hey I say, I saw a saw. A saw, I say, in Warsaw and I never saw a saw to saw quite like that saw I saw in Warsaw. Repeat that.'

That's another one we children always say wrong.

There's another one too, another conundrum: what was I doing in this big windy house, with all its strange inaccessibility? And all its high furniture staring at me and saying I don't know you.

But right then I knew who I was. And said so.

I am Lally. Who lives beneath a grand piano, who looking up can see its smooth curvy mahogany legs going up and up, and chinks in the sky of its body out of which tiny musical pings come whispering down the wind. Lally William John Jameson Winter's Tale Connell Connaughton. That's who I am. Eldest son of Lally Connell Connaughton, or whatever he calls himself. Stepson of Mam. Stepson, stony cold word that doesn't make a nice sound. I am.

And if anyone comes in here and lifts me out I am.

THE BLESSING

I T WAS A SUNDAY, SOMETIME between Easter and summer holidays, closer to summer holidays.

My father, who is called Lally too, like me, got out of the car to look at the ditch the new dredgers were digging in these fields. We all got out too, but when we started shoving one another and sliding down the steep banks Lally made us all get back in the car again.

The fields looked strange with the wide steep ditches running across them: big fields, no fences, only ditches, like fields in another country, I didn't know where.

Then Lally said that if he had the money he would get our fields at home drained like that. This is the modern age, he said. This country could be every bit as productive as Belgium or Holland. I knew then what country the fields around here reminded me of: Belgium or Holland. And I thought that the mountain I could see in the distance was exactly as a mountain in Belgium or Holland would look.

I don't know how many of us in the car were listening to Lally. The girls, I'm fairly sure, couldn't have been because they were fighting over space on the back seat. And as most of the boys were too young they wouldn't have been listening either but gazing out the window at the countryside that looked like Holland. Only my elder brother Richie and I, who were sitting in the front seat, would have been listening.

Lally continued talking whether we were all listening or not, and pointed at pools of water in a field. Look at that wet land, he said, as we drove past and a bird with big flappy wings rose from the field. The co-operative movement was the only chance for this country, he said. And he wasn't talking about communism. 'Changes will come,' he said cheerfully. 'Probably not in my lifetime. You'll see them in yours.'

Yes, Lally was fairly happy as he made these observations. Then the row got worse because the girls discovered some of the boys had muck on their shoes from the ditch and had got it all over the girls' dresses, ruining them. Lally became sad and said he didn't know why we couldn't be quieter.

We drove on then in silence and I thought again about the ditches. It surprised me they should have to be so deep considering the small trickle of water that flowed through them. And the black clay that had been brought up from the bottom and banked at the sides didn't look too good. And, could anybody tell me, were cattle going to climb down those steep banks to drink the water? I didn't want to ask Lally that because Richie would only jeer and smirk at my foolish question, especially if Lally gave me an answer that I should have known myself anyway.

We drove into a village. It was empty. The white sky dazzled down upon it. One shop was open and somebody in the back of the car said, 'Look, there's a shop', but Lally drove on. He said he had an appointment and he was late but if we waited until we were on the way back he'd stop and buy us something we could divide up among ourselves.

He did stop at the church, however. He said maybe we should go in and say one prayer. Lally threw himself down on the pew and prayed fervently. We prayed too for a minute but then we got up. The old church seemed nicer than Sunday-Mass-morning churches. The light coming through the windows softened everything, made everything warm; it showed the paper quietly peeling off the walls and paint fading off the statues so that you saw they were made of wood. We found the stairs to the gallery but Richie and the elder girls would not let us go up. Mam never allowed us in galleries of churches. The gallery, she said, was the place for people from council houses.

When we left the church Lally was thoughtful a few moments as he always was when he left a church. The big crows in the trees around the graveyard were setting up a racket that I hadn't noticed on our way in and suddenly Lally returned to the present and bustled us all into the car saying he would be dead late if we didn't hurry. We were off to Father Phil Ryan's.

I knew Father Phil Ryan's: a bungalow about a mile from the church. A place that was always open, doors and windows always flung wide and people just walking about and sitting in the armchairs that were falling asunder, both inside and outside the house. There were horses on the lawn and horses in the yards. The saddle room was the most orderly room in the house. I knew all these things because every summer I went on holidays to Father Ryan's. Great holidays these were. Along with his other boys I went on long horse-riding treks.

Men were always wandering about Father Ryan's house, making tea or polishing horse tackle. These men were usually very quiet, usually jockeys who had been told to take a rest, but sometimes they went into the village and then when they returned Father Ryan took them into a room and spoke quietly to them for hours. Once I heard one of them shout, 'Fuck off Phil with your pledge, fuck off with your blessing, do you know who you're talking to? You can't tell the best jockey in the country to stay on the dry.' Then he broke down the door. I was surprised when he was still there the next morning, quieter than ever, sitting beside the open window in the dining room, waiting for breakfast. And that evening again he was playing Bucking Broncos with us on the dining room carpet. Crouching on hands and knees on the floor, bucking and twisting his back like an unbroken horse, and whichever of us stayed on the longest before crashing onto the carpet was the winner. Sometimes travellers came to the door. The men hunted them away, but if Father Ryan was about he gave them whatever money was in his pocket. I told Lally once that I had seen him give away all his money to a tinker man that called. 'He gives away every penny,' Lally said sadly. 'His connections always bail him out.'

All of us jumped out of the car when we got to Father Ryan's so that we could run at least once through the house before Lally would be off again. We were like wild Indians. I hung back a bit from the others, not wanting to seem as excited. Richie, being too old to get excited, hung back too. A record played in the dining room but there was nobody there.

Then Father Ryan came out of his room. I had come in the nick of time, he said, because he was having trouble studding on his collar. He gave me that smile of his which always so attracted me. He had a gold tooth which shone like a flashlamp in his mouth, and he wore gold-rimmed glasses. When I told Lally once that I would like to be a priest and have a gold tooth like Father Ryan's, he laughed and said for that I would have to get a richer parish than Father Ryan had. Father Ryan hadn't got his tooth from working in this parish, he said. His tooth was a legacy of the silver spoon he had been born with.

Father Ryan had been using the wrong stud, that was why he could not stud his collar. I went into his room and rummaged around in his bedclothes where I knew I would find the right one. Then I fixed the collar round his neck, feeling privileged in front of Richie. 'I have a smashing pony for you,' he said to Richie, 'a smashing little jumper.' Father Ryan was very cute. He never let one of us think himself any more favoured than the rest. It was the same when he came around to our house and gave the blessing: everyone received the blessing. He hung the crucifix around his neck and everybody got it. The quick blessing. And after it was over he was always first to recover. While Lally kept his eyes shut and looked mournful, Father Ryan would wink at Mam and ask her was someone after biting her husband or was it the world's end or what. He liked keeping Mam and Lal married together.

Father Ryan told me to get his stole. 'Now where is that impatient old father of yours?' he said. 'We'd better go or he'll be gone without us.'

We children were piled like firewood, one on top of another, as we whizzed back through the village. The men sat in the front and Lally told Father Ryan about the big ditches he had seen. Father Ryan turned back to us. All I could see through the pile of bodies was the twinkle of his gold tooth. 'Not too wide a ditch, at the same time, for your father not to leap across on a good horse.' He was always reminding us of how good a horseman Lally was. They were horse-crazy, both of them. He loved to tell us stories about Lally and we loved to hear them: 'Haha, your father. When your father was only a tot he drank down a bottle of sherry. Oh lally stuff, he called it. Bet ye didn't know that's why he's called Lally? He told us that one day, and we all laughed. Lally, never a great smiler, smiled when Father Ryan spoke about him like that.

As we passed the church Father Ryan said it was a pity some of the money for ditch digging couldn't be spent on decorating the church. Lally said he should run whist drives and get the people interested and working together if he wanted the church done up. Father Ryan laughed: 'A progressive man, your father!' I knew he wasn't that worried about the state of his church. In a quieter voice he told Lally something about the farm on which the wide drains had been dug. 'It's having a contributory effect on the man we are going to see,' he said.

The house we drove up to was big and old. Ivy covered its walls and the white sky reflected from its windows, making it seem empty inside. I knew it was George Corcoran's house because I had been overhearing a lot of talk between Mam and Lally about George Corcoran. Mam said he was reckless and Lal said he was unfortunate in his weakness. I thought I knew what he looked like: a tall thin man with a brown coat and wide-brimmed hat who sometimes appeared at gymkhanas in the same part of the field as a woman who ran with buckets and currycombs amid ponies and children. She was as thin as he. She was Mrs Clodagh Corcoran, I was sure of that, but I wasn't sure if the man with the long coat was her husband, because he only hung about the horsebox and didn't help.

Father Ryan did not knock on the front door, and as we went round the side of the house he joked to us about the young Corcorans we were going to meet who he said would knock the stuffing out of the young Connell-Connaughtons.

We went through a cement yard at the back of the house. Dogs rose stiffly from every side; the yard was cluttered with the smell of sour milk and rust-rimmed milk churns. Father Ryan opened a door and led us into a wide room which seemed not to belong to the house but to have been built onto it.

What surprised me was how little furniture was in it. We found it so crowded with children that we had to remain at the door. But Father Ryan called us in. 'The Connell-Connaughtons are afraid of the Corcorans,' he said.

The Corcorans, boys and girls, were eating bread. At the sight of the wide cuts of bread I was suddenly starved. Some of the girls were big and I decided it must have been they who had sliced it since there was no sign of a woman. I envied how they could cut bread for themselves and did not have to wait for adults to cut it before being allowed to eat as was the way in our house. They looked eagerly at us, I think they had been told we were coming, and within moments the girls had taken our girls away somewhere and the boys took Richie and me and my younger brothers out to the orchard.

'Don't go far,' Lally said. 'I won't delay long.' Father Ryan had his stole and crucifix out.

I think Lally must have delayed. We were shown all round the farm by the Corcorans. It was one of those places with lovely wooden railings dividing the fields, but many of the railings were broken so that cattle strayed from one field to another. The Corcorans showed us the part of the farm they had sold. I was surprised to see the same fields with the wide ditches in them we had earlier seen from the road. I looked about and sure enough there in the distance was the mountain I had seen earlier. The sun had found a way to it through the cloud so that it was now in light. This time, the countryside no longer reminded me of Holland.

When I said this to the eldest of the boys – he was my age – he told me that his father was going to live in England. He said he was going to work there because he was selling the rest of his farm to the man who dug up the wide ditches. He said he had been staying with Father Ryan but that he had had enough of staying there because it was like prison and now he was going to England where he would become a bloodstock agent. This boy's name was Toppy. Toppy couldn't stay still. He would tell us something and run away, then run back to us and tell us something more, laughing all the time. 'Fff-fuckin' Jesus.' He sucked his breath in nervously and pointed at rocks piled by the far-off drain. 'You should have heard the explosion of dynamite when they blew up the rocks.'

He wanted us to walk across the field to where the big dredger stood. I looked at Richie, thinking he would be against the idea, but I should have known better: Richie loved anything to do with machinery and so we set off across the field. I told the others to fan out and to pretend we were a cavalry charge. The Corcorans were delighted with this; I think they had never played games before. The grass was white and spiky because silage had just been cut from it, and for a moment, with the yellow light and the flat sky, we could imagine ourselves riding across the prairies.

We were in sight of the ditch when suddenly, from the side of the field nearest the house, we saw a man running. I had been right in thinking the tall man I had noticed at gymkhanas was George Corcoran because here was the same man, and he was running straight at the ditch. All of us pulled up in a group and watched in amazement as the man sprinted over the ground and made no attempt to slow up. Then he jumped. His legs came apart and I saw a flash of sky between them. I thought for one second he was going to land on the far side but then he disappeared. The younger Corcorans took fright when they saw their father disappear. They ran back towards the house. Richie and I turned to Toppy. He seemed puzzled for a moment but then the brightness I had earlier liked about him returned and lit up his face. 'Did you see Daddy?' he said. 'He leaped like a racehorse.' A moment later he was crying and running towards the place into which his father had jumped. Richie and I followed.

By the time we reached the bank George Corcoran was standing upright in the muddy bottom. He must have fallen lengthways into the stream because one side of his brown coat was now, from collar to hem, an even darker brown. He held his hat in his hand and looked dazed. With a white handkerchief he wiped a spatter of mud from his forehead. Then he saw us. He looked at us a moment as if surprised by the silence between us. Then he made shapes with his mouth and we could almost see something moving up, making the long journey through his body before it reached us and became words: 'Look at me.' He raised his arms with the mud dripping off them; they were like wings. 'Useless blasted river, there was a time a decent man could drown himself in this river. There might have been weed in it but there was good deep river flow. Now look at me, my shoes are destroyed.' We couldn't see his shoes; they were covered in the river.

He pointed up the bank at the broken-necked dredger. 'Thirsty bugger,' he said. 'Pretending to lie idle today. But waiting, waiting, to dig up my whole farm.' He tried to walk but the mud must have sucked at his feet, for he lost his balance and sat back in the stream. He didn't try to get up again, but rubbed his chin. Suddenly he shouted up: 'But he's giving me good money, I'll sell every field I have to him if I want to. Nobody tells me my business.'

Toppy was sobbing. 'You're getting wet, Daddy. Mammy says you're to come home.' I felt very sorry for Toppy.

'Leave me in peace,' his father said. 'A man can't even drown himself. But I'm not beaten yet, I'll drown myself on Slievenamon.'

He pointed towards the distant mountain that looked so sunny. I didn't know how he could drown himself up there.

We walked back to the house with Toppy, none of us saying a word.

Father Ryan and Lally said nothing either as we drove back to the village. They stopped outside the closed door of a pub. Lally said he wouldn't be a minute and they both went in. A while later Father Ryan came out on his own with the brown parcel. 'Your father said you are to divide these,' he said. He had brought us bars of chocolate and we were surprised. The words he used had been Lally's all right but it was he who had bought the chocolate. Looking suddenly concerned, he placed his hand on the shoulder of one of my brothers. Then, as he was about to go back to the pub, he turned to us and gave us his big smile. 'Your father and I are cleaning muck off a man's coat in here,' he said. 'Did you like the Corcorans? They'd knock the socks off you!'

My eldest sister divided the chocolate, and Richie for once did not puck her but accepted his share. I never had less appetite for chocolate. I slid out of the car while the others ate theirs. The noise of the slurping and sucking was making my mouth dry and sticky and I thirsted for fresh air.

I don't know how it happened but I found myself in the church. There wasn't any other place in the village to go to, I suppose. It was evening and very quiet, the sun had come out just as it was about to sink below the edge of the land. It could not reach into the body of the church but lit up the gallery and filled me with an urge to climb into it.

Some presence in the church was watching every movement I made. It followed me in the dark up the stairs. But when I got to the top and crept out beneath the high windows and saw all around me the light and the dust and how it stood in the air I forgot about the presence, distracted instead by the light.

Down in the body of the church everything was dark brown. I tried to make out where it was my family knelt when we turned up for Mass at this church, which sometimes we did when it was too late to go to our own. Then I tried to remember where it was George Corcoran knelt with his family. I took out some chocolate. It stuck to the roof of my mouth. I tried to free my mouth of the clinging chocolate and wondered why we all had to kneel down there in the dark floor of the church.

I fancied the idea of the gallery. My new friend Toppy and I in the gallery. I wondered would I see him again. I probably would, in a few weeks' time, during holidays at Father Ryan's. Once his father had stayed there Toppy would probably go there on holidays. That was the way it worked.

I stood, looking down at the bare altar, hearing the flicker of the sanctuary lamp, and a picture of Father Ryan came to my mind: Father Ryan rushing out from the sacristy to say Mass. It made me laugh. I could almost see the trailing robes and the undone vestments, and the altar boy straightening them as he tried to keep up behind. I thought about what Lally said: 'He's better than a darn lot of priests, even if during Mass you can see the riding jodhpurs beneath his soutane.'

I thought about that. The jodhpurs and the smell of horses. But then another image came to me: it was last summer, the day at the end of my summer holidays at Father Ryan's. Lally had come to collect me: he stood beside the car on the dusty road – the weather had been good. One of Father Ryan's men stood nearby, grooming dried mud off a mare and smoking a cigarette. I stamped my feet in the dust and looked at the prints my sandals made. Then Father Ryan ran in for his crucifix and ran back out to bless us. First he blessed me. That presence had got into him – the church presence – that got into him whenever he gave the blessing. That turned him into someone

SALUTE THE CHAMP

COYLE SAID WE HAD TO WRITE an essay about the circus or else we would be in trouble. We had been listening for the sound of the lorries on the street. When they passed, the windowpanes jumped and if Coyle had had any brains he would have let us out on the road to watch. It would have been a good start to the essay; it might go like this:

The Circus: A motley cavalcade drove through the street this morning. Romany faces peered from caravan half-doors. They laughed and signalled, they blew balloons and whistles. 'The circus,' to the young and gay they called. But the young were all in school. The town peered back. The circus closed its eyes against the meanness, pretending to keep them open and to laugh.

That's what I felt like writing. But then Coyle would say I had strayed completely off the tracks and Colm Holland would be told to stand up and read his. Colm's essay would have strayed completely off the tracks too but it would be perfect. Besides, Coyle had arithmetic to do right at that minute and so we had to keep our heads down and try to concentrate. You never knew who he was liable to pounce on. He stalked between the desks. Whether or not there was a circus outside didn't matter: 'I'll see you crowd get jobs when you get out of here, even if I have to beat knowledge into you.'

I must say Coyle did have a feeling of something in him where the circus was concerned though. Go down and watch them put up the big top, he said as he let us out from school. And excitement puffed up his cheeks. But only for a second, before they collapsed again in threat. 'And don't hand up mere copies tomorrow of the essay in the *Forty Specimen Essays* book.'

I couldn't watch the big top go up because I had to go home and do my farm jobs. Then the carload of us headed back to town; we picked up an old neighbour on the way who said thanks a hundred times and said she never missed the circus. Mam asked her if she had enough room in the car and she said she had plenty, if she had half as much room in heaven she'd be happy. I knew Mam didn't like her, a nosey-bag she calls her, yet she offered her a lift home after the circus was over. And I wondered did the woman feel as bad as I at the reminder that it would end and all of us would return home again.

When we got there the little triangular field in which Joe Shelly keeps his donkey was no longer recognisable. The smell of sawdust went up my nose and the air between the caravans was powdery and even darker than the air of oncoming night. A generator shook so much from side to side it could hardly stay on its wheels. A fan belt running from a drive on the side of a tractor slapped through a hole in the tent.

Colm Holland and the town boys ran up to us and told us we could see the six-legged calf without paying if we wanted to. They lifted the rim of a brown canvas screen but two things stopped us from looking. One, Mam was with us and would not leave us on our own until we were safely within the tent, when she would be able to go down the town to her sister's house, my aunt the creamery manager's wife, and there they would talk and smoke cigarettes and eat salted monkey nuts and try out new lipstick shades at the mirror, and necklaces. The other reason was the man with the big head and shoulders who ran shouting after the town boys. Although I can't really say he ran. He rolled. And then, when he had stopped shouting, he did a somersault to let us know he wasn't really cross. He even stood on his head and made faces until the boys laughed. I think he was cross though.

When we got our tickets I ran to where the town boys sat but a man stopped me. This man was looking at tickets and telling people where to go. 'You no want to sit on the bench,' he said, 'when you pay for the best seats.' It was the same man who had done the somersault a few minutes earlier but now he was dressed in a maroon coat and had waxy stuff on his face. I had to follow my brothers and sisters, and when I looked again at the boys they were on the far side of the big top, high up. Just a row of faces in the crowd they were, but they were together.

Everybody from the village must have been at the circus because all the seats were filled. I was surprised at how many people turned up, people you would never have expected would go to a place to laugh or to enjoy anything. They were all around where we sat, those kinds of people, their stern watching faces like dark trees around the excited breathy laughter I could hear pour out of my little brothers beside me. And I knew I sounded the same as my brothers. Here we are surrounded by these people lighting their pipes or eating sweets out of paper bags. People like Eric Scott the newsagent, for example, who says very doleful things to shoppers when they buy the papers on Sundays. And the librarian Miss Pearl Tutty who insists on silence not just in the library but everywhere she goes. The ones who make the village the dreary place it is.

On the far side my friends were all laughing. I would like

to have been among them but Mam does not allow us to mix.

The band started up in a little balcony, curtains opened beneath it and out galloped the horses. The Arabian troupe, the ringmaster called out over the sound of music, and cracked his whip until all the horses stood in a circle. Then the music speeded up. He cracked his whip again, the horses peeled about, their manes streaming behind.

That was the moment when the daylight of the village, and everything within it, slipped away. In the big top there lived the whole world. Running into this world, running and somer-saulting at great speed, came the little man who had chased the boys away from the six-legged calf. Without slowing down he sprang and instead of landing out among us as we expected he landed on the back of one of the galloping horses. He raised his arms and the ringmaster called for a big hand for Lev the Cossack Cavalryman. He wore a black furry cap, a tunic and a sort of dress and every time the ringmaster cracked his whip he jumped from the back of one horse to another. The ring-master asked for a volunteer. A boy from the audience to assist Lev the Cossack. I knew the moment he said it the boy would be me. Something jumped up inside my head and I had to force it down. It was giving me pain. Everybody in the school knew the boy would be me. Everybody in the school knows I am supposed to be good at horses. The Horse Protestants, Coyle calls my brothers and I. Whether in mockery or in praise I can never tell but I think Coyle does not like us. (Coyle conducts this competition at the end of term: Best Patch in the Trousers Competition, he calls it. It may be my imagina-tion but he seems to take pleasure in shaming my brothers and I with the knowledge that we can never win it.)

Anyway, I knew the boys on the bench opposite would

be shouting for me and they did. I'm glad Mam was not there. 'Ask Connaughton,' they shouted. 'Go for it young Connaughton, boy,' they shouted, and I had to stand up.

If you ever don't want to do something at a circus don't stand up. Don't even half stand up. Like I did. Because as soon as you stand everything happens to you, suddenly and outside of your control. A light dazzled into my eyes. Hands hauled me into the ring. Not the hands of the Cossack; he was still bouncing up and down on his horse, his arms outstretched in my direction. A rope was tightened round my waist. The ringmaster said, 'Don't worry.' Then the clown said, 'Hi hup.' The first minute I was swinging above the crowd – I just had time to see white faces circling below me – the next I was standing on a horse's back and the Cossack had his arms round my waist, steadying me. I couldn't look round but I figured he and I were on the same horse and I didn't know how it had all been managed. 'It's OK, sonny,' he was saying to me in a strange accent. 'Make the feet straight please.' I did as he commanded. So mesmerised I was I would have done anything he commanded. The rope loosened round my waist and I felt the horse beneath me. Even though my feet were like jelly. 'It's good,' he said and jumped off and left me on my own, circling the ring without time to think of anything except to stay on the back that was running away beneath me. Then the horse did run from under me. I fell backward, expecting to hit the ground but instead the rope grabbed around my waist and pulled me forward like a puppet, in position again.

When I realised that I wasn't going to fall, that I was safe in the hold of the rope, I began to grow in confidence. My feet steadied and I felt myself respond to the movement of the horse's broad back. Just as I knew I no longer needed the rope, and I looked around me to find where the boys sat so that I could wave, something happened. I was no longer on the horse's back. I wasn't on the ground either. I was swinging high in the air again.

They had pulled the rope on me. I was disappointed because I knew I had mastered the art of standing on a horse's back. And now here was everybody laughing at me. Here was I swaying helplessly above them.

Then the rope seemed to let go of me and I fell from my heights. I was falling on faces and arms that stretched up towards me. Something thumped me in the side of the head, I didn't know what: the Cossack's knee maybe as I cracked down on him, or something hard like a bottle in the pocket of the clown. I was stretched on the ground, and looking up I saw the opening of the big top and outside a pool of dark that I seemed to be swimming towards. 'You be OK, sonny?' I heard a voice. It was drifting away from me. The next thing I remember I was toppling back to my seat, quickly as I could over the low wall of the ring, spitting out sawdust, somebody behind me still saying, 'You be OK, sonny?'

I couldn't tell whether or not I was OK, and the centre of the ring was not the place to find out. But I felt let down; not just let down by the rope, let down. There I had been: part of the speeding merry-go-round. Only to have been hurtled from it. I think the shock of being so suddenly flung out was greater than that of being hurtled in.

'Give him a big hand,' I heard the ringmaster say. 'Now on with the show.' And the show went on: Irene's Performing Poodles performed, the clowns kicked one another up the backsides, the Turkish Jugglers came and went. But I was not noticing. I was back at the first act. Balancing. Legs straight as poles, arms out. Applause from the crowd holding my body steady even while my mind wobbled on the brink of failure. The first act played and replayed in my head, like the circular procession of the horses.

Then the ringmaster announced a challenge: 'Meet the Weather-weight Champion of the World,' he said. 'Meet a man for all weathers. A boxing cyclone who has thrown down his challenge in every snowy town and every sunny town of Scotland, England and of Ireland. He has never been stopped. Is there anybody in this town to stop the Weather-weight Champ?'

And like everybody else in the audience, I died to know what next was about to happen.

'Stand up the local prizefighter,' the ringmaster called and held a pair of boxing gloves above his head. 'Surely there is somebody.' But nobody stood up. Nobody else was about to do what I had done and be picked out by the spotlight as I had.

'A quick five-pound note for whoever defeats the Champ.' The ringmaster snapped a note between his fingers.

Then the cries started. 'Ruction Dunne. Stand up Ruction Dunne.'

I knew Ruction Dunne. I suppose you could call him a prizefighter. He was born with only one arm, his other arm but a stump. He had as much strength in the stump, everybody said, as any other man would have in an uppercut. There were reports about Ruction. He was dangerous. Once, in a pub, he so badly injured a man that he was up in court. The judge let him off on grounds of compassion. Every afternoon after school we saw Ruction Dunne. We passed him as we walked around Miner's Corner to where Mam waited for us in the car. He stood among the line of idle men that Mam said she did not wish to be stared at by. They stood there every day even though the coal mine was long closed and the dust-covered bus no longer came to pick them up for the night shift. Ruction seemed always to be dazzled by the sun, and his tongue, like the soapy underpart of a snail, always hung out of his mouth. We were under orders, always, to pass him by and not to look; not to look at him, or at any of the street-corner boys. Right now, Ruction was not standing up.

Then the Champ appeared. In his red boxing gown he look-ed great. I had never seen boxing gloves before and I was sur-prised at how big they were. As big as heads. The Champ punched and pawed the air and the ringmaster said, 'Whoa, big boy,' and ran away from him, pretending to be afraid. The Champ looked so strong you didn't notice how small he was. Until someone shouted, 'He's only a midget.' And after that no matter how much he punched the air it didn't matter. Because some expression had come across his face. Bedlam took over from the hush when he had first come out: 'He's only a midget. You'll dust him, Ruction.' The Champ no longer looked impressive.

Ruction rose. The hush returned again. Everybody fears Ruction. 'Oh Jaysus,' somebody said, 'where's the ambulance?' The ringmaster took a quick look at the stump of Ruction's right arm – the arm that was supposed to pack the knockout punch – and said, 'A southpaw, I see, the local champ are we?'

At that moment Ruction looked anything but the local champ. He was dazed, either by the lights or by the shouts from his friends in the audience. At the same time, however, in some sort of dull and dangerous way, he responded to their shouts and you felt a little sick at the thought of what might happen.

Ruction would not take the single glove offered him by the ringmaster. The Weather-weight Champ took off his cloak and sweat was running down his skin. 'Queensberry Rules,' the ringmaster said, 'first man down for a count of ten is out.' A clown sounded a gong. The Champ wore a red bandage round one knee. He skipped across the ring. Ruction stood, looking baffled. As the Champ sprang on his feet, the red bandage kept jabbing into my mind. I couldn't work out why, but then I remembered: I remembered the horses' hooves, circling about me, kicking up sawdust. I remembered looking up, seeing someone's bare legs, seeing a red bandage around one knee. And an anxious voice: 'You be OK, sonny?' – the Cossack's. And then my mind had sailed away somewhere, on air that smelled of wintergreen, and words sailing through it: '. . . not fuckin' funny . . . the ringmaster he let go the rope . . .' '. . . he let go the rope last night too . . .' Two people talking.

I decided I must have been knocked out. For a few seconds, lost my memory. And that nobody knew it, except maybe for the Cossack.

Queensberry Rules was something Ruction knew nothing about. Everybody could see that but nobody seemed to mind. 'Go on, Ruction' – they were delighted when Ruction got the Champ's head in an arm hold. He turned round to his friends and when they shouted again he tried to twist the Champ in two. The Champ's hands were bound inside his gloves and he could do nothing to release himself except beat his fists against Ruction's side. That didn't help because Ruction wore so many clothes he would have felt nothing. The only effect was to make him beat down on the Champ's head with his stump arm while he tightened his grip on it with the other. Nobody could see the Champ's head. The Champ's legs began to sag like those of a tired animal. And then, because his head was pressed into Ruction and it couldn't be seen, people began to get worried. 'He's a goner,' they said. 'Give him air.' A man in a seat just behind me jumped up. It was Eric Scott, the newsagent. 'This is no boxing match,' he said, 'stop it.' Other men jumped up too but just then the Champ managed to swing his fist up and smack it into Ruction's mouth. The next second he was free, and blood was pumping from Ruction's mouth.

Now the Champ darted in and hit Ruction and darted away before Ruction could grab hold of him again. He did it a few times and it looked like real boxing and the crowd shouted, delighted. But Ruction didn't like it. He made one furious charge on the Champ. He caught him up, ran across the ring with him and thumped him against the centre pole. The pole shook, some ropes that had been tied to it dangled loose and the Champ dropped to the ground. I couldn't see what happened next because all around me people were up on their feet and shouting. I caught a glimpse of Ruction kicking the Champ. The ringmaster and one of the clowns ran in and got between the contestants. Ruction tried to get at the Champ again but when the ringmaster caught his arm and lifted it, shouting, 'The new Weather-weight Champ', he calmed down. People sat down again and, wiping blood from his mouth, Ruction returned to his friends who laughed and clapped him on the back. 'Your fiver, Ruction,' they shouted when they realised he had not received his prize money. 'The final act, ladies and gentlemen,' the ringmaster shouted above them. 'Be seated please.' They shouted a few minutes more, but the ringmaster said there could be no prize money for a brawl. They stood on the bench and then got off it and threw it into the ring. The ringmaster waited in the centre of the ring, surprisingly patient, as if there was nothing unusual happening, and did nothing. I thought they were not going to allow the circus to continue, but in the end the trapeze artists came out and they stopped.

The trapeze ladies were beautiful. They had long legs and wore the tightest of bathing togs and gold dust shone off their skin. It was the sight of them, I think, that stopped the shouting. And yet the men did not begin to wolf-whistle as you would expect. The ladies kicked and stretched hands above heads and gave little shouts and did other circus things. The men were gone dumb. They were looking at the ladies as if they were tropical birds or jungle animals or something. And not ladies. Or else they were overcome by them. As I was. The Champ was forgotten.

Some people were afraid to look at the trapeze artists. A man with black hair dangled high up in the big top. He dangled by his legs from a swing and caught in turn each of the women as they dived at him from different swings. There was the split second when they dived, before he caught them, when the 'oh' went up from the crowd and everybody looked away.

But people got used to the split-second movement because everybody was looking when the accident happened. One of the women, the youngest and most daring, instead of clasping the man's hand as she dived, she kept going. I think she was supposed to catch a trapeze swing that should have been pushed out for her. That was the idea. But the swing wasn't there. I think it got dislodged the time Ruction belted the Cossack against the pole. Then she was no longer diving but falling. The audience rose. She must have caught a rope as she fell because her fall was checked. But only for a second. Just in time for a man to run out beneath her. I saw the flashing red bandage, his upturned arms, the rope she held come loose, her fall, and then the two of them flat on the ground. That was the end of the performance. The ringmaster thanked us for coming and wished us a safe journey home.

Everybody left, wondering would the man be all right and would the woman ever perform again. One person said that if she stood again it wouldn't matter because her nerves would be shot for all time. Somebody else said they would be OK. Acrobats had their backbones extracted when they were born so that they could bend backwards. There would be no damage...

Colm Holland and the town boys ran round as we left. I didn't know what they might say about my horse riding. They said nothing about it, just said Ruction was done out of the fiver and said I should go with them and see the six-legged calf. He was a monster, they said, four legs on the ground, two sticking out of his hole, stiff as snails' horns.

I stood with them in the line that formed outside the cabin where the six-legged calf was kept, hoping something would happen so that I didn't have to go in. I didn't want to see whatever two-headed thing was in there; a foul smell was coming from the cabin.

At the door, selling tickets, stood a man in a maroon coat. It was his voice I recognised: 'Not to miss. Nowhere in the world you see such a calf.' It was the same coat he had worn when showing us to our seats at the beginning of the show. The same man, nobody else seemed to recognise him – the Cossack who had caught the girl beneath the high trapeze. It amazed me he could stand. I thought he was bent a little, I thought his face dark with shadows. But maybe that was the poor light.

Then I got to the door and looked in and what I saw sent new thoughts about the man shooting through my brain. The man who could be the owner of such a terrible sight, who could show to people such naked injury. I backed away, hearing people say things in hushed tones. 'It's a sort of two Siamese twins stuck in one.' 'It's a shocking cruelty to animals,' I heard Miss Pearl Tutty say.

When my sisters came running for me I was glad, for once, to be told my mother was ready to go home. I was able to get away. Mam packed the old neighbour into the car amongst us and asked her if she had enjoyed the circus. 'Grand,' she said. She began to talk of the six-legged calf. She knew all about it. It was a cow really. She had seen it before. A young girl in the middle of labour that the Lord's design had struck in the same way it had struck this cow. She wondered how this cow was kept alive. 'God bless the mark.'

Mam was furious when she dropped her off. 'How she could look at such a thing,' she said. 'And talk about it like that. Dirty old nosey-bag. Old Holy Joe. I hope none of you saw it.' She looked back in the darkness at me. The smell of the cabin rushed at me and I just managed to hold in the sickness that squirted up through me.

My essay about the circus. I was pleased with it. It was the story of a circus man. He performed many acts, assumed many guises, but none which involved ownership of a six-legged calf. 'When the young Russian boy Lev visited the circus he had been smitten. In a spirit of adventure he ran away from the dull town in the Steppes where he had grown up. He was but eleven years old.' The story went on like that . . . describing the exciting life he lived, the sights he saw on his travels, his delight the first time he stood bareback on a galloping horse. The great friends he made. The story was not about the performance we had seen. But I knew it was good. Coyle liked imagination – 'use your meagre imaginations,' he always says – and this was the first essay in which I had used mine. I knew he would not say that it was completely off the tracks.

When he came into the classroom, gripping the corrected essays beneath his arm, I even thought I stood a good chance of a prize.

He laid the copybooks on the table. He puffed his cheeks as he always does, his warm-up exercise: the same when he is either about to erupt in anger or to single out someone for praise. This time, I thought, it was praise that filled his cheeks.

A look of mystery came over him. 'Salute the Champ,' he said. His voice cracked with something that sounded like either happiness or madness. We looked at one another. We looked up at the sky outside the high window. We didn't know what he was talking about. Nobody ever knew what to expect from Coyle. It could be a prize, it could be a puck. 'Stand up the author of a prize-winning essay entitled "Salute the Champ",' he said.

I was right. It was praise filled his cheeks. But it was not for me. Colm Holland stood up. Colm, who never has to make an effort, but spends all his time instead making jokes about the master. Laughing, always laughing at him, even when he is being praised, but never letting himself be caught at it. Or else quietly reading books beneath his desk. As he read his essay I could only marvel at how brilliant it was. Like me he had recognised the circus man in all of his different guises.

Colm's essay was brilliant, but there was also something else. 'Salute the Champ,' it ended. 'Salute the man who must place his life at risk in every dangerous little, shoddy little, town. Who is shackled by the hideous beast he must haul with him, shell on a snail's back, wherever he goes. And for what end? For small-town applause? Yes, for bruises and for insults and for small-town applause. And because he must keep heart and soul and body together, and curtains on his caravan.'

Oh God, with every word of Colm Holland's essay my embarrassment increased. How could I not have seen it like he did? So exactly how it was. So obvious and so real. Why was it I could never see things for real? Coyle held up Colm's arm. 'Salute the Champ,' he said.

And I knew it would be only a matter of a few minutes.

Once he had released Colm's arm, and the proud quivering in his cheeks had stopped ... then he would turn to me. 'Completely off the tracks,' he would say.

ALL ETERNITY

THIS MORNING MAM SAYS WE shouldn't go. The snow is too bad. We'll never get there. We can listen to it on the wireless. Lally asks her what is she suggesting: 'What, and have Holy Communion flown in on a helicopter to us?'

And so we set out. Lally, Mam and Mam's eldest, Richie, in the front of the car. All of us other children, Mam's by her first marriage, Lally's by his first marriage, the children of their joint marriage, in the back. Shovels and sand in the boot. It is early light.

There is not a car track on the road when we come out on our lane. Not a mark in the snow.

'You're a madman to attempt it,' Mam says, but Lally drives on, keeping to what he judges to be the road's centre.

We children look out the back windscreen in wonder at what we are doing: at the single car tracks across the surface of a vast unknown. 'Daddy look back,' one of the girls says. 'Oh never look back,' he laughs. 'Always look ahead in this life.' He is pleased we have set off, he is trying to make Mam smile, so she will be pleased about it too. 'Don't distract your father while he's driving,' Mam says crossly.

Twice, on Copper Hill and on the hill by the parish priest's house, the car skids and will not carry on. We children jump out, Mam doesn't, Lally lets the car run back a little. We dig out the snowdrift. Lally says push. And on we go again, clambering, one on top of the other, into the back seat.

The church sits on top of a hill. We see its yellow walls but not its roof. The roof is the same colour as the sky. The village too is rubbed out and there are fewer cars than normal converging on it.

There are tractors. Some have come to Mass on tractors this morning, hunched and frozen. 'That's how we should have come,' Lally says.

'Wouldn't I look a picture coming to Mass on a tractor,' Mam says.

Lally does not see the joke. 'It's practical,' he says. 'The Son of God went on a donkey.'

'I fear Hill Street is too slippery.' He parks up a laneway at the bottom of the village and says we can walk up a short cut to Mass.

'I'm not walking,' Mam says, so we drive up the street and again we skid and have to get out. This time fellows who are walking up the street tell us to get in again. They'll push, they say. They nearly lift the car off the road and then they bang on the roof when it gets going. We look back at them skidding and laughing, some of them lying on the snow. We find it strange. They are the coal miners. The miners never laugh; the miners have no confidence above ground.

The congregation is sparser this morning and so the church is more draughty. And the coughing almost an epidemic.

'Listen to the flock of old crows' – the parish priest turns round to us once. 'The Gathreen swine. Would ye not be such molly-coddles? Would ye not one hour at least bear witness with me? Ye sorry lot.' Everybody feels bad then. I feel personally mortified, but after a few minutes the coughing starts up again.

Then he reads out the parish collection: 'Patrick Webster, Lisnamrock, two-and-six. Richard Ivors, Lisnamrock, two-and-six. Thomas Considine, Lisnamrock, two-and-six.' I am listening for Lally's name: 'L.W. Connaughton, Barnane, five pounds.' There are lots more two-and-sixpences: 'Gerard Connors, The Commons, two-and-six. Anthony Shaw, Colliery Road, two-and-six.' The two-and-sixpences are the miners, Yorkshire names, immigrants of the distant past, of a time dimly remembered except within the hills. Some of them contribute five shillings. The pounds and five pounds are the farmers and town merchants.

I find it interesting. It stops the throat-clearing competition.

Another diversion this morning is the presence of the coffins. There are three, end to end, alongside the altar rails. I have never before seen more than one.

The Mass carries slowly on; then Jamesy, my brother Jamesy who is one of the altar boys, he allows the Host to drop to the floor while the priest is distributing Communion.

Candles have to be lit; incense is stoked up. With a tiny brush the priest sweeps all the dust off the carpet into a chalice and he drowns the lot with holy water. Altar boys are tripping over one another, the priest in a state.

At this stage, Communion time, I am primed. Ready to make my dart. It is a skill. To get first out the door but not to make my move until the priest has given the blessing and turned his back.

There are some miners who have left the pews before he has turned back to the altar, who don't care about him. I have to get ahead of them, but today they beat me to the door.

Sunday morning. An anxious time. Mass is anxious. Lally and Mam are both anxious. So much rushing. The papers to be got, the shopping. Such fuss to get home quickly to the

Sunday jobs. Such speed. Quick dart to the holy water fount. Sidestep a few bodies ...

I suppose the lengthened stay in church is responsible. Imagine forgetting that on the other side of the doors, all across the countryside, there lies this continuous carpet of snow. Over hill after hill.

My fingers skid across the frozen holy water fount. I am dazzled. A little flurry of snow has just tailed off over where the yew trees and the cemetery should be. Then the Mass leavers are pushing out behind me, sweeping me, like a stone on a landslide at the colliery pit, down the steps towards the street. There is the sun, the sun just arising out of the white hills. But I cannot delay, I must not let the crowd get ahead of me to the shops.

I pass a newly dug grave at the edge of the cemetery. All alone, brown gash in the snow. No other graves are visible, no headstones, all snow-covered; I think it might easily be in a field.

The gravediggers stand; they have cleared away a space of grass, a platform for the mourners to stand on and look down from.

I pass two women. They link arms and one holds the rails that run the length of the steps down from the church. She moves carefully in the snow, stooping, sort of like a rat. A tall man with a long, dripping nose walks behind them. His hands are held before them, as if to catch them in case they should fall.

'Missis Butler' – the woman holding the rails nods towards the open grave.

'Which Missis Butler is it Mary?' the man asks.

'Renée, Billy's wife, Billy Butler's wife.'

The man looks at the grave. 'Is it Billy's wife. I heard she wasn't well, but I didn't know ... God I'm sorry. She was only a young woman. Was it, was it you know what?' (I realise at this stage that I am delaying, but conversations always slow me down.)

'Oh you know what, you said it,' the old woman called Mary says. 'And she has to go in today, snow or no snow.' She stops walking. For what she has to say next she has to look up at the man. 'For she's lying in the church since it started falling. Three days she is.'

The man sniffs as if smelling something putrid. They both nod. I speed on then, keeping to the untrodden snow at the outside of the rails. 'May she rest in peace,' I hear the other woman say. I am glad to get away from their voices that seem to know so much.

I am not first into George Bishop's, the newsagents. The conversation on the steps has delayed me. Two women, of about nineteen or twenty, stand before me at the counter. They wear high heels, very short coats, and they hold the coats tightly about them, both shivering and clattering from one shoe to the other in their attempts to warm.

Then some men come in. This means further delay because George Bishop serves only grown-ups. And his daughters, behind the counter with him, serve only when loudly spoken to. They are impossible to speak to: they give you the impression, if ever you do speak, that you should be about to marry them.

'Bloomin' freezing,' one of the chattering women says with a twang in her voice. 'Bloomin' fridge that church. They still haven't heard of such things as heaters in the churches this side of the Pool.' They buy cigarettes.

'Cold weather to be on holidays,' George Bishop says. As people walk in behind me I hear the greetings, low, as if intended not to disturb the weather further: 'Fierce fall of snow, how are you keeping?' George Bishop turns to other customers. 'Will it ever stop? We're cut off entirely. Will we ever get

back to normal tell me? And get about a day's work again?'
He piles papers on the counter for a customer, 'Express, News
of the World, Weekend, is that it?' and pulls in money, telling
his daughters to serve others.

'Was it the God above dropped you down the papers, then,
George?' a man says and there are some titters. I think it is
a risky thing to say, as George Bishop does not go to our church
up on the hill but to the little Protestant church in the hollow.

'Anyone take us dancing tonight?' One of the women, still
at the counter, is laughing when I leave. 'Is there anywhere
there's no snow?'

I hurry past the local boys back to the car. They scrutinise me.
I am different ... The derision with which they stare. I wish,
as I do every Sunday, I could be just like them. Fling off my
good clothes and stand as they do, tight-eyed and close-fisted.
But even that would not be enough. Even then they would
want to fight. They come from the coal mine cottages. All
the times we are told about the broken bottles and knife fights
in the pubs.

Mam is seated in the car and so I hand her the papers. There
is no sign of Lally but after a while I see him. 'The funeral
will take place after second Mass today of Missis Renée Butler
née Ryan, Mardyke, may she rest in peace.' It has been announced during Mass. Missis Butler's funeral today, the two
others after Mass tomorrow. 'Have to be buried,' the priest
said, 'snow on the ground or not.' Lally is standing, head
lowered, at the graveside. On his own. He returns.

Driving down the street then ... A tricky business any Sunday, but this morning, what with fresh drifts of snow, and Lally
such an impatient driver ...

I don't know why we drive to this out-of-the-way place for
Mass. When our nearest town is only two miles from where
we live. 'Fashion, God help them,' Mam says of the women

of our nearest town. 'Mutton dressed up as lamb.' There is little fashion up here in this exposed place. Those girls in high heels, home from England, I saw in Bishop's. That's it. Maybe she and Lally fit in better up here. 'With honest-to-God people,' as she says herself.

The commotion starts up in the back of the car. 'Can you not control yourselves?' Lally pleads and in the end shouts uncontrollably. 'Stop it.'

'Give me the sweets,' Mam says calmly. 'I'll divide them.' She stuffs them in the glove compartment where they stay and that is the end of the row.

It isn't that she is not generous. She is. In a practical sort of way. She is noted for helping people in trouble. With marriages, with drink and so on. Once she used to fry rashers and sausages on arriving home from Mass. But then one Sunday, the day Lally said 'it's too expensive', she realised her family was far too big. That put a stop to the fries. Now we only have toast. But that is another story.

Mam is not reading the papers this morning. She rubs the windscreen for Lally. We are out of town again and heading home. Uphill, downhill, past the creamery, past the convent.

'Driving is not so difficult today,' Lally says. 'Wait till tomorrow when the snow is packed.' He is in good humour. He has received Communion.

'Wait until it turns into slush, the land will be as wet as sponge,' says Mam.

'Yes, it will be a late spring,' he says.

She and he don't usually chat as agreeably as this. I think the silence in the back seat has given them the chance – we are all looking out the window.

Right now it doesn't matter whether the land is wet, dry, late or early. It is covered and forgotten. There are six or seven car tracks on the road. 'Careful at this bend,' Mam says.

'We got stuck here on the way. Don't brake whatever you do.' Mam is not just a backseat driver. According to Richie she is a better driver than Lally.

'Look, there's where we dug ourselves out.' We point, amazed at the mound of snow we dug on the way up.

'Accelerate, accelerate,' Mam suddenly screams. 'You're going into the ditch, get out.'

'No need to shout.' Lally drives himself into the middle of the road again. The car skids and then settles down to its crawl.

'I don't know where the road ends and the ditch begins,' he complains.

We are catching up on the car ahead. We drive slowly behind it a while, watching it churn up the snow in its wake. Until Lally grows suddenly impatient. 'Would he not go a little faster, does he not know I have work to do when I get home?' He revs the engine. We crunch up alongside but cannot pass. We hear the wheels skid. 'Jesus, trust it to give up on me now.' He throws the steering wheel round to his right. The car surges forward, getting a grip on something, and rises in the air.

'You're up on the ditch,' Mam roars. 'Get down, get down!' We in the back seat are both petrified and delighted.

'I'll pass him,' Lally grits. He accelerates again. The car slumps down on one side and fails to move any further forward.

'I told you,' Mam says.

'Told me what?' He blows the horn at the other car but it putt-putts steadily forward. 'The bloody so-and-so' – he is bitter. 'Knocks us off the road and won't help us back on it. Talk about neighbours!'

He revs the car again. The wheels sing in their tracks and we laugh, half in dread, at the height the snow is thrown into the air.

We open the doors and fall out in the drifts and exhaust fumes. We dig with cold-handled shovels and find the wheels on one side are not even touching the ground.

'Holy God, the chassis is sitting on the ditch. Look what he has made me do.' Lally shakes his fist at the snow before him but the other car is gone. He is in despair. 'Lift.' He gets us all together, our hands gripping the side of the car. 'When I count to three.'

We children giggle and flounder in the snow. We heave, puff, and laugh at our pretentious puffing. You might think Mam would tell us off. But no, she finds it amusing when Lally is laughed at. Having us on her side she can feel she is right and he is mad. Lally gets furious but the car does not budge.

Mam returns to the car and picks up the papers, reading them in a menacing sort of way that means she is not to be disturbed. 'Everybody get in the car.' It is just as the first snowballs are about to fly.

Lally stamps his feet a few times. 'Will there be anybody else along this road this morning?'

'There would be if you hadn't gone praying at an empty grave. Now everybody is ahead of us,' Mam says sweetly. 'Whatever you were praying so long for. Father Glee is the only one behind us now.'

'Oh God help me.' Lally throws his head in the air. 'A great assistance he'll be.'

It is up to each one in the back seat to claim his or her space. This involves a certain amount of squirming and shoving. When the car is in motion the struggle is not noticeable; the car's movement jolts us into position. But now territorial war has broken out all over the back seat. What has begun as silent pinching, elbowing, erupts into vehement whispers: 'That's not fair –' 'Move over –' 'You're hurting me –'.

Mam looks over her front seat and silences us. She knows that if we aren't silenced and the squabbling increases, Lally will lose his temper; she doesn't want his roars carrying across the snow-covered countryside.

We sit on. We are, I assume, awaiting the arrival of Father Glee.

Richie is the eldest of us children. That is why he sits in the front seat between Mam and Lally. He turns round now and smirks and returns to his reading of the paper. Richie bosses the rest of us about.

'It's clouding over again,' Lally says. 'More snow. We'll have to get a tractor and some planks and get out of here.'

'Wait till Father Glee,' Mam says. 'That car of his is as strong as any tractor.'

'Blasted extravagance it is,' Lally says.

I don't know how long we sit there. I think of the sweets in the glove compartment. Mam must have forgotten about them.

There is a building on our right. The snow has drifted over it, smoothing it so that the only edge left is a lip right around it. I realise after a long time it is the tennis pavilion. The lip is the verandah roof under which club members sit in the summer. I stare in awe at my discovery: the summer pavilion, secret beneath the awning's shade, where there are glimpses of open-necked shirts, of bare legs, of drinks in hands. I can't imagine the smack of summer sun, ever, upon its wooden walls again. Lally once asked Mam if she should like to join the tennis club. 'Wouldn't I look nice?' she answered.

Suddenly, and silently, a long ghost of a car passes. We see the white face of the priest, the hat. We are given a slow wave.

He drives on. Slows to a stop before his driveway. The brake lights shine pink on the snow and then he is gone through a bank of snow. 'Does he think he's the Pope?' Lally fumes. 'Does he think we have been waiting here to witness his passing?'

'He didn't see us.'

'In my hat he didn't, he waved at us.'

'He couldn't stop.'

'He couldn't stop because he'd be late for breakfast.'

'And he deserves it.'

'And others deserve it a lot more.'

'He has to eat too.'

'He didn't stay on to bury that poor Butler woman.'

'The curate will do it, doesn't take two.'

'Indecency. Imagine telling the bereaved their dead are a hindrance about his altar.'

'He's a fat ...'

'The children are listening.' Mam's voice remained calm. 'I don't know why you are so overcome. I didn't know you disliked Father Glee. He visits us ...'

'He doesn't visit the miners ... I don't know why he was appointed to this parish. He should be in Thurles, where he can discuss his theology till the cows come home, and sit in drawing rooms on his fat backside.'

'Enough. Scandalising the children. You who go to Mass every day, standing before empty graves saying prayers.' Mam shakes her paper and the discussion is closed.

Lally leaps out of the car and walks back towards the tennis pavilion.

'Let him cool off,' Mam says, 'or fall into a snowdrift.' She laughs nervously.

When he returns the sun has gone in and the sky is again become the same colour as the land, snow flurring again on the breeze. His face seems to have turned blue.

He has made a decision. 'Richie, like a good lad, go and get help. There's a farm up there on the hill. He'll drive you back on his tractor. Bring a rope, some planks. I'll stay here with your mother and stop the car covering over.'

He is never afraid to ask favours of farmers. He believes in good neighbours. How many times he has set me on the road with a request to some farmer . . . a loan of hay, a trailer, a buck rake, help at cattle testing. It embarrasses me; Richie too I think. Though sometimes I am not sure but that it is Lally who is embarrassed and gets us children to do the asking for him.

Richie sets off. Once he looks ruefully behind. His coat is black, then grey, the colour of the falling snow, then he is gone.

'We may wait now,' Mam says, 'until dark.'

'Why? That farmer's place is not far, what's his name do you know? Is it Kiely?'

Mam shakes her head. 'He won't go into Kiely, or anybody else. He'll walk home and drive back on our own tractor.'

As soon as Mam says it I know she is right. So does Lally.

'Why he couldn't go and ask someone . . .' He creases his face as if he is about to cry. But he is resigned. He will never openly quarrel with Mam over any of her children. There is this line beyond which he will never step.

The windscreen has snowed over. He gets out. We hear the grumbling sound of snow as he pushes it off with his coat sleeves. When he returns to the car his mood has completely changed. 'You know I think I might have a sweet. Could you fiddle out a soft one for me dear?' I have never seen Lally eat a sweet before. He has become quite jolly.

Mam divides the sweets, saves for Richie his two. There is silence then for a while but for the chewing of sweets and the squeak of seat leather.

Richie is some time gone when Lally starts it. He has been silent. Mam is reading. We are whispering loudly to one another in the back of the car. We have invented a game. The snow is a massive sheet covering everything. Like a sheet that drapes all the furniture in a room during painting the ceiling.

And we have to imagine what lies beneath all the fantastic shapes. The tennis pavilion for example, it is a giant mushroom. Father Glee's turreted presbytery is a large-beaked bird. The snow-covered trees are ... there are so many shapes.

Like a clock Lally suddenly starts it up. Like a clock that has sprung into action and then goes tick tock, tick and on and on. Mam doesn't appear to be listening. Lally's voice is even. 'The snowdrifts ... You know what lies beneath the snowdrifts ...? What lies in the deep of the earth ...? In the coal veins ...? Beneath these hills where the miners are at work even now while we sit in the car above them ...?' None of us says anything.

'Do you not feel it? Ticking away. Ticking our lives away. Every second of our lives? It occurred to me this morning when Jamesy here dropped the Communion plate. Don't ask me why.'

We look at Jamesy, our altar boy, expecting that now at last he will receive his reprimand.

'Every second ... Every second that passes is another that will never be repeated. Never.' Lally grows almost terrified. 'Eternity. Eternity is what lies under the snowdrifts. Time, the passage of time. We only imagine the snow stops time,' he says theatrically and then his voice evens out again. 'It will not stop.' He turns around, pleading, to us. 'I can't believe the age I am. I can't believe it ...'

'Stop it, stop it,' Mam suddenly shouts. 'I can't stand any more of this. Why do you look into graves?' If Lally has been able to control the fear that has almost erupted in his voice Mam cannot conceal hers. 'I've never heard such rubbish. Frightening the lives out of the children. I'll tell Father Glee what you're saying.'

'But it's true,' Lally says. 'Oh God so little time. Such a depth of eternity. Oh don't remind me.' He cups his face in his hands and holds it there a long moment.

'I'll tell you a story,' he says at last. He has made himself look happy again, as when he asked for the sweet.

'When I was a young boy' – he looks longingly at Jamesy – 'about your age. And size. Did you know I was an altar boy too one time?' He tells his story:

'My father was coming home from Kilkenny. In those days there were very few cars on the road. He hired a hackney to bring him home to Cranagh. The weather was just as it is to-day. Brighter maybe. The roads and fields, after a long hard winter, still covered in snow. Weeks on the ground it was and all that time cattle had to be kept indoors. The road they travelled was a main road and so I suppose the snow had been cleared somewhat off it. Driving along, somewhere between County Kilkenny and Tipperary, they suddenly saw, in all that white country, a patch of green. They drew nearer. It was a field. A green field without a spot of snow on it and drifts all about, feet deep. Well they drove into the next town and told everybody what they had seen and where. Hordes of people went back with them to look at that field. They were as excited, my father said, as if they had never seen a field before. No one could tell why there wasn't snow on it. 'Some energy in the ground,' they suggested. 'A stir of life.'

Lally turns round to us in the back seat. 'Now wasn't that a nice story?' He looks into our puzzled faces. It takes a few moments for all of us to return to the present. Then the cars start to arrive for second Mass.

They help release us. We are off again. Mam says, 'Stop speeding, you'll kill us.'

And Lally says, 'I have to, I have to save time.'

We stop only once. And that is to pick up Richie, who will not look behind so we can smirk at him from the back seat. He keeps his head down. Between Mam and Lally. She sometimes looks over his head at Lally. Every time she does so Lally is looking elsewhere. Every time he looks at her she is looking elsewhere.

I am thinking of all these things. The green field with the men looking down on it and so on. The snow falls again and collects on the windscreen slowing us to a crawl. It darkens in the back of the car. My stomach is tightening in a hungry knot. I am thinking of the toast and suddenly I think that this journey is going on for ever.